Sab and *Autobiography*

The Texas Pan American Series

Sab and *Autobiography*

——— • ———

By Gertrudis Gómez de Avellaneda y Arteaga
Translated and edited by Nina M. Scott

University of Texas Press
Austin

The Texas Pan-American Series is published with the assistance of a
revolving publication fund established by the Pan American Sulphur
Company.

⊗ The paper used in this publication meets the minimum requirements
of American National Standard for Information Sciences—Permanence of
Paper for Printed Library Materials, ANSI Z39.48-1984.

Library of Congress Cataloging-in-Publication Data
Gómez de Avellaneda y Arteaga, Gertrudis, 1814–1873.
    [Sab. English]
    Sab ; and, Autobiography / Gertrudis Gómez de Avellaneda ; edited
and translated by Nina M. Scott.—1st ed.
        p.   cm.—(The Texas Pan American series)
    Includes bibliographical references (p.   ).
    ISBN 0-292-70442-9 (pbk.)
    1. Gómez de Avellaneda y Arteaga, Gertrudis, 1814–1873.
2. Authors, Spanish—19th century—Biography.   I. Scott, Nina M.
II. Gómez de Avellaneda y Arteaga, Gertrudis, 1814–1873.
Autobiografía. English. 1993.   III. Title.   IV. Series.
PQ6524.S313   1993
868'.509—dc20
[B]   92-21961

To Jim, and to our children: Catherine, Chris, and Sam

Contents

Preface

After many years of teaching Spanish American Literature, especially that of women writers, as well as Comparative Literature of the Americas and Spanish American Literature in Translation, it became more and more obvious to me that the time for an English translation of *Sab* was more than overdue. In comparison with both the colonial and the contemporary periods, where many translations are now readily available, relatively few texts produced in nineteenth-century Spanish America have thus far been available in English. And few are as interesting and thought-provoking as this text, a youthful, sometimes flawed, but always passionate work, in which a talented writer began to spread her literary wings and dared to articulate human feelings in a mulatto slave—and in a white woman—that in her native Cuba were literally unspeakable. It is my hope that this translation of *Sab* will reach new readers unfamiliar with this Cuban woman who, eleven years prior to *Uncle Tom's Cabin* (1852), created a feminist/antislavery text, a work in many ways more radical than that written by Harriet Beecher Stowe.

For my translation I have used two different editions of *Sab*: the 1914 text published in Havana by Aurelio Miranda, and Mary Cruz's edition, also published in Havana by Editorial Letras Cubanas in 1983. Whenever there were discrepancies in these editions—as, for example, in the verses of Carlota's ballad, which Miranda publishes as one long verse and Cruz divided into four-line stanzas—I have gone with the Miranda edition. Avellaneda's *Autobiography*, also from the *Complete Works* published by Miranda, was written at approximately the same time as *Sab*, when the author was about twenty-five; I believe that a comparative reading of the two works is mutually enlightening, especially in the author's use of the epistolary mode in creating the narrating self.

In the translation, I have attempted to preserve the tone and vocabulary of nineteenth-century literature, high-flown and rhetorical as it may sound to the modern reader's ear. In some instances I have changed the tense of the original text when its use would sound awkward in English. Other than that, I have tried to remain as true to Avellaneda's original as possible.

A number of friends and colleagues deserve my thanks, most especially Pauline Collins, bibliographer extraordinaire, and Doris Sommer, who gave me much encouragement and support. Luis Harss, Margo Culley, Antonio Benítez Rojo, and Evelyn Picon Garfield offered helpful advice. I was particularly inspired by Susan Kirkpatrick's scholarship and also wish to pay tribute to Carmen Bravo-Villasante, my professor of long ago who, along with Pedro Barreda, did much to focus attention on Avellaneda when few others were interested in her. Others I wish to mention are Janet Gold, David Gies, Asunción Lavrin, Jill Netchinsky, and Elizabeth Ammons. It has also been a great pleasure to work with Theresa May, Carolyn Wylie, and Robert Fullilove of the University of Texas Press, and I wish most particularly to thank my anonymous critical readers for extremely helpful and encouraging comments. My deepest debt, however, is to my husband Jim, to whose faith and enthusiasm, to say nothing of his defense of my time and space, this project owes a great deal.

Nina M. Scott
Amherst, Mass. 1992

Introduction

——— • ———

Gertrudis Gómez de Avellaneda

Gertrudis Gómez de Avellaneda y Arteaga was born in Puerto Príncipe (today Camagüey), a provincial capital in central Cuba, in March 1814, the eldest child and only daughter of Manuel Gómez de Avellaneda and Francisca de Arteaga y Betancourt. Her father was of aristocratic Spanish lineage, an officer in the Spanish navy in charge of that area of the island (Cuba remained a Spanish colony until 1898). While stationed in Puerto Príncipe, he had met and married Doña Francisca, a wealthy Creole from a socially prominent family;[1] Gertrudis was the first of five children of this marriage, of whom only she and her younger brother Manuel survived. She was raised much like other privileged daughters of the slaveholding landed gentry, except that her education was extraordinary for the times. Drawn to literature and especially to poetry from a very early age, Gertrudis was encouraged in her early writing by one of her tutors, the Cuban patriot and Romantic poet José María Heredia, whose influence on her poetry is evident.

Gómez de Avellaneda's life is extraordinarily well documented, especially by herself. She was a consummate letter writer, and her voluminous correspondence provides much personal information. Early in her life (1839) she wrote a short epistolary autobiography for Ignacio de Cepeda, with whom she had fallen passionately in love in Seville; this document not only contains important details about her childhood, adolescence, and early adulthood but also constitutes the backdrop against which she wrote *Sab*. Judging by her own statements—and by the kind of woman she subsequently became—one gets the impression that the young Gertrudis was intelligent, headstrong, highly imaginative, and spoiled. From the beginning Avellaneda was convinced that hers was a "superior soul," a term much in vogue during the Romantic period, but which in her case was not so much posturing as a genuine expression of an intensely sensitive and emotional self. On the other hand, she was also aware that she was often her own worst enemy, as she confessed to Cepeda in a letter written in 1839: "There is something so unstable, so capricious and so fickle in my character that it will cause me much grief in my life" (*Diario íntimo* 54). Prophetic words indeed.

When Avellaneda was nine her father died, and her mother remarried ten months later, a—for then—scandalously brief period of time. Don Isidoro de Escalada was, like her father, a Spanish officer stationed in Cuba. Whether because of his personality or the emotional shock of losing a dearly loved parent, Gertrudis disliked Escalada from the beginning. She particularly resented having to obey his wishes because of her financial dependency upon him, a topic which comes up in *Sab,* and rejoiced when she came of age and became financially independent.

Within a few years of his marriage to Doña Francisca, Escalada began to make preparations to return to Spain, principally because he feared that the 1791 slave uprisings on the neighboring island of Haiti/Santo Domingo—then called St. Domingue—might spread to Cuba as well. His fears were not without substance. In 1798 there had been a slave rebellion in a sugar mill in Puerto Príncipe itself (Barreda 6), in 1812 black freedman José Antonio Aponte had attempted to organize both slaves and free blacks to take over the entire island—he failed and was hanged—and in the 1840s there were numerous other uprisings, culminating in massive reprisals after the Ladder Conspiracy of 1844, so called because accused blacks were tied to ladders and whipped (Luis 15–18). Thus, after Escalada sold off his wife's property and slaves, the family set sail for Bordeaux in 1836. Upon her departure Avellaneda wrote a fine sonnet which lamented leaving her native land, but she was also excited at the prospect of the voyage and at seeing Europe.

She recorded impressions of her travels for a cousin back in Cuba, which give some insights into the young woman's character. Describing a storm at sea, she maintains proudly that it exhilarated rather than terrified her and garnered her the distinction she perennially craved: "That night was dreadful, Eloísa! The captain took down the sails until the ship was left with bare masts, and all the passengers were in the grip of such terror that I was the calmest person [aboard], and perhaps the only one who enjoyed herself in that terrible clash of two elements and the sublime impressions this incites. For many days my serenity on that occasion was the topic of conversation" (Figarola 252). (All translations, unless otherwise noted, are mine.)

The notebooks record some attacks of homesickness, positive first impressions of France, and negative ones of Galicia, in northwestern Spain, where the family stopped to visit Escalada's relatives. Avellaneda detested his family as heartily as she did Escalada himself, a feeling which was quite mutual, especially since the women criticized her for paying more attention to her books than to household chores. In spite of chafing under their criticism, she does admit that they had reason to take umbrage at her behavior:

> In Galicia we American women are thought of as lazy, idle, and little suited for domestic duties; and I believe that it is undeniable that we, perhaps because of climate, perhaps of education, really are— the Cubans at least—more indolent than the Galician women; it would be the rare woman in our country who would willingly allow herself to get all smoky in the kitchen in the morning and spend the evening with her knitting in her hand . . . among the women of Galicia I have admired a strength and a vigor that copes with the hardest tasks. (Figarola 265)

As La Coruña, with its damp climate and lack of cultural life, soon stifled Avellaneda, she and her brother Manuel left their mother, Escalada, and three step-siblings to travel by ship to Cádiz and thence to Seville to visit paternal relatives. Andalusia was much more to her liking. Not only was the city beautiful, society lively, and cultural life thriving, but Avellaneda found fertile ground for her own initial literary endeavors. Her home became a place where the literati gathered, and she was soon publishing poetry in a number of newspapers. She organized subscribers to help her with the publication costs of *Sab* (on which she was at work at that time) and of her first play, *Leoncia*, which she wrote under her *nom de plume* "La Peregrina" (The Pilgrim); it was produced in June 1840. The play did well, and Avellaneda began to achieve a certain local fame. But she had set her sights on going to Madrid, the center of Spain's literary scene.

When one first looks at Avellaneda's life, one wonders how she as an outsider managed so deftly to infiltrate the masculine literary world and establish herself as a successful poet, playwright, and novelist. She soon learned to parlay her physical attractiveness, her exotic background, and an undeniable literary talent into useful connections with men of influence in the world of letters. A case in point is her strategy with Alberto Lista (1775–1848), thinker, educator, and "unquestionably the most learned and influential critic of the day" (Shaw 3). In his mid-sixties when she made his acquaintance in Seville, she dedicated *Sab* to him, a gesture which apparently nonplussed Lista to some degree. In his courtly letter of thanks to the young author, he admits that whereas he is flattered, "it is a little strange that you have shown preference for an old man now abandoned by the muses" (Figarola 150). Avellaneda, however, knew what she was doing. After being left an inheritance by recently deceased members of her father's family (Harter 30), she finally had the economic means to move to Madrid and asked Lista for a letter of introduction to Nicasio Gallego, a well-connected poet and member of the Madrid Lyceum. Another poet, José Zorrilla, left a famous account of her initial entrance into this select group of writers. Avellaneda, now in her mid-twenties, appeared incognita at a gathering of the Lyceum, whereupon her escort asked Zorrilla if he would read some of her poems in public. As he was impressed by their quality, he did so, and the audience responded with enthusiasm, all the more so when he introduced the stunning young poet:

> She was a beautiful woman, very tall, with sculptured contours, well-turned arms, her head crowned with abundant chestnut curls that reached charmingly to her shoulders. Her voice was sweet, gentle, and feminine; her movements languid and measured; the gestures of her hands delicate and supple; but the firm gaze of her serene blue eyes [which in reality were dark], the flourish with which she wrote on the paper, and the manly thoughts of those vigorous verses through which she revealed her talent showed a virile and strong dimension to the spirit enclosed in that voluptuous young phenomenon. There was nothing harsh, angular, or in any way masculine in that womanly and very attractive body: no ruddy complexion, nor too heavy eyebrows, nor down to shadow the freshness of her lips, nor brusqueness of manner; she was a woman—but undoubtedly only by an error of nature, which had absentmindedly placed a manly soul in that vessel of womanly flesh. (Cited in Bravo-Villasante 57–58)

Making a smashing first impression was one thing; sustaining acceptance in the literary world of Madrid and becoming economically self-sufficient through her writing was another, but Avellaneda succeeded. She published her first—highly successful—volume of poetry and her first novel, *Sab,* in 1841, followed by another novel, *Dos mugeres* (*Two Women*), in 1842, and a number of commercially successful plays, as well as poetry and novels, in the years that followed. She in fact became one of the most famous authors of the nineteenth century, claimed by both Spain and her native Cuba. As Beth Miller observed: "From a historical and feminist perspective, probably the single most important thing Avellaneda achieved was endurance. She is one of a meager number of female Romantic poets to appear in anthologies a hundred years after first publication. . . . Avellaneda became a celebrity, a successful and envied literary artist, a woman of letters" (203).

But these achievements were not without cost. As a woman who had to negotiate societal expectations of femininity while endowed with a spirit which rebelled against the gender inequalities endemic to her times, Avellaneda was often in the forefront of establishing the right of women to see themselves not only as narrated objects but also as writing subjects. Susan Kirkpatrick's outstanding scholarship on the problematic role of women authors during the era of Romantic literature makes patent the "tension between the desire-driven, egocentric self projected in Romantic discourse and the passionless, other-directed female subject defined by bourgeois gender ideology" (34). By nature Avellaneda was endowed with just such a "desire-driven, egocentric self" which sublimated into writing her desire for freedom from a variety of social constraints.

Her first two novels are probably her most radical expressions of this rebellion and, for that reason, among the most interesting of her works for a modern reader. Given her early negative experiences with the tyranny of matrimony, the young Avellaneda was openly gun-shy when it came to wedlock, advocating free and open relationships with—or preferably without—benefit of clergy (Miller 207). In *Sab* she equated marriage to slavery, and in *Dos mugeres* presented a tolerant view of an adulterous relationship; if change is a law of nature, she queried, why should human affections be exempt? Although Avellaneda managed to publish these works in Spain, they were banned by the censors from sale in Cuba; a royal decree in the Cuban National Archives classifies the first (*Sab*) as containing "doctrines subversive to the system of slavery on this Island and contrary to moral and good habits; and the second [*Dos mugeres*] for being plagued with doctrines prejudicious to Our Holy Religion and attacking therein conjugal Society and canonising adultery" ("Documents" 350).

Predictably, Avellaneda's personal life was stormy. After the amorous entanglements she describes in her 1839 *Autobiography,* she had a number of other relationships. Shortly after she arrived in Seville, she was smitten with the aforementioned Ignacio de Cepeda—a wealthy, well-educated, and socially prominent young man, but desperately ordinary, conservative to the point of prissiness, and visibly overwhelmed by her tropical passion. His reluctant courtship may also have been based on other concerns: Avellaneda's biographer Cotarelo y Mori maintains that Cepeda did not wish to marry her because she had no money (37). Her infatuation lasted many years, as can be seen in her many letters to him, all of which he saved and ordered published after both had died. The on-again, off-again correspondence with Cepeda lasted from 1839 to 1854, at which time, with no prior notice to Avellaneda of his intentions, he married someone else.

In 1844 the thirty-year-old Avellaneda embarked on a torrid love affair with poet and diplomat Gabriel García Tassara, with disastrous consequences, for when she became pregnant, her lover abandoned her. Tassara refused to acknowledge paternity of the child, who died less than a year later; a heartbreaking letter from Avellaneda, begging him to see his infant daughter before she died, brought no response from him. In 1846 she married Pedro Sabater, of whom she was fond but did not love; already seriously ill with cancer, he died four months after the wedding. In her sorrow she took refuge for several months in a convent in Bordeaux.

In spite of personal unhappiness, her literary successes continued, and when her friend Nicasio Gallego died in 1853, she decided the time had come for her to storm the ultimate male bastion and solicit his chair in the Royal Spanish Academy. She had many powerful backers, and extant letters record her frantic lobbying for admission, but when the vote was taken among the membership on the issue of admitting women, Avellaneda's faction lost.[2] Apart from the generally conservative attitude many academicians held on the gender issue, her defiant independence and flaunting of social convention very likely also influenced the vote. One of her supporters, the Marquis of Pezuela, had to break the news to her: "We did what we could. The majority defeated us. In my judgment, almost all of us are worth less than you; but, nevertheless, because of the question of gender (and talent should not have any), we supporters must bear the sorrow of not counting you among our academicians for now" (Figarola 172). Avellaneda was more than bitter. In her essay on "La mujer" ("Woman"), written seven years later, she still fulminated against the "bearded academies" from which women were barred because "unfortunately [even] the greatest intellectual prowess is unable to make that animal abundance that requires cutting by a razor sprout on a [female] face" and so "this has become the only and insurmountable distinction of the literary males" who control the rules of admission (*Album cubano de lo bueno y lo bello* 261). Avellaneda had other reasons for being angry: exclusion from the academy also meant exclusion from financial benefits paid to writers by the Spanish government (Figarola 214), and she was, after all, dependent on her pen for her livelihood.

These events took their toll on her. Though she was always ambivalent about marriage, in 1853, when she was forty-two and her voluptuous figure had gone to fat, she and Antonio Romero Ortiz, a newspaperman eight years her junior, began a flirtation.[3] One senses Avellaneda's fatigue and despondency in some of her letters to him. She confesses to feeling "a barren tedium" in her existence which affected her writing (*Cartas inéditas* 19). Although love had always been the principal emotion in her life, now she felt some apprehension toward new relationships. "I have never been happy nor have I made anyone else happy" (35), she wrote, but knew much of the fault was hers for always tending to extremes: "I would like to be prudent and I get angry at myself when I feel that I am not. . . . I don't dare trust even my own heart which has been wrong so many times before" (36). At bottom she still felt the irreconcilable difference endemic to her character: "In me there are these two powerful natures, that of the poet and of the woman" (43); as Kirkpatrick noted, "The rift between the author's 'male' character or subjectivity and her female social identity con-demns her to unhappiness in Spain as well as Cuba" (140).

There is some mention of matrimony in her correspondence with Ro-mero Ortiz, and after all Avellaneda had been through in the past few years, part of her longed to be conventional, to be settled and taken care of, while the other feared the curtailment of her freedom and a husband's possible tyranny. Initially drawn to Romero, Avellaneda subsequently changed her mind about the possibility of marriage. In any case, she man-aged to frighten him off in much the same way as Cepeda, with bouts of jealousy and public scenes.

Nevertheless, after breaking with Romero Ortiz, Avellaneda did decide to marry again. Colonel Domingo Verdugo had connections at the court of Isabel II (as did Avellaneda), so the two were married in April 1855 at the Royal Palace with the queen and her consort as witnesses (Harter 41). Three years later Verdugo was stabbed, almost fatally, after an altercation with a man who had attempted to disrupt one of Avellaneda's plays by heaving a live cat on stage; though Verdugo recovered from the wound, his health was permanently affected, and he died four years later.

In 1859 Verdugo had been posted to Cuba, which allowed his wife to return to the land she had left so long ago. For Avellaneda the return to the island was a triumph. She was celebrated everywhere, and at her in-duction into the Lyceum in Havana, she was even presented with a crown of gold laurel leaves, which she claimed was her heart's dearest treasure. As her piety increased with age, Avellaneda bequeathed her golden crown to the Virgin Mary and left it in a church in Havana before departing for Spain in 1864 (Figarola 34).

Avellaneda wrote actively during these years in Cuba, turning out a number of novels, plays, and folk legends. In 1860 she also founded a short-lived women's magazine, the *Album cubano de lo bueno y lo bello* (*The Cuban Album of the Good and the Beautiful*). She was the only woman to found and direct a magazine for women in Cuba at that time. The ex-tant issues offer a fascinating compendium of topics important to her and to her female contemporaries. Avellaneda was both editor and occa-sional contributor, composing poetry, essays, short biographies of famous women of the past, including her four-part essay on "La mujer," in which she examines the roles of women in religion, history, government, and intellectual life.

After Verdugo's death Avellaneda returned to Spain via the United States. She wrote little more but instead assembled material for the publi-cation of several volumes of her collected *Literary Works,* which appeared between 1869 and 1871. Avellaneda herself decided not to include either *Sab* or *Dos mugeres,*[4] partly because she had grown more conservative with age and partly because she was anxious to sell her books in Cuba. In spite of her status as the island's most famous daughter, the political climate in Cuba was still extremely repressive, as slavery was not abolished until 1886 and government officials would not have tolerated any book with openly antislavery views.

Avellaneda's turbulent life came to a quiet end when she died of diabetes in Madrid in 1873. Even though she had achieved great fame during her lifetime and was celebrated in both Cuba and Spain, a reporter for a Madrid newspaper noted sadly how few people attended her funeral:

> We thought we would see all the writers of Madrid there; we could not suppose that there would be even one who would forego the duty of paying his respects to the earthly remains of this most distinguished lady, the famous writer, the inspired poetess who has given the country such glory, who esteemed writers so greatly, who had such a noble and Spanish heart; but this belief of ours was an illusion. There were only six writers there. The academicians, the artists of the Madrid theatres, the poets, the novelists, the playwrights we hoped to see on this sad occasion didn't want to take the trouble or thought themselves excused from dedicating a few moments to the illustrious lady, whose loss leaves a void in our literature, one that will never be filled. (Figarola 21)

Avellaneda was ultimately laid to rest in Seville.

Background to Sab

In past discussions of *Sab* with scholars of abolitionist literature of the United States, I noticed that few of them knew that a contemporary school of antislavery literature existed in Cuba; they were also unaware that Avellaneda published *Sab* eleven years prior to Harriet Beecher Stowe's *Uncle Tom's Cabin; or, Life among the Lowly* (1852). For this reason some background on the novel and on its critical reception seems appropriate.

In Cuba as in the United States, opposition to the institution of slavery became more vocal as the nineteenth century wore on, but in Cuba these views were severely repressed by Spanish officials anxious to preserve the island's colonial status, and most wealthy Cubans preferred "to keep the protection of the Spanish armed forces rather than risk ruin in a possible republic teeming with free Blacks" (Netchinsky 1). In most other Latin American countries, where political independence had been achieved early in the century, abolition followed soon thereafter, but in the Cuban struggle for independence "abolitionism becomes a *condition,* not a result of independence" (Sommer 118). Its fixed geographical boundaries put the island in a particularly explosive situation.

At the beginning of the nineteenth century, Cuba found itself in an enviable economic position. The successful slave uprising on St. Domingue took that island out of the lucrative Caribbean sugar production, thus raising both the demand and the prices for Cuban sugar; in fact, in the first forty years of the century, Cuba supplied almost a quarter of the world's sugar (Rodríguez 41). Huge fortunes were made during this sugar boom, accompanied by a sharp upturn in the importation of African slaves to the island, despite the abolition of the slave trade to Cuba by treaties between Spain and England in 1817 and 1820. Statistics record a significant rise in the black population of the island; by 1827 slaves and black freemen together comprised 56 percent of Cuba's inhabitants (Barreda 7). Sugar, coffee, and tobacco, all crops produced by slave labor, drove the flourishing colonial economy while Spain tacitly ignored the illegal slave trade, and the interests of the sugar oligarchy (sacarocracy) determined what Antonio Benítez Rojo terms Cuba's "discourse of power" (12–14). Nevertheless, in the 1830s there were some Cuban whites who were genuinely concerned with establishing a counterdiscourse, which, as we shall see, was antislavery but not abolitionist in nature. I am referring to the gathering of intellectuals and writers around the wealthy, Venezuelan-born planter Domingo Del Monte (1804–1853), a group whose activities began in Matanzas in 1834 and moved to Havana the following year. Del Monte and his followers were genuinely alarmed by the huge increase in the island's black population as well as by the inhuman working conditions in the sugar mills. They used their writings to plead for the curtailment of the illegal slave trade and pointed out the injustices of the institution of slavery on human and moral grounds, yet never went so far as to openly advocate emancipation. In this counterdiscourse, scholars like Benítez Rojo (as well as Schulman, Netchinsky, and Luis) see the roots of the incipient Cuban identity and literature.

Del Monte's influence over his followers was enormous. He shared his extensive library of contemporary European authors and was in active contact with English abolitionists like Richard Madden, once British consul in Havana and still a judge on the Mixed Court, the arbitration tribunal of the slave trade. Del Monte not only commissioned antislavery texts from members of his group, but he and the authors conferred among themselves and critiqued each other's works as they were being written, in effect producing a series of collective texts. In 1835, in a kind of forerunner to today's Latin American testimonial literature, Del Monte found a literate mulatto slave, Juan Francisco Manzano, and urged him to write his autobiography. Manzano had already published poetry in Cuban newspapers, which was very unusual for a slave, and at the time of his interaction with Del Monte was a fugitive. Manzano had been promised his freedom in exchange for his text (the original is housed in the National Library in

Havana), so that he quite literally wrote his way out of bondage (Netchinsky 27); the group subsequently raised the sum needed to buy the slave and free him (Luis 36). Since Manzano's manuscript was full of orthographic and grammatical errors, one of the group's members, Anselmo Suárez y Romero, undertook to correct these mistakes; it is obvious that the autobiography heavily influenced Suárez y Romero's subsequent antislavery novel *Francisco,* as well as some other, later works (see Netchinsky's chapter on Manzano for a thorough discussion of the manuscript's many incarnations). Suárez y Romero's corrected version was also given by Del Monte to Madden, who translated and published it in English in 1840 (it did not appear in Spanish for another eighty years).

In order to elicit the sympathy of Cuban readers, the Del Monte authors often dwelt on incidents where innocent and submissive slaves were barbarously mistreated, but given the prevailing fear of slave uprisings among their readership, they never dared to present a rebellious slave who might resort to violence. For all of his activism against the continuation of the slave trade, Del Monte himself never openly advocated either abolition—he realized that this would destroy his personal fortune—or political independence from Spain (Rodríguez 52, 47). However, in spite of the group's essentially conservative stance, their "antislavery narrative represented one side of a dialogue on slavery which directly threatened slavers and Spanish officials in Cuba" (Luis 61), and after two serious slave uprisings in 1843 and 1844, the group was placed under such political pressure that it disbanded. Manzano, who was jailed for a year before being freed, never wrote again, while Del Monte was exiled and died in Spain in 1853.

Ivan Schulman's key article on the origin of the novel in Cuba points out that this genre has its roots in these crosscurrents of debate surrounding the institution of slavery (356–357), a view shared by Netchinsky, who shows how novels like *Francisco* and *Sab* "map the frustrations of youthful development for a human being and a nation," both longing to be free from outside control (263). Schulman establishes two generations of abolitionist novels, with the earliest ones being written (but not necessarily published) about 1838 and the last (*Cecilia Valdés*) making its appearance in 1882 (365).

Avellaneda was not part of the Del Monte group for a variety of reasons: her youth, her gender, and the fact that she came from central Cuba, which was a fair distance from Havana and whose principal industry was cattle, not sugar. Antonio Benítez Rojo points out the implications of this fact by noting that "since Puerto Príncipe did not depend on sugar for its economic development, its mode of slavery was much less intensive than the east, with the result that the proportion of slaves in relation to the total population was considerably less" (15). But the principal reason why Avellaneda had no contact with the Del Monte group was that she left for

Spain in 1836, only one year after it had relocated to Havana. She started work on *Sab* possibly as early as 1836, definitely by 1838, and published first in 1841 (Morejón 34). It should also be noted that her novel is her text alone, not a collective effort as was the case with the literature of the Del Monte writers. In launching a controversial novel like *Sab*, Avellaneda had the advantage of being in Spain and living under the generally liberal government of the Regent, Queen María Cristina; publication of an anti-slavery work was possible in Spain, as opposed to Cuba, where it was not.

Being her earliest novel, the one closest to her departure from the island, it is also her most American, especially in her description of the Cuban landscape.[5] In spite of Avellaneda's having adopted an American setting, critics are right in underscoring that her text is responding more to European than to autochthonous Cuban influences (Guerra 710), and indeed *Sab*'s literary ancestors are recognizably European.[6] Avellaneda was a voracious reader who was fluent in French and was conversant with such authors as Rousseau, Lamartine, Mme de Staël, George Sand, and others. Three writers influenced Avellaneda in particular: Chateaubriand, Aphra Behn, and Victor Hugo. The young François René, Vicomte de Chateaubriand, had spent seven months in the United States in 1791, and on his return he wrote the famous *Atala; or, The Love and Constancy of Two Savages in the Desert*[7] (1801), featuring a pair of star-crossed Indian lovers and containing long descriptive passages of the fauna and flora of tropical Florida and Louisiana. Avellaneda's descriptions of her native island in *Sab* (as well as the idea of a pre-European utopia of peace and harmony with nature) owe a clear debt to *Atala*; it is also more than likely that the raging storm so important to her novel's plot development has its roots in a parallel episode in Chateaubriand's work.

Whereas Chateaubriand's lovers were Indian, Avellaneda responds more to her Cuban roots by creating a hero who is mulatto. The black character in Hispanic literature had its roots in the Spanish Renaissance, and in the plays of Lope de Vega, not to mention *Othello,* to whom Sab refers in his letter to Teresa. Shakespeare aside, one of the first European writers to present a black protagonist in an American setting was the Englishwoman Aphra Behn.[8] Early in her life Behn had traveled to Suriname and claimed that her novel *Oroonoko; or, The Royal Slave* (1688) reflected some of her experiences there. It is almost certain that Avellaneda was familiar with a French translation of *Oroonoko,* which apparently was widely read in eighteenth-century France (Jackson 26); furthermore, Mary Cruz cites Avellaneda's reference to "Oroondates" in the *Autobiography* (letter of July 25), which Cruz feels is a misspelling of "Oroonoko" (9). Behn's text, like Chateaubriand's later *Atala,* abounds with descriptions of tropical American nature and her cast of characters—white colonists, Indians, and black slaves—reflects the multiethnic nature of the Caribbean. Her hero is an African prince who is sold into slavery to the Americas; as Jackson noted, "It is probably due to [the popularity of] Oroonoko . . . that there are so many royal slaves in literature and that such a large percentage of black slaves were kings in their native countries or sons and grandsons of kings, persons of quality and natural goodness" (25). Sab certainly fits into this convention. Oroonoko's rebellion against his enslavement is also much like Sab's: "Reduced to the impotence of a plantation slave, he pits his personal code of honesty, honor, loyalty and fortitude against the social order that sanctions self-interest, arrogant power, and sadistic brutality" (Metzger xiv). However, *Oroonoko* is a far more violent text than *Sab,* for the hero does in fact organize a slave rebellion, is defeated, and dies a ghastly death by dismemberment. Prior to his own death Oroonoko kills his beloved wife, the princess Imoinda, to spare her a similar fate.

Violence is also prevalent in Victor Hugo's very early novel *Bug-Jargal,* which he allegedly wrote in two weeks when he was sixteen (1818) and published in 1826. *Bug-Jargal* was all the rage in France just when Avellaneda arrived in Europe, and its influence on *Sab* is unmistakable.[9] Though Hugo had never been to the Americas, he set the novel in St. Domingue and described events related to the slave uprising in 1791. Like Oroonoko, Bug-Jargal is an African prince who leads a slave rebellion and is ultimately executed; unlike Behn's hero (who had a black wife), he is in love with Marie, the daughter of the white French planter who owns him. Hugo thus presented rivals in love similar to those that Avellaneda created in *Sab,* with conflicts that cross both racial and social lines (Cruz 9). Nancy Morejón rightly urges the modern reader not to underestimate the radical nature of *Sab*'s plot: Avellaneda raised a slave, considered by most of her fellow Cubans to be not a person but a *thing,* to the status of protagonist; furthermore, the very idea that he could love a white woman was considered nothing short of heresy (35–36).

Aside from the black/white love triangle, there are other instances of intertextuality with Hugo's work: Bug-Jargal on several occasions saves the life of his white rival, like Sab he has a loyal dog, and his speech is totally correct and cultivated. As was the case with *Oroonoko* and *Atala,* Hugo's novel also dwells on the exotic aspects of tropical American nature, and the particular episode of Carlota in the garden may well have its roots in Hugo's text, where the lovely Marie, too, retreats to a leafy bower on her plantation to dream of love. In short, a reading of these three novels makes patent just who *Sab*'s principal literary ancestors were, though none of these texts developed their female characters anywhere nearly as well as Avellaneda did.

As was said earlier, Avellaneda had worked on *Sab* intermittently for several years before deciding to publish it. Barreda perceptively points out that "when she began a more independent life around 1838, the form of

Sab started to gel and to acquire contours" (72). By 1841 she had achieved
a number of literary successes, found the subscribers to help her pay the
publication costs and thus launched a book which would help to under-
score her own exotic background.[10] The edition was a small one, however,
and Avellaneda's Spanish relatives, scandalized by her antislavery stance,
reportedly bought up a large number to take them out of circulation (Figarola 77). Nevertheless, her book made its mark. Though the novel was
officially banned in Cuba, chapters of *Sab* were copied and clandestinely
circulated on the island (Portuondo 212). As Cubans became more and
more restive about their colonial status in the last years of the century, *Sab*
resurfaced in the 1870s, "serialized in a Cuban revolutionary journal in
New York [which] suggests how important an ideological weapon this
novel must have been" (Sommer 119). Avellaneda did not live to see slavery
abolished in 1886 or independence come in 1898, fifteen years after her
death. *Sab* was finally published in Cuba in 1914, on the centennial of
Avellaneda's birth, in what is still the definitive edition of her complete
works.[11]

For a long time *Sab* received minimal critical attention.[12] Standard reference works on Spanish American literature of just a few years ago (cf.
Torres-Ríoseco, Franco, and even Arrom, who is himself Cuban) barely
mentioned Avellaneda, and *Sab* not at all. Literary historian José Antonio
Portuondo noted the stance of fellow Cuban critics toward the novel: as a
rule, it was "elegantly dismissed in two words. . . . What is necessary is to
read *Sab*, which is what the majority of our literary historians usually fail
to do" (211–212).

Portuondo's remark dates from the early 1980s. Since then a number of
feminist critics have paid serious attention to *Sab*, as they have to many
other examples of women's literature of the nineteenth century. Unaccustomed to the extreme sentimentality of these works and to the copious
tears shed within their pages, which make for rather soggy going at times,
the modern reader must learn to penetrate below the surface and to realize
that some extremely important, even radical issues are being discussed.
With respect to the literature of the United States, Jane Tompkins has
pointed out "[that] the popular domestic novel of the nineteenth century
represents a monumental effort to reorganize culture from the woman's
point of view, that this body of work is remarkable for its intellectual
complexity, ambition and resourcefulness; and that, in certain cases, it offers a critique of American society far more devastating than any delivered
by better-known critics such as Hawthorne and Melville" (83). As Tompkins says, what makes this discussion different from other literature of the
time is that it is being carried on by women, and from a woman's view of
the world. The same is true for Spanish American works, so that comparative research into the literature of this hemisphere is very productive. Case

in point: the recent feminist revindication of *Uncle Tom's Cabin* as a serious work in the United States is paralleled by the critical attention accorded *Sab* in Spanish American literature, and the conclusions drawn often transfer very well. Elizabeth Ammons, for example, has focused on the radical nature of Harriet Beecher Stowe's text, on the way in which it lays bare the "root evil of slavery: the displacement of life-giving maternal values by a profit-hungry masculine ethic that regards human beings as marketable commodities" (156), an observation which can be applied equally well to *Sab*.

Another topic common to many nineteenth-century women's texts in both North and South America was the attack on the institution of marriage. In the United States, involvement in the abolitionist movement made many women conscious both of their own lack of human and legal rights and of the similarity between the bondage of the slave and that of the woman whose need for economic security frequently forced her into analogous situations of dependence and servitude. Indicative of this awareness is southerner Mary Chesnut's bitter comment at witnessing the auction of a black woman: "You know how women sell themselves and are sold in marriage from queens downward, eh? . . . Poor women, poor slaves" (10–11). Spanish American authors, such as Mercedes Cabello de Carbonera, Clorinda Matto de Turner, and Flora Tristán, were often even more mordant than their North American counterparts, since divorce did not exist in their Catholic countries. Avellaneda was no exception: she was among the most outspoken of these women, and critics have rightly noted that in *Sab* her feminism consistently overshadows her denunciation of slavery (Kirkpatrick 156).

Recent, principally gender-oriented criticism has contributed a number of other insights, as for example some of the differences in narrative structure between Avellaneda's novel and other Cuban antislavery texts (cf. particularly Netchinsky). Whereas most male writers favored panoramic portrayals of race relations in their society, Avellaneda's stage was a smaller one, as she chose to make a personal love story the central focus of her novel.[13] Therefore, the issue of Sab's race comes to be both a Cuban social problem and the determining factor which raises him to the tragic Romantic hero in pursuit of an unrealizable goal (Barreda 71–72; Guerra 709). Another aspect unique to her text is the parallel which Avellaneda draws between women and slaves, as is the interplay between issues of gender, race, and types of social marginalization. It is evident that Avellaneda used the figure of Sab not only to protest slavery but also to vent many of her own particular frustrations. "In the imagined expression of a slave's outrage speaks, in fact, the anger of a young colonial woman who aspired to pour out her own subjectivity in writing capable of captivating the great centers of civilization and culture, but who was told to be silent and resign herself to the self-abnegating virtues of the angel of the hearth" (Kirk-patrick 157).

This topic of Sab's rage is an important one. European-authored *Oroon-oko* and *Bug-Jargal* present black characters who led bloody slave uprisings and did not hesitate to use violence to fight the enslavement of their minds and bodies, but in America Sab—like Uncle Tom—refuses this course of action. This stance has bothered a number of critics, for given the forceful articulation of Sab's anger against society, his refusal to fight seems incon-sistent, unless one recalls the perennial Cuban fear of slave uprisings, which made the rebellious slave a forbidden topic; black literary characters had to remain "nonthreatening and acceptable to white readers" (Luis 53).[14] However, several gender-oriented critics have looked at this issue from their particular angles. Netchinsky feels that Avellaneda's work throbs with "a sense of power that is dormant, repressed, bound," and although "Avellaneda and her protagonist are quick to rescind the lan-guage of active protest, the words have been pronounced" (208–209). In Kirkpatrick's opinion, Sab's avoidance of violence reveals "a narrative im-pulse divided against itself in the attempt both to justify and contain an-ger" (155). Sommer has gone a step further in showing that in fact there is considerable violence in *Sab,* but that it is rhetorical and not physical. Although Avellaneda simultaneously violated accepted codes of language, race, class, and gender, she was ultimately unable to make a definitive break with convention (113–116).

The fact that Sab is a mulatto (unlike Bug-Jargal and Oroonoko who are pure African) is also significant. "Cuba," Barreda maintains, "is a mu-latto nation, and the Cuban is, if not biologically, at least psychologically a mulatto" (1). Antislavery literature reflected the broad spectrum of racial blending that characterized Cuban society, and in Spanish—as opposed to English—the designation "mulatto/a" was a commonly accepted term.[15] Sab, then, is not an African who had been transplanted to the New World but an American, a Cuban, born in the Americas of the two races domi-nant in Cuba. Although a slave, he is an aristocrat through both of his parents and is, in fact, Carlota's cousin.[16] Despite her abolitionist stance, Avellaneda has been taken to task by contemporary critics who point to instances of unconscious racism, such as, for example, Sab's remark that "in spite of her color, my mother was beautiful." The same might be said for the description of Sab's own physical features, but in both of these cases we are in danger of reading this novel out of context. As William Luis rightly maintains:

> It stands to reason that antislavery, as a concept or as a literary, po-litical, or economic movement in Cuba, could only exist as a white movement. The white dominant perspective . . . which helped to

formulate the antislavery narrative could only be expressed by using the mechanism available to white or Western culture. Language and writing, as a bourgeois means of expression, can only be in the form of a dominant white aesthetic. A slave or a black described as having white characteristics may suggest, to a contemporary reader, assimilation. But within a different context, the same description was, in fact, aggressive and daring and challenged the slavery system. (65)

Sommer is also intrigued by the author's problems in classifying Sab's exact racial status. For example, when Avellaneda describes the slave's features, she maintains that Sab was neither a white *criollo* nor a perfect mulatto, "as if the inherited signs of a European language could not catch up with an elusive American referent . . . this racial indefiniteness, this new shade of social meaning . . . may be among the most radical features of this novel" (113).

Feminist critics (Gold, Schlau, and Kirkpatrick in particular) have also called attention to the importance of female friendships and female bonding as a weapon—or at least a consolation—against marginalization and powerlessness, a theme that appears in other of Avellaneda's works as well. I feel that Avellaneda also has a marked tendency to subvert the role of the innocent child/woman who functions as the quintessential heroine in many male-authored Romantic texts. Avellaneda creates a different kind of woman: in *Dos mugeres* it is the adulteress Catalina who claims center stage, and in *Sab* it is Teresa, the poor, unattractive, and illegitimate relation. Aside from their innate nobility of spirit, these two women are seen as exemplary because of their intelligence and experience in the world, qualities that Avellaneda herself had had to acquire in order to survive as a writer and to maintain her independence as a woman.

In a related vein: what has always struck me about Avellaneda is her insistent concern with the economic realities that determine a woman's status in the world. Her *Autobiography* gives us ample clues why she should think this way. Gertrudis was a child of privilege, but her refusal to marry the man her family had chosen for her had dire economic repercussions when her grandfather altered his will. Her lack of personal means forced her to obey Escalada, thwarted her plans with Ricafort, and very likely cooled Cepeda's lukewarm ardor further still. At first she disliked thinking about money. For example, when the young Gertrudis disembarked in France, she registered her disapproval with the dockside scene, where hotel keepers, porters, and fruit sellers competed for her family's attention. "This hunger for money was a disagreeable shock, for it is still quite unknown in our rich Cuba" (Figarola 253). Once she was on her own, however, it did not take her long to realize that she could not ignore material concerns. In *Sab* one still notices her ambivalence toward the topic of money—she detests the materialistic Otways but also realizes that Don Carlos's lack of business acumen has dire consequences for his daughters—but this disappears in *Dos mugeres,* published only a year later. Her heroine Catalina is not only lovely and accomplished in all social and cultural graces but also is an efficient manager both of her own fortune and that of a woman friend whom she saves from financial ruin.

A word about the *Autobiography.* I have included it in this translation not only because Avellaneda wrote it at about the same time as *Sab* and readers will notice the intertextuality between Avellaneda's life and novel but because in both cases the author was engaged in writing a fictional self through the medium of epistolary autobiography (cf. Kirkpatrick, Netchinsky, and Sommer). I am also fascinated by her style. In the *Autobiography* one gets to appreciate the mercurial temperament of the young writer, as well as her transparent efforts to manipulate and seduce her reader. It was a good thing that she failed or that Cepeda was too terrified of her to let himself be ensnared, for at heart she knew that her independence was her greatest strength. Later, when she rejected Antonio Romero, Avellaneda again realized this fact. I particularly remember a sentence with which she ended one angry letter to him, a sentence which could well be an epigraph for her whole life: "I feel . . . that true freedom is never enslaving yourself to anyone in anything" (*Cartas inéditas* 39).

Autobiography of
Gertrudis Gómez de Avellaneda

The twenty-third of July [*1839*], *at one in the morning*

I must attend to you;[1] I offered to do so, and since I cannot sleep tonight,
I want to write; I am attending to you while writing about myself, as I
would only consent to do this for you.

The confession which a superstitious and timid conscience wrests from
a contrite soul before a minister of God was never more sincere nor more
open than the one I am disposed to make to you. After reading this notebook you will know me as well—and perhaps better—than you know
yourself. But I demand two things. First: that fire may consume this paper
as soon as it has been read. Second: that in the whole world no one but
you must be aware that it ever existed.

You know that I was born in a city in the center of the island of Cuba,
where my father was employed in the year 1809 and where a little while
later he married my mother, a native of that country.

As extensive details regarding my birth are not necessary for the part of
my history which might be of interest to you, I will not burden you with
useless trifles but, on the other hand, will not suppress some others which
may help to give you a clearer idea of later events.

When I began to reason, I realized that I had been born into an advantageous social position, that my maternal family occupied one of the highest ranks in the country, that my father was a gentleman and enjoyed all
the esteem he deserved for his talents and virtues and all the prestige which
employees of a certain class enjoy in a small and growing city. No one,
neither his predecessors nor those who succeeded him, had this degree of
prestige in his position as commander of the central island ports. By means
of his distinguished talents, my father excelled in his profession and had
known how to acquire the most honorific connections in Cuba and even
in Spain.

Soon it will have been sixteen years since he died, but I am very, very sure that his memory lives on in Puerto Príncipe and that his name is never uttered without praise and benedictions: he did no harm to anyone and did all the good he could. In his public and his private life he was always the same: noble, intrepid, truthful, generous, and incorruptible.

Nevertheless, Mother was not happy with him, perhaps because there can be no happiness in an arranged marriage, perhaps because as she was too young and my father more mature, they could not get along. But even though they were unhappy, both of them were at least irreproachable. She was the most faithful and virtuous of wives and could never once complain of even the least insult to her dignity as wife and mother.

Forgive me these praises; they are a tribute I must bring to my progenitors, and when I recount the qualities which made my father so esteemed, I feel a definite pride in being able to say: I am his daughter.

I was not quite nine years old when I lost him.[2] Of the original five children only two remained when he died: Manuel and I, and thus we were tenderly loved, with some preference of Mother's for Manolito and my father's for me. Perhaps because of this, and because I was older than he by three years, my grief at Father's death was greater than my brother's. Nonetheless, how far I was at that point from realizing the full extent of my loss!

For several years my father had been planning to return to Spain and settle in Seville; this plan was most definite and uppermost in his mind during the last months of his life. He complained of not being laid to rest in his native soil and, predicting that Cuba would suffer the same fate as that of a neighboring island, seized by the blacks,[3] begged my mother to come to Spain with their children. No material sacrifice, he said, was too great: the advantage of settling in Spain was never too dear. These were his last wishes, and when I learned of them later on, I wished to comply with them. Perhaps this is the reason for my affection for this country and for the desire with which I sometimes longed to leave my homeland in order to come to this old world.

Mother was left a widow when she was still young, rich, and beautiful (for she was extremely so), and presumably she had no lack of admirers who sought her hand [in marriage]. Among them was Escalada, a lieutenant colonel of the regiment that back then was stationed in Puerto Príncipe, also young, not bad-looking, and attractive because of his gentle manners and cultivated spirit. Mother perhaps fell in love with him far too quickly, and scarcely ten months from the time we were orphaned we had a stepfather. My grandfather, my uncles, and the whole family took this marriage very badly; but in this matter my mother showed a firmness of character she had never exhibited before nor has since. Although very young, this was a blow to my heart; however, it was not base considerations of a material nature that made me so sensitive to this marriage: it was the grief of seeing my father's bed so quickly occupied [by another] and a premonition of the consequences of this precipitous union.

Fortunately we were with my stepfather only a year, for although an iniquitous and arbitrary royal law obliged us to remain under his guardianship, luck separated us. His regiment was sent to another city, and Mother refused to leave her home and her property in order to go with him. This separation lasted eight years: each year Escalada would spend only two or three months of his furlough in Puerto Príncipe, and during those times he behaved very well toward Mother and toward us. As a result we were happy! Although Mother had other children from her second marriage, her affection for us remained the same. She has always idolized Manuel in particular and loved me enough so that I have not the smallest complaint. I was given the most brilliant education possible in that country, was praised, spoiled, indulged even in my whims, and experienced not the slightest care in the pleasant dawn of my life.

Nevertheless, I was never carefree and reckless as children are wont to be. From my earliest years I showed an inclination for study and a tendency to be melancholy. I found no kindred spirits in the girls who were my age; only three, neighbors of mine, the daughters of an émigré from Santo Domingo, warranted my friendship. They were three pretty creatures with a clear natural intelligence. The oldest was two years older than I, and the littlest two years younger. But the latter was my favorite, for although the youngest, she seemed to me more sensible and circumspect than the others. The Carmona girls (this was their last name) readily approved of my wishes and shared in them. Our games consisted of acting out plays, making up stories, competing to see who could think up the best ones, playing charades, and having contests to see who could draw the best flowers and birds. We never participated in the noisy games of the other girls with whom we had contact.

Later, our dominant passion came to be reading novels, poetry, and plays. When we were already somewhat older, Mother would sometimes scold us for not taking greater care of our appearance or for avoiding society like wild creatures. But our greatest pleasure was to be shut up in the library, reading our favorite novels and weeping over the misfortunes of our imaginary heroes whom we adored.

In this way I turned thirteen. Happy days, never to return! . . . Cepeda! Tomorrow I'll continue to write. I am tired and this pen is dreadful; what will you do now? Sleep, perhaps! I hope so!

The twenty-fifth, in the morning

I imagine I won't be seeing you today, because according to your system I believe you are not planning to attend the opera I will be going to. I believe, however, that the reason you are not going cannot be that you are indisposed, as this thought would upset me greatly, leading me to think that it was caused by the impertinent demands I made on you last night to go to Cristina.[4] —— I shall continue my story and will try to be brief.

My family arranged my bethrothal to a local gentleman, a distant relative of ours. He was a man of good personal appearance and was reputed to be the best match in the country. When I was told that I was to be his wife, I saw nothing in that plan which was not advantageous for me. At that time I began to make my appearance at balls, strolls, and social gatherings, and my feminine vanity awakened. To marry the wealthiest bachelor in Puerto Príncipe, whom many women were after, to have a sumptuous house, magnificent carriages, rich finery, and so on was an idea that appealed to me very much. On the other hand, I knew nothing of love except what I gathered from the novels I read, and I convinced myself that naturally I was madly in love with my intended. As I had little contact with him and knew him hardly at all, I could freely choose the character I most wanted him to have. It goes without saying that I convinced myself that his was noble, great, generous, and sublime. My fertile imagination endowed him with ideal perfections, and in him I saw combined all the qualities of the heroes of my favorite novels: the valor of an Oroondates, the cleverness and passionate sensitivity of a Saint-Preux, the graces of a Lindor, and the virtues of a Grandison. I fell in love with this consummate being, whom I envisioned in the person of my betrothed. Unfortunately, my enchanted chimera was not of long duration; in spite of my preconceived notions, it did not take me long to find out that the man in question was great and kind only in my imagination, that his talents were very limited, his sensitivity very commonplace, his virtues very problematic. I began to grow sad and to consider my marriage from a less flattering point of view. About then my intended had to go to Havana, and his absence, which lasted ten months, gave me the advantage of being able to forget my bethrothal. As I didn't see my fiancé and he was almost never spoken of, I hardly remembered that he existed, and that only vaguely. At that moment friendship absorbed me completely. I made a new friend in a cousin who had been educated in a convent and was just coming out in society. She was an adorable creature; I, who cared for none of my other female cousins, was drawn to her from the first moment I saw her.

I have noticed in the course of my life that although every now and then my heart has been wrong, most often its first impulses have been instinctively excellent and felicitous. Rarely have I liked those people who displeased me on first sight, and often I have discerned in the abovementioned first impression the object of my future affection.

I liked my cousin right away, and she did not take long to gain a prominent place in my heart. Only Rosa Carmona came close, as I liked neither of the other two Carmona girls as well as I did her. When all of us were together, we talked about fashion, dances, novels, poetry, love, and friendship. When Rosa, my cousin, and I were alone, we usually spent our time on things that were more serious and on a higher plane of intelligence. Many times our conversations dealt with religion, death, and immortality. Rosa was very perceptive in what she said, and I always admired the precision of her reasoning. As for my cousin, she, like me, was a mixture of depth and frivolousness, of joy and sadness, of enthusiasm and dejection. Like me, she combined the weakness of a woman and the frivolity of a child with the elevation and profundity of emotions that are characteristic only of strong and virile natures. I have never found in anyone greater congeniality!

As we five girls were not unattractive and had a reputation for being talented, we were very soon the ladies of fashion in Puerto Príncipe. Our get-togethers, which took place in my house, were extremely brilliant given that setting: the cream of the youth of the opposite sex and the most outstanding young ladies met there. All strangers of note who came to Puerto Príncipe vied to be introduced into our group, and we were the center of attention at promenades and dances. We attracted the envy of the women but enjoyed the preference of the men, and this pleased us.

Then my fiancé returned, but I could not look at him without a kind of horror: stripped of the brilliant plumage of my illusions, he appeared to me a hateful and despicable man. My great defect is that I can never choose the middle ground but always tend to go to extremes. I despised my fiancé as much as I had previously thought I loved him. He could not appreciate the change in me because I had never shown him my affection. My illusions were born and perished there in the secret recesses of my heart because, as shy as I was passionate, back then I could not imagine how one could say *I love you* to a man without dying of shame. As I was not to marry until I was eighteen and was then but fifteen, and as my fiancé visited me very little, the marriage bothered me less than it should have. I looked on it as far off, enjoyed the present, and did not question the future.

Lola (the second of the Carmona girls) and my cousin fell in love almost at the same time, and this circumstance, which seemed so unproblematic to me, nevertheless had a profound influence: they loved and were loved fervently, and I was confidante to both of them. Then I underwent a sudden and puzzling change. I became unsociable and capricious. Amusements and study ceased to attract me: I avoided social gatherings and even my friends; I sought solitude in order to cry without knowing why and felt an abyss in my heart. I was no longer the person my two friends loved best: they took delight in another feeling which I did not know. I felt jealousy and envy! Thinking about that happiness which my imagination magnified even further, I invoked the person who could bestow this on me: the same person whom I created in the first dreams of my fervor! I thought I saw him in the Sun and the Moon, in the green of the fields and the blue of the sky: the nighttime breezes bore me his breath, the sounds of music the echo of his voice; I envisioned him in everything which was great and beautiful in Nature; I carried on as though I had a fever!

However, the situation was not devoid of attraction. I enjoyed weeping and hoped someday to realize the dreams of my heart.

Cepeda! How wrong I was! . . . Where is the man who can fulfill the desires of this sensitive nature which is as fiery as it is delicate? For nine years I have searched in vain! In vain! I have found men! Men who are all alike, to none of whom I could submit with respect and declare ardently: You are my God on this earth, and the absolute master of this passionate soul. For this reason my affections have been irresolute and short lived. I searched for a goodness I was unable to find and which perhaps does not even exist on earth. Now I no longer search for it nor desire it: for that reason I am more composed.

This afternoon or tomorrow I shall continue to write. Good-bye!

The twenty-fifth, in the afternoon

A young man I barely knew was introduced to our group. An old enmity, passed down from fathers to sons, divided the Loynaz and Arteaga families. The young man belonged to the former, and Mother to the latter; for that reason we had had no contact prior to that time. One of my male cousins was the first to breach the wall, becoming a friend of one of the Loynaz family members. The families, who in the beginning looked askance at that friendship, ended by ignoring it, and Loynaz, taking advantage of this, asked to visit me. Mother avoided the issue for a while, but my cousin insisted so strongly and I made such fun of that ancient and childish enmity that she finally gave in, and Loynaz was able to come to the house. He wasted no time in ingratiating himself with Mother and in becoming the most sought-after member of the group. Although he was very young, his talent was extraordinary, his appearance extremely handsome, and his manners attractive.

My engagement and the enmity between our families were two powerful reasons for him not to harbor any hopes concerning my person, but without assuming the role of suitor, he knew how to show me attention that flattered me. Our relationship was purely friendly, and the whole group considered it as such. As for me, I did not stop to examine the nature of my feelings: I read poetry with Loynaz, I sang duets on the piano with him, we did translations, and I had no time to think of anything except my joy at having acquired such a friend.

In the summer we went to the country, to a place not far from the city, and I took Rosa Carmona with me, who, from the time my cousin had a suitor, had become my best friend. Loynaz, my cousins, and many friends of both sexes often came to visit us. I spent delightful days there! Nonetheless, even then I felt reasons for unrest and worry. I was enchanted with Loynaz, but I was far from believing that he was the man my heart had chosen. I felt he had more talent than sensitivity, and in his character there was an undertone of superficiality that disturbed me. As a suitor he did not fit my dreams, but I saw him as a friend and had become accustomed to his presence. Rosa made me become apprehensive. She was determined to persuade me that our supposed friendship was no more than a disguised love, and because of this, more dangerous. She reminded me constantly of my engagement and sang praises of my betrothed which I had never heard her utter prior to this. Weighing the advantages of that marriage, she simultaneously cowed me into thinking that it was inevitable, because only by creating a scandal and making my family suffer could I break such a serious and long-standing commitment.

By dint of telling myself that I loved Loynaz, I was able to convince myself thereof; but as always I knew that he was not the one who could understand me, and he inspired in me neither esteem nor fervor. That love did not make me happy in the way I desired, and in place of the pride a heart that finds what it is searching for should feel, I felt the kind of humiliation caused when we allow ourselves to be drawn to a person unworthy of us.

We returned to the city in the month of September to attend my cousin's wedding; she was marrying the man she loved. As I said previously, her courtship and Lola Carmona's had begun at the same time, and they also married almost simultaneously, although in very different ways. The whole family approved of my cousin's choice; Lola, opposed by her family, married against their wishes and left immediately for Havana with her husband. Thus I found myself deprived of one of my friends.

I accompanied the newlyweds to the country, and when I returned a month later, I found an enormous change. Loynaz had been forbidden to call on me, and under the pretext of wanting to leave with her husband, my mother had arranged for the date of my wedding to be within three months, whereas previously it was to have been when I turned eighteen. The bridegroom agreed to everything: he neither loved me (just as I had always thought) nor hated me. He wanted to settle down with a girl of his family who was innocent and to some degree pretty. My grandfather had told him that I was the one he was looking for and that he would leave me his entire fifth[5] (certainly no paltry amount) if I married him. This was what had convinced and motivated him.

When I arrived and found out about these new events, I was crushed, not knowing why they had occurred. But it did not take me long to find out and to suffer the first and most terrible of my disillusionments.

It is late, Cepeda; I shall continue later.

At one at night

I saw Curro[6] at the theatre but not you, but then I didn't expect to. But are you going to continue this sort of life? It can't be, it simply can't, that a distaste for society induces you to this kind of misanthropy. One has to have suffered greatly, been a victim of society in order to despise it to that degree. You, who have no real motives to complain, you can know its vices and injustices and not give in to it with the imprudence of inexperience and naiveté; but it is not possible that without overpowering reasons you avoid society this stubbornly at the age of twenty-three. If not society, the music itself might attract you to the opera. I, who have undoubtedly suffered more real cares than any you might have, who knows the world and Society at least as well as you do, do not feel this misanthropy; and although I do not regard either society or the world through the enchanted glass of illusions, I still know that I have need of both: why is it, then, that you enjoy my trust yet deny me yours? You call yourself my friend and dissemble with me! Listen. I don't ask you to tell me your secrets; no, I respect them; but ask God if I have not guessed them.

If the idea which has pursued me since last night is not a figment of my imagination; if the seclusion, in which you live, has the motive I suspect . . . I will always be your friend, but I will know that you are not mine. Furthermore: I will know that you are capable of deceit and minor falsehoods, I will know that you have not understood me, and . . . I don't know! I will see in you *a man* like all others. Since last night, you have fallen so much in my estimation that . . . (why should I not say it clearly?) that I am almost afraid I will have to add your name to the list of my disillusions. If this were the case, I would lose, lose an illusion, a last illusion that has brightened a few of my days, but you would lose even more: yes, you would. For where will you find another friend like me? You have no idea, you can't possibly know how pure, how selfless, how tender the affection is that you inspire in me. But where will this lead me? I'm contradicting myself! —— No, dear Cepeda, you will never lose my friendship as long as it means something to you, but I beg you in the name of Heaven and the sincerity of my soul, I entreat you that if this friendship destroys interests which are dearer to your heart, that if you are afraid it would result in jealousy and cause unpleasantness to a beloved person, don't use pretexts to avoid them. Listen. Our friendship is too pure and noble to have to endure the shadows of mystery; I certainly can't bear that, but if the manifestation [of the friendship] might offend love, love comes first:

friendship will have to be sacrificed, and so it shall be, for I will demand it. My heart will not change because of this, and Cepeda will always have a special place therein.

Tomorrow I will continue my story and perhaps finish it; but you will not have it that soon, for tomorrow we will not see each other. We must avoid such frequent contact because your company would make me dislike any other, and I don't want to reduce but rather enhance the realm of my pleasures as much as possible. Good-bye, until tomorrow, I mean [whenever it's] tomorrow for this letter, for I repeat that I will try, even if I absolutely need your company, to spend as many days as I can without seeing you.

The twenty-sixth, in the morning

Loynaz's being sent away and the proximity of my wedding were for me two blows which were as painful as they were unexpected: but you should have seen how I felt when I found out by whose hand they had been inflicted on me! . . . Rosa, my friend, my confidante Rosa had convinced my mother that a love relationship existed between Loynaz and me—that he was urging me to break my engagement—and, knowing better than anyone else the purity of my feelings and the rectitude of my intentions, was sufficiently evil to pretend that she was terrified that I, carried away by the passion she supposed I felt, would take some foolish and irremediable step. She was completely successful in achieving her purpose! Cepeda! And that girl was only fifteen! What can she have become afterward!

I had no knowledge either of the world or of men: I was as innocent and inexperienced as the day I was born; I had thought that Rosa loved me and that her heart would be incapable of treachery. The knowledge of that first deception was for me a mortal blow which fell squarely on my soul.

But just observe my naiveté and ingenuousness! Rosa was able to convince me that only my best interests and the tenderness of friendship had made her take this step, and she swore to me that her intentions were the purest and most selfless. I believed and forgave her!

Loynaz wrote to me and for the first time failed to use the term "friendship" for the feeling I inspired in him. He told how Mother had forbidden him to keep on visiting me and complained of a snub he did not deserve. "I do not disregard," he told me, "the commitments your family has made on your behalf, and you know better than anyone how scrupulously I have respected these, but since my conduct has not been properly appreciated, I do not wish to intrude where I am no longer wanted: I want you to know that I love you and am ready for anything if I find you feel the same way."

It seemed to me that his letter contained more pride than love, but I was moved nevertheless. Had I been able to see the young man, I never would have loved him, because his very evident frivolousness was a happily placed antidote to whatever sweet sentiments he might have aroused in me: but when I couldn't see him, when I thought him unjustly snubbed and unhappy on my account, my feelings for him took on an intensity they probably would never have had otherwise. Nevertheless, I had enough sense to control myself and in my answer told him that I was resolved to sacrifice myself to please the family by marrying a man I detested. "I am not unmoved by your affection," I told him at the end, "but I plan to respect my promises, and I beg you not to write me again."

He paid no attention to this request: he wrote me twice more, very passionate letters asking me to break a resolution which was making him and me equally unhappy, but I didn't answer him and he stopped writing.

In spite of my very sensible conduct and the resignation with which I was willing to enter into an abhorred marriage, I suffered, mostly because of my family. Mother was and is an angel of goodness, but her great defect is a character that is so weak that it becomes the plaything of the people she is with. My aunt and uncle induced her to treat me with severity and were constantly turning her against me, hatefully interpreting my smallest acts. And do you think my relatives sincerely wanted my marriage to take place? Nothing of the sort; they pretended they did but would have given anything to prevent the wedding in question. In the first place, they resented the advantages my grandfather was disposed to bestow on me; secondly, they wanted my fiancé for their daughter, and perhaps in using such unwarranted severity with me, they had no other motive than to make me rush into some reckless act which would aid their secret intentions. They certainly achieved this!

I was on the eve of my wedding; house, dowry, certificate of dispensation—all was ready. But there came a moment when I lacked the strength to go through with the sacrifice, one of those moments when one acts without thinking. I secretly left my house and sought refuge with my grandfather, who lived in a villa near the city. Disconsolate, I threw myself at his feet and told him that I would kill myself before I would marry the man they had chosen for me.

That break produced a huge uproar: my entire family pronounced itself totally surprised and indignant at my decision; my aunt and uncle, who were inwardly rejoicing, were the first to declare themselves against me. Only my grandfather showed me goodness and indulgence, although no one was sadder than he at the breaking off of a marriage he had arranged. I suffered so much! I was aware that public opinion condemned me. To have spurned such an advantageous match! To have the impudence to break such a serious, long-standing, time-honored promise! To inflict a mortal blow on my family! This seemed unpardonable: naturally it was said that I had a bad streak, that my cleverness was ruining me, that what I was doing then was a good indication of what I would do in the future, and how sorry my mother was going to be for the extravagant education she had given me. Then my stepfather came to Puerto Príncipe, and the cup of my tribulations ran over.

I am always pursued by a kind of fatality which causes ill-fated circumstances and [bad] luck to make my indiscretions seem much more serious; I say indiscretions, although I certainly think it was more than that to have broken off an engagement of which my heart disapproved.

Circumstances entirely beyond my control brought on quarrels between my grandfather and my stepfather. These became so serious that my grandfather moved out of the house, where he usually stayed when he was not in the country, and went to live in one which belonged to my aunt and uncle. The people who knew about my marriage being called off, but not about the later quarrels which broke out between Escalada and my grandfather, wasted no time in saying that my grandfather had moved out because he was so terribly disappointed in me. My uncle and my girl cousins, who had always looked with envy and apprehension on the preference which my grandfather felt for my mother and me, took advantage of his presence in their house to undermine this preference and make him believe that I was undeserving. I was portrayed as an inconstant and capricious harum-scarum; they maintained that Mother was ruining me with her excessive indulgence and the freedom with which she allowed me to follow my extravagant and dangerous inclinations; in short, they wasted no opportunity to rail against my mother and me to the paralyzed old man who, lacking physical and moral strength, was pliant wax on which they could stamp their impressions. They achieved their goal! My grandfather died three months after the marriage was called off, and a will appeared which annulled the one he had made benefiting my mother and me, leaving his third and his fifth to my Uncle Manuel, in whose house he died.

My stepfather, to evade the guilt of being the cause of this change of heart and of the injury done Mother, announced that because of the vexation caused him by my calling off the marriage, my grandfather had left our house and had changed his will in my uncle's favor, [thus] casting the blame on me when it was all his own fault. My uncle and my cousins (who could not pardon my having any merit at all even after they had deprived me of my grandfather's affection) maintained that the mortal blow I had dealt the old man had brought on his death: in short, everyone said that my foolishness in breaking off the marriage had deprived Mother of Grandfather's third and me of his fifth.

I had a soul which was above material interests of this kind, and God knows that of the tears which I shed not one went to mourn the loss of that greedily sought-after inheritance! But my heart was broken by the injustices of which I was the target. I was totally convinced that my grandfather had not left our house because I had called off the marriage: I knew very well how much kindness and affection I had found in him after that so-called rashness they claimed had made him so angry. I felt not the least reproach for being the cause of his death, but nevertheless I was tormented by grief and repentance. How many times did I shed tears of bitterness and ask God to end my life, a life I had not asked Him for and for which I could not be grateful! How often did I envy the good fortune of those women who neither feel nor think; who eat, sleep, vegetate, and whom the world often calls sensible women! Overwhelmed by the sense of my superiority, I began to suspect that which later I have come to know very well: that I have not been born to be happy, that my life on earth will be short and tempestuous.

There was only one last straw to add to the full measure of my cares, and Fate did not deny me. I found out, with no room for doubt, that Rosa Carmona and Loynaz were in love. Only then did I understand the motives of that perfidious woman's previous conduct, and in my heart the despicable betrayal of a friendship gave way to profound contempt.

These, oh Cepeda, were the first lessons the world taught me! This is what I found when innocent, pure, trusting I sought love, friendship, virtue, and pleasures: inconstancy! treachery! sordid material interest! envy! crimes, crimes, and nothing else. Am I to blame for not loving [the world]? Can I have any illusions? . . . But I live as though I had them, because the world, my friend, takes cruel vengeance on those who scorn it. One must feign life even when bearing death in one's heart.

Cepeda! Dear Cepeda! Is it true that, just as I, you feel how little the world and its corrupt pleasures are worth? Won't you be yet another disappointment for me? Who can assure me that you are no hypocrite? Who guarantees your sincerity? . . . Cepeda! Cepeda! If you are not first among men, then you must be last, and . . . I confess my mind vacillates between those two extremes. But you see how my imprudence carries me away: this notebook is an example thereof. Perhaps someday I will be sorry that I wrote it. What does it matter! It will be one more disillusion, but it will be the last.

In the afternoon

My only friend now was my cousin Angelita; like me she was unhappy, and like me wept because of a disillusion. Her husband, that tender suitor, had changed into a tyrant. How that poor victim suffered! And with what heroic virtue! My affection for her became fervor; my aversion to marriage was born and grew rapidly. I saw no one save my cousin, and that sedentary, unhappy, and contemplative life-style affected my health. I became so thin and ill that my worried mother took me to the country. There I spent three months in solitude: physical solitude and solitude of the heart! I grew no better and we returned to the city. That time in my life was unhappy, very unhappy! It still hurts me to remember it. I hoped to die soon, but I had moments where the progression of my illness seemed too slow to me, and I felt the temptation to accelerate the end result myself. My religious principles and the deep affection I felt toward Mother and my brother stifled this impulse.

My stepfather's health was also broken, and he attributed it to the climate. He convinced himself that he would die if he did not return to Spain, and as he did not despise life the way I did, he was determined to do so. This plan countered my despondency; I looked forward to another sky, another land, another life: I loved Spain and was drawn to her with all my heart. Disappointed in my maternal family, I longed to know my father's, to see his native land and to breathe the air of his youth. I therefore became determined to convince Mother to settle in the Old World. Escalada, for his part, used all of his influence in order to convince her, pointing out a thousand advantages in the move. But Mother, influenced by her relatives, resisted.

In spite of this Escalada went to Puerto Príncipe and began to sell property and slaves and to transfer all possible cash to French banks. Then, thinking that it would be easier to convince Mother if he took her away from her home and her family, he proposed to spend some time in Santiago de Cuba, where his regiment was stationed. We all supported his efforts and were successful.

Painful, far more painful than I had thought, was the separation from my home and my cousin, but when I got to Santiago all sorts of new distractions gave me new life.

Santiago is a city more or less like Puerto Príncipe, but uglier and less orderly. But its gorgeous sky, its picturesque and magnificent environs, its busy port, and the culture and pleasant nature of its inhabitants make it quite superior in some ways. I had such a kind welcome in that city that within two months of being there, I was no longer a stranger. Never has a woman's vanity had so many reasons to feel pleased with itself. I was appreciated and entertained everywhere and will never be able to forget the kindnesses I owe the inhabitants of Santiago. Once again I was able to take pleasure in study and society.

I wrote some verses which were enthusiastically received; I gave myself over to amusements in which I was sought after and heaped with compliments. You might well suppose that I had no lack of admirers; I feel some pride in saying that the most distinguished young men in the country vied for my favors. Not one, however, had exclusive rights. At a ball my favorite would be the best dancer, during a promenade the one who sat his horse most elegantly, at a gathering the one whose conversation was the most amusing and varied. I had no illusions of love in Santiago and as a result left with no disappointments. Perhaps that's why I'm so fond of it.

Loynaz arrived in Santiago four months after we did and attempted to renew his suit. He apologized for his flirtation with Rosa saying that somehow she had gotten him into it and vowed both that I was his first and only love and that the only reason for his trip was to gain my forgiveness and to make up. I didn't say no to one or the other; I forgave him and offered him my friendship but was inflexible on the subject of love. Before he returned to Puerto Príncipe, he asked for my promise to keep writing to him, and as he promised that his letters would be merely friendly, I acquiesced to his demand. Indeed, both of us continued the abovementioned correspondence until his death, which occurred halfway through the year 1837, when he turned twenty-five and I was already in Spain.

My stepfather knew very well how to exercise his influence over Mother, and I backed him to such a degree that we finally convinced her to come to Spain. —— On the ninth of April, 1836, we boarded a French frigate to Bordeaux and, sorrowful and teary, ungratefully left behind that beloved land we perhaps may never see again.

Forgive me! My tears are staining the paper; I am unable to recall without being moved that memorable night when I saw Cuba for the last time.

The voyage was for me a source of new emotions. —— "When we sail on the blue seas," Lord Byron has said, "our thoughts are as free as the Ocean." —— His sublime and poetic soul must have felt thus: mine felt so as well. Nights in the tropics are beautiful, and I enjoyed them, but nights at sea are more beautiful. There is an indefinable enchantment in the stirring of the breeze as it fills the lightly quivering sails, in the pale brilliance of the moon, reflected in the water, in the immensity of what we see above and below us. It seems that God reveals Himself better to the receptive soul in the midst of those two infinite elements—sky and sea!—and that a mysterious voice makes itself heard in the sound of wind and waves. Had I been an atheist, I would then have stopped being one. We also had some storms, and with Heredia[7] I can say:

When the furious hurricane hurled itself down,
When over my head the lightning crashed,
I trembled with joy. . . .

At last, after good weather and bad and all the ensuing impressions of a long voyage, on the first of June we jubilantly greeted the pleasant coast of France.

The days I spent in Bordeaux now seem like a lovely dream. My soul unfolded in that land of reason and enlightenment. I neither loved nor suffered, I hardly know if I thought. I was charmed and my heart and eyes were not able to take it all in. We had to leave that captivating city, and I could not do it without shedding tears.

I was unable to find anything agreeable in Galicia, and coming from one of the principal cities of France, La Coruña seemed even worse to me than it really is, because today I think it is one of the most attractive cities in Spain. But I found the Galician character unpleasant, and the climate disagreed with me. Nevertheless, I might have been able to get used to it and then the negative first impression I had felt on arrival might have dissipated, had not unexpected reasons caused me real and indisputable problems. Good-bye, until later.

At night

Up to that time, my stepfather had behaved well toward us; now he showed his true face. He was in his country and with his family, while we had left everything behind. His mean spirit made bad use of this advantage.

I will not burden you with vexing details of our domestic situation; let it suffice for you to know that in secret I ruminated upon all kinds of burdens and humiliations. Mother was very unhappy, and I lacked the strength to take on her cares, although I steadfastly bore my own. My stepfather put Manuel in such a difficult situation that he was obliged to leave Galicia. Oh, I could go on forever were I to enumerate in detail all the absurd, tyrannical, and base actions of that man, whom I still ought and wish to respect as my mother's husband. God knows this and someday will judge us both.

In that disagreeable domestic situation I met Ricafort and was loved by him: I, too, loved him from the first day I met him. There can be few hearts as beautiful as his: noble, sensitive, unmaterialistic, full of honor and gentleness. His intelligence did not measure up to his heart: to my dismay it was quite inferior. I found out about this disadvantage very quickly: although generous, Ricafort seemed humiliated by the superiority which he attributed to me; his ideas and inclinations were always at odds with mine. He did not like my fondness for study, and for him it was a crime that I wrote poetry. My ideas about many things caused him grief and worry. He was terrified of public opinion and told me many times: "What do you expect to gain when you achieve literary fame and a reputation for talent? You will attract envy and provoke criticism and gossip." He was right, but that cold logic chilled me.

Although he had the highest and most favorable regard for my heart, he did not hide the fact that my character displeased him and used to repeat that this character of mine would make both him and me unhappy. I made an effort to control it and stifle my inclinations in order to please him, but this continuous repression affected my spirits, and when he saw it he convinced himself that he could never make me happy. In spite of this we were more in love every day.

My troubles at home came to affect me so much that I needed to unburden myself and told him about them. I shall never forget that moment! I saw his eyes brim with tears! Then, with a tone that falseness could never achieve, he implored me to accept his heart and his hand and to give him the right to protect and avenge me.

I vacillated for many days; my horror at the idea of marriage was very great, but in the end I gave in: my situation at home was so unbearable; my helplessnes, his love and mine, everything conspired to convince me; and when I told him that I agreed to be his wife, I resolved to dedicate my life to make his happy and to sacrifice my own the moment I could no longer meet this objective. Talent, pleasures, nothing mattered to me any longer; I only wished to fulfil those grave obligations I was promising to take on and to do everything in my power to lighten the chains which these imposed on Ricafort. Oh God! Why couldn't I do it? . . . You know if my promises were pure and sincere! Why didn't You hear them? I will not say that I would have loved Ricafort forever (who can answer for one's heart?), but I am sure I would always have respected him, and I would never have made him rue the day that he bound himself to my fate, because even though I am not responsible for my feelings, I can at least be responsible for my actions. But none of this was to be: the unfortunate weakness of my character was to ruin everything.

Our union could not take place right away. He was proud and so was I: neither one of us wanted to be dependent on our families for even a single day, and thanks to my stepfather my property was all tied up, while Ricafort had only an irregularly paid salary. I made some reasonable proposals to my stepfather, who would not hear of them! I went to court to ask that they declare me of age, explaining my exceptional circumstances, but before any decision was reached, Ricafort Senior was deposed and his son received orders to join his regiment. I spoke frankly to the General: I knew his character and openness and had no doubts that I would find a father in him, but I was too proud to come into his family like a beggar and resolved not to marry until my property was cleared up and I could tell Ricafort of what it consisted and the greater or lesser security this implied.

In any event, after many vacillations and painful scenes, Ricafort went on his way. This separation was very, very painful, even though I was far from thinking it was forever; but after the first months went by I thought hard about the differences which existed between Ricafort and myself and asked myself if that superiority which he attributed to me would not sooner or later produce a rift, and reflecting on the disadvantages of marriage and the advantages of freedom, I congratulated myself on still being free. About that time my brother came to Coruña . . . and now I will need your indulgence, dear Cepeda, because I am still ashamed of my fickleness. My brother came and disapproved of the relationship. He described the sad lot of the soldier in today's times: he told me enthusiastically of a trip to Andalusia he wanted us to take together to meet our father's family (on whom he heaped praises which today I know are undeserved) and how happy I would be when I was of age, able to enjoy a comfortable and independent life and able to do what I liked; above all he told me, and this is what made the greatest impression on me, that if I married Ricafort he and I would have to separate, perhaps forever. What can I tell you to justify my actions? . . . nothing, nothing is enough. I was weak and inconstant. I left with my brother for Lisbon: I never heard anything from Ricafort again.

Except for the pain of leaving Mother, I can say that I departed from Galicia with pleasure. There were precious few people there who deserved any of my affection, and I knew that I had many enemies: among these were all of Escalada's relatives. Thank God they could not hurt my honor no matter how hard they tried, but in another guise they inflicted a thousand pinpricks on my reputation. They said I was an atheist, and the proof they gave of that was that I read Rousseau's works and they had seen me eat [something] with butter one Friday. They said I was the cause of all the problems Mother had had with her husband and I was the one who advised her not to please him. The education which young ladies receive in Cuba is so different from that in Galicia that a woman of my country, even one of the middle class, would think it degrading to perform some duties which in Galicia even the most socially prominent women look on as an obligation of their sex. My stepfather's female relatives therefore maintained that I was good for nothing because I didn't know how to iron or cook or knit socks; because I didn't wash dishes nor make beds nor sweep my room. According to them, I needed twenty maids and assumed the airs of a princess. They also made fun of my love of study and called me *la Doctora*. One of Escalada's sisters boxed a housemaid's ears, because when she questioned her about me—in a house where the sister had spoken so *brilliantly* of me—the poor woman committed the folly of saying that I was an angel and that, far from being imperious or demanding in the household, all the maids were fond of me for my agreeable ways.

You can imagine how little I would mind leaving that place. [I don't think] I could ever go back willingly, especially if I had the bad luck to have my family return there as well.[8]

After I had broken my engagement and found myself free, though no happier, convinced that I should never marry and that love caused more grief than pleasure, I proposed to adopt a plan I had been thinking about for some time. I wanted pride to take the place of feeling, and it seemed preferable to me to be agreeable to many rather than be loved by only one: all the more so when this one would never be a person who could meet my expectations. I had lost hope of finding a man my heart desired. I no longer looked for either love or friendship: I wanted ephemeral, superficial liaisons that would keep me from boredom without arousing my feelings. In any case, I could not find even such distractions no matter how I tried. Separated for the first time from Mother, with no hope of seeing Ricafort again (whom I still loved), feeling more than ever the emptiness of my soul, disappointed in a world that did not fulfill my dreams, disappointed in myself for my inability to be happy, it was totally in vain for me to even try to become distracted or have to stifle within me the fertile source of emotion and grief.

I had another disappointment besides, and not one of the least painful. I loved my brother very much: with him I had shown such selflessness that others chided me for it; with him I had always been affectionate, obliging, and gentle. When I was alone with him in the world, I expected that his conduct toward me would match mine toward him. I soon learned better! I found out that a man always takes advantage of defenseless goodness and that there are few souls great and gentle enough not to want to oppress when they know themselves to be the stronger.

I would have liked to have altered my nature. I thought that I would only be less unhappy when I succeeded in not loving anyone very fervently, distrusting everybody, scorning everything, burying all manner of illusions, controlling all events by having foreseen what would happen, and taking all the good things life had to offer me without, however, giving them great importance. I was already embarrassed by a sensitivity that perennially made me the victim.

I have been working on realizing my goal for a year; I don't know if it's wasted effort. During this time I have twice had fleeting relationships, so fleeting that one did not last two weeks. They did not come from my heart; it was only my head, the need for amusement, the example of the society in which I lived: nothing more. They were more social commitments than love.

I soon got tired of this and broke off those bland semiloves with as much frivolousness as I had begun them. I won't even tell you about my Uncle Felipe's plan to marry me off to one of the landowning sons of Constantina,[9] or of how my brother, who was so opposed to my marrying, all of a sudden became my suitor's supporter. This does not merit further details, for the plan in question in no way influenced either my heart or my future. But I should explain more fully the story of a recently concluded relationship, which you know about. It is important not to hide anything, for you should know my reasons for entering into it and for breaking it off. My reasons for entering into it! I will be embarrassed to tell them—but that's not important. My openness demands that I tell them; your scrupulousness will order you to forget them as soon as you have finished reading this.

Good-bye, I need a moment to rest. Besides, it's ten o'clock and I'm going to get dressed to fetch Concha and go to the Plaza Duque. I hope that by going this late I won't meet you at Concha's house.

At one at night

I indeed did not find you and learned that you had not been there. Thank you so much! Now I know that there really is an enormous affinity between the two of us. I can see that we have reached a decision at exactly the same time. Yes, we must, we absolutely must see each other less frequently. Otherwise we would become ever more unsociable and strange. Consequently, I am telling you that I will avoid you scrupulously. Both of us are too unhappy and disillusioned to want to be even more so. You must seek out more cheerful society, and so must I. But do not look for a sincere soul: that is a title I claim for myself, do you understand? In short, I have decided to break my resolution. Yes, I am offering you *my friendship*. But understand that I can be your friend without seeing you every day, or even at all; and that you shall be my friend, my *only friend,* but I do not wish—nor should you—to have you be my escort or accompany me to social gatherings. I'll finish this tomorrow: I don't know when I'll give it to you. Good night, I have a terrible headache.

Today, the twenty-seventh, in the afternoon

At the same time Méndez Vigo began to court me, *someone else* [10] paid me some attention. This *someone* pleased me more than I wanted. I felt drawn to him by a strange, capricious force, and I trembled at the thought of still being able to love, all the more so when, believing there to be an enormous difference between the personality and inclination of the abovementioned person and myself, I foresaw a new disillusionment in a new love. Nonetheless, my heart instinctively seemed to tell me that the time had come when I should put my former inconstancies behind me, and without knowing why I felt myself overwhelmed.

I know how much stronger an inclination can become when opposed, and I had no wish to fight mine; but I also did not want to give in to it completely, because I feared that in this way it would become overpowering. It was thus necessary to fight emotion with pride and find some amusement to distract the excessively keen interest which I felt.

Cepeda! I am holding nothing back to be frank: for Heaven's sake don't judge me harshly.

The man in whom I was interested avoided me, and the one I did not care for redoubled his courtesies and assiduousness. Because of his influence over my heart, the first caused me great turmoil and stung me with his indecision; the second flattered and amused me with his juvenile devotion and did not seem a bit dangerous.

I did what appeared more advisable to my peace of mind and what I supposed would have lesser consequences. I accepted the affections of one and attempted to suppress those which the *other* inspired in me. Now everything is out in the open! Now forget it.

I will not pretend that I failed to be moved by the candor, the enthusiastic love, and the many fine qualities I discovered in my young suitor. Poor boy! How he did love me! Why was this capricious heart unable to return his affection in a worthy manner? . . . I don't know!

He inspired in me an affection without illusions, without warmth, an undefinable affection that sometimes seemed to me similar to what a mother must feel for her child—don't laugh at the comparison. Why had this young man failed to make me feel another kind of love? I couldn't tell you, because on my oath I have no idea. As you know, he is not badlooking, nor stupid, and I can even say that there were certain points of compatibility in our ways of feeling, but he loved me the way I would love, were I to find the man of my dreams. But he was not that man. I tried in vain, and by telling him I loved him I tried to convince myself that I did; inside I reproached myself in vain for being capricious and thankless: in vain! I will confess to you what I didn't want to confess to myself at that moment: when I was with that young man I felt moments of unbearable boredom, and his most passionate words left my heart cold and at times made me feel indescribable tedium.

This was an inexplicable caprice of the heart, because I cared for him! God knows! I repeat that I cared for him, but I cannot, without proving my inner conviction false, say that I loved him. I cannot explain this difference, but I understand it perfectly.

He was too much in love to limit his wishes to a simple relationship, doubtless of short duration. He wanted to wrest from me the promise to be his wife, and I absolutely refused. I made my aversion to marriage clear to him and did not hide from him that my love was not of such a nature as would inspire in me the desire to be his. He called me a strange woman, cold, heartless. The tears! The tears! The recriminations!

I would have broken off with him had compassion not moved me to wait so that he could get over this amorous exaltation which possessed him, as I had no doubt he would. I saw him suffer so much that I was moved, and just as one promises the moon to the child who is crying because he wants it, I promised that someday I would be his.

Some silly thing caused him to get in Mother's bad graces, and she treated him with such disdain and even rudeness that I, feeling offended, forbade him for his own good to come to the house for a few days, so that Mother might calm down and I could make her understand how rude she had been with him for such a childish reason. The poor boy thought that now he would never see me again; I have no idea what went on in his head. What is certain is that he did a thousand foolish and irreparable things. After a couple of days of fretting and mortal anxiety, which even my tenderest letters could not assuage, he committed the rashness of speaking to his father and of writing to my brother, explaining the desire and the firm intention he had of marrying me, without prior consultation as to what my wishes might be, probably because he was unsure of them.

Questioned by my family, I of course declared very seriously that I was not considering marriage of any kind, and my brother wrote as much to Méndez Vigo.

Then all hell broke loose! I will not burden you with unpleasant details. I think the poor boy became unhinged, for among the many foolish things he said and did, he wrote me a letter (which I still have, as I do almost all his others) in which he vowed to me that he would shoot himself if I did not marry him within three months.

I was afraid he was capable of anything, all the more so when I found out (Bravo knows it, too[11]) that he was weeping like a madman in the cafés and on the streets. I felt great sympathy for his plight, I wrote him letters full of tenderness and promised that sometime later on I would be his.

But nothing was enough: I don't know what evil spirit had come to possess that poor young man. His friends know to what degree his reason on occasion wandered.

Perhaps I might have been moved to marry him out of pity (in spite of the fact that such a weak character and fragile mind have never caused me to feel esteem or confidence), had family pride not absolutely kept me from doing so.

The father of this young man who, as I understand, owed his son the considerable dowry his first wife had brought him (and who doubtless did not want to part with it, as he would have to if his son married) said that he would not agree to the marriage any sooner than three years, for he [Méndez Vigo] was still very young to enter into such a serious commitment. As a result of this declaration, he refused to come and ask for my hand, as it appears his son wanted him to do, and he threatened his father that he would go to the provincial governor to ask for the permission his father was denying him. You can imagine my indignation at the first bit of this to reach my ears! I became more distraught and broke completely with this rash young man, writing his father a letter in which I declared that I had never had any intention of marrying his son, with his permission or without it. Consequently he ought to look upon all the things his son had done with respect to this matter as a young man's folly, and I advised and implored him to send his son on a trip to distract him.

Few people in Seville know these details, but many have been aware of Antonio's desperation and of the reproaches he hurled at me in his over-wrought state. It seems to be my fate that appearances always incriminate me and that I am judged without an understanding of my motives. I know that I am criticized for having toyed with this young man's feelings and labeled as being inconstant and flirtatious. You already know my trans-gression: I have committed no other but that of beginning a relationship (as everyone does in Seville) that I supposed would be nothing serious and have no repercussions of any kind: this is the extent of my fault, and God knows how sorry I have been for it! If after all was said and done I could not resolve to sacrifice my freedom and my scruples by marrying him without the official approval of his father, I certainly don't deserve to be criticized for that, and in my opinion it would have been most despi-cable had I acted any other way. If passion could not induce me to com-promise my decorum and force my way into a family, how much less would I do it out of pity!

Antonio finally departed, and I breathed a sigh of relief: I felt I was seeing the sun again after a long term of imprisonment, or had thrown off a weight borne for eons.

I confess it: I was tired of love. That delirious and frenetic love, which I had not shared, made me weary.

For this reason I focused more than ever on my plan of never falling in love. I have sworn never to marry, never to fall in love; and now I even propose to renounce any involvement as well, even the most superficial and transient. —— One month after Méndez Vigo's departure you re-turned from Almonte.

My story is at an end! Earlier I thought of not writing it except during your absence, for I wanted to start to exchange letters with you; but later I changed my mind because I don't think we even ought to begin the abovementioned correspondence.[12]

There is no more for me to tell, dear Cepeda; now remember my conditions. —— This [document] will be reduced to ashes as soon as it has been read, and only you in the whole world will know that it ever existed.

Farewell: I don't know when we will see each other and I can give you this little notebook.

Perhaps because of it I will lessen the esteem with which you favor me and undermine your friendship: no matter! Should I be sorry to have given you the weapons to combat a friendship that would perhaps be better for both if it ceased to exist? I will always be your *friend* even when there is no *friendship* between us. What I mean is that I will always esteem you even should I stop expressing [this feeling] to you.

Farewell, my dear: shake off that melancholy which troubles me. Believe me: to be happy, moderate the loftiness of your soul and try to adjust your existence to the society in which you must live.

When injustice and ignorance pass you by and trouble you, then say to yourself: There is one being on this earth who understands and esteems me.

Yes, I do think I understand and esteem you. What if I am wrong? if you were other than the one I believe you to be? . . . It would be but one disappointment more—and what does one more matter to the woman who has suffered so many?

[here follows Avellaneda's signature]

P.S. I have read this over, and I am almost tempted to burn it. Aside from being poorly organized, badly written, and so on, should I give it to you? I don't know: perhaps not. Before God and men, I certainly have nothing to be sorry for. My soul and my conduct have been equally pure. But so many vacillations, so many foolish acts, so much inconstancy—will they not produce a very unfavorable opinion of my heart and my character in the one to whom I am confessing them?

Should I perhaps not be exposing the defects of the people who are close to me, as I have done? . . . Certainly not, Cepeda; I should not. To convince me to give you this notebook, I have to esteem you so much, so much that I believe you to be not a man but a superior being.

Therefore I don't know what to do: I will put it away and will follow the impulse of my heart—to give it or to burn it—when next I see you.

[Avellaneda's signature]

Sab

An Original Novel
By Señorita Doña Gertrudis Gómez de Avellaneda

Dedicated by its Author
to her Honorable Friend
Señor Don Alberto Lista

Translated by Nina M. Scott

A Word to the Reader

These pages were written for amusement during moments of leisure and of melancholy: at that time the author had no intention of exposing them to the public's unforgiving eye.

For three years this little novel has slept almost forgotten in the bottom of her writing case. It was subsequently read by a few intelligent persons who have judged it kindly, and as many friends of the author expressed an interest in possessing a copy thereof, she made up her mind to have it published, believing herself excused from having to make a formal statement of the idea, the organization, and the purpose of the work by stating that she is publishing it without any sort of pretensions.

If this little novel were written today, the author, whose ideas are now somewhat different, might perhaps make some changes therein. But whether out of laziness or our unwillingness to alter something we wrote with real conviction (even when the latter might vacillate to some degree), the author has made no changes in her original drafts, and hopes that if judicious persons find some mistakes scattered among these pages, they will not forget that the latter were composed by the at times exaggerated but always generous sentiments of early youth.

Chapter One

Who are you? What is your homeland? . . .
The tyrannical influences
of my guiding star formed me
into a monster of such rare quality
that while I am of heroic lineage
in the endowments of my soul,
I am also the scorn of the world.

—Cañizares

——— • ———

Twenty years ago, or thereabouts, late on a June afternoon a young man of handsome bearing journeyed on horseback through the picturesque country watered by the Tínima River and in leisurely fashion guided his spirited sorrel along the path known in these parts as the Cubitas Road, leading as it did to the villages of this name, which were also known as the red lands. The young man in question was four leagues from Cubitas, from whence he appeared to have come, and three from the city of Puerto Príncipe, at that time the capital of the central province of Cuba, though only a few years earlier it had been but a humble township.

Perhaps because of his scant knowledge of the road, perhaps because of the pleasure he took in appraising the landscape before him, the traveler gradually slackened his pace and from time to time reined in his horse as through to scrutinize the places through which he passed. Quite possibly his repeated stops had as their sole object the fuller savoring of the richly fertile earth of that privileged country, which most likely attracted him all the more if—as his fair, rosy skin, blue eyes, and golden hair seemed to indicate—he had been born in some northern region.

The brutal sun of the torrid zone was sinking into dusk among undulating clouds of purple and silver, and its last rays, already feeble and pale, bathed the virgin fields of that youthful nature in melancholy hues. It was a landscape whose vigorous and luxuriant vegetation seemed eagerly to welcome the afternoon's balmy breezes which began to flutter through the leafy crowns of the trees, parched by the day's heat. Flocks of swallows crossed and recrossed in all directions in search of their night's refuge; the green parrot, banded with gold and scarlet, the crow, distinctly black and lustrous, the royal woodpecker, of iron tongue and muted plumage, the blithe macaw, the swift *tomeguín,* the iridescent butterfly, and a whole host of native birds alighted in the branches of tamarind and aromatic mango trees, ruffling their variegated feathers as though to imprison therein the comforting breath of the gentle breeze.

After having crossed immense savannas where the eye encounters but the dual horizon of earth and sky, and pasturelands crowned by palms and gigantic ceiba trees, the traveler at last reached a fence, which indicated that this was someone's property. And indeed one could discern in the distance the white façade of a farmhouse, toward which the young man immediately directed his mount. But suddenly he reined in his horse and pulled him over to the side of the road, apparently intending to wait for a country fellow who was approaching with measured step, singing a folk tune whose last verse the traveler's ear was able to catch perfectly:

> A dark woman is my torment
> Have pity on me—
> For she whom my heart adores
> Has none at all for me.[1]

When the man was but three paces from the stranger, noting that the latter was waiting expectantly, he stopped, and both men regarded each other for a moment before speaking. Perhaps the uncommonly handsome appearance of the traveler caused the local man to hesitate, while in turn the eyes of the former were just as strongly drawn to the latter.

The newcomer was a tall young man of average build but with striking features. He did not appear to be a white *criollo;*[2] neither was he black nor could one take him for a descendant of the indigenous inhabitants of the Antilles. His face was a singular composite which revealed the mingling of two distinct races, an amalgam, it could be said, of the features of the African and the European yet without being a perfect mulatto.

His coloring was of a yellowish white with a certain dark undertone; his broad forehead was half-hidden under irregular locks of hair as lustrous and black as the wings of the raven; his nose was aquiline, but his thick, purplish lips revealed his African heritage. His chin was triangular and somewhat prominent, his slanted eyes large and black under straight eyebrows; in them shone the fire of early youth, despite the slight lines that etched his face. The sum of these traits formed a face of distinctive features, one of those countenances which instantly attracts the gaze of others and which, once seen, is never forgotten.

The man's clothing was in no way different from that which is generally worn by farmers in the province of Puerto Príncipe and consisted of trousers of cotton ticking with wide blue stripes and a linen shirt, also striped, secured around the waist by a belt from which hung a wide machete, his head covered by a floppy hat woven of *yarey* leaves[3]—quite informal clothing, but comfortable and indispensable in a scorching climate.

The stranger broke the silence and, speaking in a Spanish so pure and fluent that it seemed to belie his northern physiognomy, said to the farmer, "My good friend, would you be so kind as to tell me if the house that can be discerned from here is that of Bellavista plantation,[4] belonging to Don Carlos de B——?"

The farmer bowed and answered, "Yes, sir, all the land you see down there belongs to Don Carlos."

"Undoubtedly you are this gentleman's neighbor and can tell me if he and his family have arrived at the plantation."

"They have been there since this morning, and I can be your guide should you wish to visit them."

The stranger showed by a nod of his head that he accepted the offer, and without awaiting a further response the farmer turned as though to take him to the house, which was now quite close. But perhaps the stranger did not wish to arrive quite so soon, for slowing his horse to a walk, he resumed his conversation with his guide, all the while casting curious glances around him.

"Did you say that Señor de B—— owns all of this land?"

"Yes, sir."

"It appears to be very fertile."

"Indeed it is."

"This plantation must bring its owner a good income."

"As far as I know there have been times," said the young man, stopping to glance at the land under discussion, "when this plantation produced for its owner some three hundred thousand pounds of sugar every year, because then more than a hundred blacks worked in the cane fields. But times have changed, and since the present owner of Bellavista has only fifty blacks, his production does not exceed six thousand loaves of sugar."

"The slaves on these plantations must have a very hard life," observed the stranger, "and I am not surprised that their number has been so considerably reduced."

"It is truly a terrible life," said the farmer, casting a sympathetic glance at his questioner. "Under this fiery sky the nearly naked slave works all morning without rest, and at the terrible hour of midday, panting, crushed under the weight of the wood and the sugarcane he bears on his shoulders, scorched by the rays of the sun that burn his skin, the unhappy soul at last gets a taste of all the pleasures which life holds for him: two hours of sleep and a frugal meal. When night comes with its breezes and shadows to console the scorched land and all nature rests, the slave with his sweat and tears waters the place where neither the night has shadows nor the breeze freshness, because there the heat of firewood has replaced that of the sun and the unhappy black walks endlessly around either the machine which extracts the cane's sweet juice or the cauldrons in which the fire's heat converts this juice into molasses; hour after hour he sees go by, and the sun's return finds him there still. . . . Ah, yes! The sight of this degraded humanity, where men become mere brutes, is a cruel spectacle. These are men whose brows are seared with the mark of slavery just as their souls are branded with the desperation of Hell."

The farmer suddenly halted, as though aware that he had said too much, and, lowering his eyes while permitting a melancholy smile to touch his lips, added hastily, "But the principal cause of Bellavista's decline is not the death of the slaves: many have been sold, as has some of the property, yet it is still a valuable enough plantation."

Having said this, he resumed walking toward the house but stopped after a few steps when he noted that the stranger was not following, and when he turned to look back at him, caught an expression of distinct surprise fixed on the stranger's features. In effect, the bearing of that farmer seemed to reveal something great and noble which attracted attention, and what the stranger had just heard, expressed in a language and with an eloquence which belied the class his dress appeared to denote, increased his admiration and curiosity.

The young farmer had approached our traveler's horse with the demeanor of a man who waits for a question he knows will be directed to him, and he was not mistaken, for the stranger, unable to quell his curiosity, said, "I gather that I have the pleasure of conversing with a distinguished landowner of these parts. I know that when they are out on their country estates, the *criollos* like to dress as simple laborers, and I would be sorry to remain ignorant any longer of the name of the person who has offered to guide me with such courtesy. If I am not mistaken, you are Don Carlos de B——'s friend and neighbor . . ."

Upon hearing these words the countenance of the one addressed showed not the slightest surprise but fixed the speaker with a penetrating glance; then, as though the mild and charming nature of the stranger's features had satisfied his inquiring gaze, he lowered his eyes and answered, "I am not a landowner, sir, and though within my breast beats a heart ever ready to sacrifice itself on Don Carlos's behalf, I am not in a position to call him my friend. I belong," he continued with a bitter smile, "to that unhappy race deprived of human rights . . . I am a mulatto and a slave."

"So you're a mulatto?" exclaimed the stranger, who, once he had heard the speaker's declaration, assumed the tone of disdainful familiarity used toward slaves. "Well, I suspected as much in the beginning, but you have a look so uncommon to your class that it caused me to think otherwise."

The slave continued to smile, but his smile became increasingly melancholy and, at that moment, held a hint of scorn as well.

"It can happen," he said, again fixing his eyes on the stranger, "that at times the soul is free and noble though the body be enslaved and base. But night is coming on and I will guide Your Grace[5] to the plantation, which is now very near."

The mulatto's observation was correct. As though it had been torn violently from the beautiful Cuban sky, the sun had ceased shining on that land it loves so well, though the altars once erected to it have long since been destroyed. The pale and melancholy moon slowly rose to take possession of its dominions.

The stranger followed his guide without interrupting the conversation.

"So you're Don Carlos's slave?"

"I have the honor of being the *mayoral*[6] of this plantation."

"What is your name?"

"I was christened Bernabé, but my mother always called me Sab, and that is what my masters have called me as well."

"Was your mother black or a mulatto like you?"

"My mother came into the world in a country where her color was not a mark of slavery. My mother," he repeated with a certain pride, "was born free and a princess. This was well known among all those who, like herself, were brought here from the coasts of the Congo by the dealers in human flesh. But although a princess in her own country, here she was sold as a slave."

The gentleman smiled indulgently when he heard Sab bestow the title of princess on his mother, but as the conversation appeared to interest him, he wished to prolong it further.

"Your father must undoubtedly have been white."

"My father! I never knew him. My mother was only a child when she was sold to Don Félix de B——, the father of my present master and of four other children. For two years she wept inconsolably, unable to resign herself to the bitter turn her fate had taken. But once this time was over, a sudden change took place within her; my mother was once again able to embrace life because she had fallen in love. A deep and powerful passion was kindled in her African heart. In spite of her color my mother was beautiful, and undoubtedly her passion was reciprocated because about that time I came into the world. My father's name was a secret which she always refused to reveal to me."

"Your fate, Sab, seems less deserving of pity than that of the other slaves, as the position you hold at Bellavista proves the esteem and affection which your master feels for you."

"Yes, sir, I have never suffered the harsh treatment which is generally meted out to slaves, nor have I been condemned to long and arduous labor. I was only three years old when my protector Don Luis, the youngest of Don Félix de B——'s sons, died, but two hours before that excellent young man departed this world he had a long and secret talk with his brother Don Carlos and, as was revealed later, entrusted me to the latter's kindness. And so I found in my present master the same good and pious heart of the kind protector I had lost. A short while later he married a woman—an angel!—and took me with him. I was six when I began to rock Miss Carlota's cradle, the first child of that happy marriage. As she was an only child for a period of five years, I became the companion of her games and her studies; her innocent heart disregarded the distance that separated us, and she bestowed upon me the affection due a brother. At her side I learned to read and write, for she refused to be instructed if her poor mulatto Sab were not with her. Because of her I grew to love reading; her own books and even her father's have always been available to me and have been my solace, though they have often stirred up disturbing ideas and bitter reflections in my soul."

The slave stopped himself, unable to hide the deep emotion which, to his sorrow, his voice revealed. Swiftly regaining control, he brushed his hand across his forehead, shook his head slightly, and added more calmly, "By my own choice I became a coachman for a few years; later I wanted to work with the land, and I have been helping on this plantation for two years now."

The stranger had smiled maliciously ever since Sab had mentioned the secret discussion which the late Don Luis had had with his brother. When the mulatto stopped talking, he said, "Strange that you are not free, seeing how much Don Luis de B—— loved you. It only seems natural that his father should have given you your freedom, or that Don Carlos should have done so."

"My freedom! Freedom is doubtless very sweet . . . but I was born a slave, I was a slave from my mother's womb and so—"

"You are accustomed to slavery," interrupted the stranger, very pleased at having articulated what he thought the mulatto must be thinking.

The latter did not contradict him but smiled bitterly and, as though he derived pleasure from the words he slowly uttered, said in a low voice, "As a child I was signed over to Miss Carlota; I am her slave, and I wish to live and die in her service."

The stranger spurred his horse lightly, and Sab, who was walking ahead of them, had to quicken his pace as the handsome sorrel of Norman stock, on which his interlocutor rode, stepped out.

"That affection and your excellent feelings do you great honor, Sab, but Carlota de B—— is about to marry, and perhaps dependence on a master will not be as pleasing to you as dependence on your young lady."

The slave came to a sudden stop and turned his penetrating black eyes on the stranger, who continued, momentarily reining in his horse.

"As you are a servant who enjoys the confidence of his masters, you cannot fail to know that Carlota is engaged to marry Enrique Otway, only son of one of the richest merchants of Puerto Príncipe."

A moment of silence followed these words, during which time there was no doubt but that an incredible upheaval was taking place in the slave's soul. Vertical lines creased his brow, from his eyes shone a sinister brilliance, like the lightning bolt which flashes from among the dark clouds, and then, as though a sudden idea had dispelled his doubts, he exclaimed after an instant of reflection, "Enrique Otway! That name, along with your appearance indicate a foreign origin. Doubtless, then, you[7] must be Señorita de B———'s future husband!"

"You are not deceived, young man; I am indeed Enrique Otway, Carlota's future husband, the same who will try not to have his union with your mistress be a misfortune for you. Just as she has done, I promise to make your sad lot as a slave less arduous. But here is the gate;[8] I can manage without a guide now. Farewell, Sab, you may go your way."

Enrique spurred his horse, which, after passing through the gate, departed at a gallop. The slave looked after him until he saw him reach the door of the white house. He then fixed his eyes on the sky, gave a low moan, and let himself fall upon a grassy bank.

Chapter Two

*I will say that her brow gleams
brighter than snow in a dark valley:
I will speak of her simple goodness,
and of the crimson of her cheek
as pure as her innocence.*

—Gallego

—— • ——

"What a beautiful evening! Come here, Teresa—isn't it wonderful to breathe such refreshing air?"

"For you the evening is undoubtedly lovely and the breezes cooling: for you, who are happy. From this window you can see your good father himself adorning the windows of this house with branches and flowers; this day, on which you have wept so much, will be one of happiness and rejoicing for you. Cherished daughter, beloved mistress, future wife of the man you have chosen—what can afflict you, Carlota? In this beautiful evening you see the precursor of an even more lovely day: the day on which you will see your Enrique here. Why do you cry, then? . . . Beautiful, rich, cherished . . . you should not be the one to weep."

"It is true that I am fortunate, my dear friend, but how could I return to this place which for me holds so many memories and not feel profound melancholy? The last time that we lived on this plantation I had the company of the tenderest of mothers. She was your mother too, Teresa, for she loved you as such: that soul was all tenderness! . . . Four years have gone by since she lived in this house with us. Here she enjoyed her last days of happiness and of life. It was only a few days after we left this property and returned to the city that she succumbed to that fateful illness which took her so prematurely to her grave. How could I not feel the influence of such dear memories when I returned to these places which I had not seen since then?"

"You are right, Carlota. You and I should forever mourn that loss which deprived us both, you of the best of mothers and me, poor destitute orphan, of my sole benefactress."

A long period of silence followed this short dialogue, and we shall take advantage thereof to acquaint our readers with the two young women whose conversation we have just relayed with scrupulous exactness, as well as with the place in which the abovementioned conversation took place.

A small, square, low-ceilinged chamber adjoined the main room of the house by a wooden door, which was painted dark green. It also had a large window which began almost at the floor and reached a man's height, with a semicircular wooden sill to the outside, as well as Dutch doors, also fashioned of wood. At present these were open in order allow the gentle evening breeze to cool the sitting room.

The room's furnishings were very simple yet elegant; in the back of the room could be glimpsed two canvas cots, side by side, of the type which are commonly used during the hottest months of the year in all the small villages of Cuba. A kind of hanging bed, or hammock, was strung obliquely from one corner of the room to the other, its soft undulations inviting the drowsiness brought on by excessive heat.

There was no artificial light in the room, lit solely by the light of the moon coming in through the window. Two young women sat facing each other by this window, seated on two wide, low-armed chairs known as *butacas*. Our readers would instantly have recognized the gentle Carlota by the sweet tears which she still shed in memory of the mother who had died four years ago. Her beautiful, pure brow rested in one of her hands as she supported her arm on the windowsill; her parted chestnut hair cascaded in a multitude of ringlets which framed a seventeen-year-old face. Had that face been scrupulously examined by the light of day, it might not perhaps have presented a model of perfection, but the combination of her delicate countenance and the soulful gaze of two large and darkly beautiful eyes gave her features, lit as they were by the moon, a certain angelic and poignant air impossible to describe. The ideal nature of her lovely figure was enhanced by a dress of purest white which called attention to the contours of her slender and graceful shape, and even though she was seated, it was evident that she was tall and of admirable proportions.

The woman who faced her presented a certain contrast. Still young, yet lacking the charms of youth, Teresa had one of those ordinary faces that fail to speak to the heart. Her features, while not repugnant, were in no way attractive either. After a close look at her, no one would call her ugly; however, on seeing her for the first time, no one would think her beautiful, for her face was so devoid of expression that it might just as well inspire hate as love. Her eyes, under thick, straight brows, were dark green and had a cold, indifferent look which held neither the fascination of sadness nor the charm of gaiety. Whether Teresa laughed or cried, those eyes were always the same. Her laughter and her crying appeared completely mechanical, so little did her features participate in the effort. Nevertheless, when a great passion or even a severe shock made her abandon her lethargy, then the sudden flash in Teresa's eyes could be astonishing. Rapid was her glance, fleeting her expression, but alive, energetic, eloquent; when her eyes then returned to their accustomed blankness, one who had seen them earlier marveled that they were capable of such an awesome language.

The illegitimate daughter of a distant relative of Don Carlos's wife, Teresa had lost her mother at birth and had lived with her father, a libertine who abandoned her utterly to the pride and harshness of a stepmother who loathed her. Thus from her birth she had been weighed down by misfortune, and so, even when Señora de B—— and her husband had taken her in after her father's death, neither the affection she found in this happy couple nor the tender friendship shown her by Carlota were sufficient to rid her character of the hardness and austerity it had acquired during her trials. Her inborn pride, continually lacerated by the stigma of her birth as well as by the lack of a fortune which placed her in a position of eternal dependence, had unconsciously embittered her spirit, and the effort of keeping her sensitive nature in check seemed to have drained her completely. At the time our story begins, Teresa had lived for eight years under the protection of Señor de B——, the only relative in whom she had found affection and compassion, and even though this was the time she might call the happiest of her life, it had nonetheless not been devoid of great tribulation. Destiny seemed to have placed her at Carlota's side to make her realize by sad comparison the utter inferiority and misfortune of her position. Next to this rich, beautiful, and happy girl who was idolized by doting parents, considered the pride of her entire family and continually showered with praise and attention, Teresa felt humiliated and fed in silence on her mortification. She learned to dissemble, to make herself ever more cold and reserved. Seeing her always serious and impassive, one might think that the icy calm, which at times resembled dullness, had been imprinted on her countenance by her soul; nevertheless, that soul was not incapable of great passions—I will go so far as to say that it was created in order to feel them. But what eyes are perspicacious enough to interpret a soul hidden under the scarred tissue of protracted calamities? In a cold, severe face we often detect the mark of insensitivity and almost never suspect that it is but a mask which hides misfortune.

Carlota loved Teresa like a sister and, already accustomed to the dryness and reserve of her character, was never offended by the fact that her affectionate friendship was not reciprocated. Lively, ingenuous, and impressionable, she could scarcely fathom Teresa's sad, profound character, the depth of her suffering, and the constancy of her indifference. Although Carlota was endowed with marvelous talent, she, as indeed everyone else, had come to believe that her friend was one of those good and serene human beings, so cold and apathetic as to be incapable either of criminal acts or of great virtues, of whom no more should be asked than that which they can give, because the capacity of their hearts is limited.

Teresa, immobile opposite her friend, suddenly shuddered convulsively. "I hear the galloping of a horse," she said. "It must be Enrique."

Carlota de B—— lifted her pretty head, and a light, rosy blush crept over her cheeks. "As a matter of fact," she said, "I do hear galloping, but Enrique is not expected here until tomorrow, tomorrow was the day designated for his return from Guanaja. Nevertheless, he may have wanted to hasten it . . . Ah! Yes, it is he! And I hear his voice greeting Father. Teresa, you are right," she added, throwing her left arm around her cousin's neck while with the other she brushed away the last tear running down her cheek. "You are right when you say I am very fortunate!"

Teresa, who had stood up and was looking attentively out the window, sat down again slowly. Her face regained its icy and almost dull immobility, and between clenched teeth she remarked: "Yes, you are very fortunate!"

Carlota was no longer weeping: the painful memories of a cherished mother vanished before the presence of an adored beloved. At Enrique's side she saw nothing save him. For her the entire universe was reduced to the place from which she beheld her beloved, because Carlota loved with all the illusions of a first love, with the confidence and the abandon of early youth, and the passion of a heart formed under a tropical sky.

Three months had gone by since her marriage to Enrique Otway had been decided upon, and in those months there had been daily vows of undying love, vows that to her tender and virginal heart were as holy and undying as though they had been consecrated by the most majestic rites. Not the slightest doubt, not the least hint of distrust had poisoned this pure affection, because when we love for the first time we make a God of the object of our infatuation. Imagination bestows upon it ideal perfections, the heart surrenders without fear, and we do not even remotely suspect that the idol whom we worship can change into the real and concrete being which experience and disillusionment will reveal to us with prompt dispatch, stripped of the brilliant raiment of our illusions.

The sensitive island girl had not yet experienced that painful heartbreak of a first disillusionment; she still saw her beloved through the enchanted lens of innocence and love, and everything in him was beautiful, grand, and sublime.

Did Enrique Otway deserve so beautiful a passion? Did he share in that divine enthusiasm which permits Heaven to be dreamt on earth? Did his soul understand that other passionate soul of which he was master? . . . We do not know: the events themselves will soon tell us and will then shape the opinions of our readers. Not wanting to get ahead of things, we will limit ourselves for now to providing some knowledge of the people who appear in this story and of the events leading up to it.

Chapter Three

I want a woman of wealth.
—Cañizares

—— • ——

It is well known that Cuba's riches continually attract innumerable foreigners, who, with middling effort and activity, soon become prosperous, in a way that astonishes the indolent islanders; these, content with the fertility of their soil and the ease with which one lives in a land of plenty, become somnolescent under the effect of their fiery sun, surrendering their agriculture, commerce, and industry to the greed and enterprise of the Europeans, by means of which numerous families become prominent in very short order.

George Otway was one of those many men who swiftly rose from nothing, thanks to the riches of that new and fertile land. He was English; for some years he had been a peddler in the United States, afterward in the city of Havana, and finally had come to Puerto Príncipe, trading in textiles. He was then over thirty and brought with him a six-year-old son, the only issue left him from his marriage.

Five years after his arrival in Puerto Príncipe, George Otway, along with two Catalonians, already owned a dry goods shop, in which he and his son waited on customers from behind the counter. Five years more and the Englishman and his partners opened a superb department store with all kinds of fine linens. But it was no longer they who attended to customers from behind the counter: they had employees and sales agents, and sixteen-year-old Enrique had been sent to London by his father for the purpose, as the latter was wont to say, of improving his son's education. After yet another five years George Otway had become the owner of a handsome dwelling on one of the city's best streets and by himself ran a vast and lucrative business. It was then that his son returned from Europe, handsome of figure and with fine and agreeable manners; thanks to these, and to the prominence which his family had begun to acquire, he was not excluded from the country's most distinguished social gatherings. If we were to let five more years go by, the reader would observe the rich merchant George Otway, moving in the highest social circles, waited on by slaves, the owner of magnificent carriages, and enjoying all of the prestige of great wealth.

Enrique was therefore not only one of the country's most elegant young men but also one of the most brilliant matches. Nonetheless, at the very time when the English peddler's fortune was reaching the apex of its rapid ascent, a number of considerable losses dealt a mortal blow to his vanity and greed. He had become embroiled in several extremely risky commercial enterprises and committed the further imprudence of borrowing large sums of money at a high rate of interest in order to cover up their lack of success and maintain his firm's credit. He who once was a moneylender found himself constrained to reduce his expenses, becoming in turn a victim of the profiteering of others. He learned very quickly that the foundation of his fortune, constructed in such short order, was threatened by a calamitous downfall, whereupon George decided that it would be to his advantage to have his son marry before the decline was publicly evident.

He had his eyes on the country's wealthiest heiresses and believed that in Carlota de B—— he had found the woman who suited his plans. Her father Don Carlos, like his siblings, had inherited a considerable fortune, and though he married a woman without means, luck had lately favored his wife: she came into a large and unexpected inheritance, thanks to which Don Carlos's house, which had fallen into some disrepair, became once again one of the most prosperous in Puerto Príncipe. Actually, his tranquil enjoyment of this rise in his fortune lasted but a short time, as a certain relative of the testator who had benefited his wife initiated a suit and, based on real or imagined rights, tried nothing less than to have the will in question annulled. But this attempt appeared so absurd, and the suit seemed to present such favorable aspects for Don Carlos, that no one doubted his complete triumph. George Otway had all this in mind when he chose Carlota to be his son's wife. Señora de B—— had already died, leaving her husband with six children. According to general opinion, Carlota, the firstborn of this union, was the favorite child and could expect a considerable bequest from her father. Eugenio, the second child and only son, who was being educated in Havana, was of a frail and sickly constitution, and most likely George did not fail to note this fact, foreseeing in the delicate health of the young man one heir less. Furthermore, Don Carlos's older brother Don Agustín was an influential bachelor, and Carlota his favorite niece. Thus George Otway did not vacillate and told his son of his decision. As the young man was endowed with a malleable character and was accustomed always to give in to his father's forceful will, he easily agreed to his wishes. This time it was without aversion, for besides Carlota's personal charms Enrique was not indifferent to her wealth, fully indoctrinated as he was by the commercial and speculating spirit of his father.

Thus he declared himself the suitor of Señorita de B—— and was immediately loved by her. Carlota was at that perilous age at which the heart feels with the greatest ardor the need to love and was, in any case, by nature tender and impressionable. A great deal of sensitivity, a lively imagination, and great spiritual activity were gifts which, when combined with a character more enthusiastic than prudent, were reason to make one fear the effects of a first love upon her. It was not difficult to foresee that her poetic soul would not long love a man of common disposition, but one could also predict that she had sufficient wealth of imagination to embellish any object she chose. For some time now, Carlota's illusions had presented her with the image of a noble and beautiful being, created expressly to be united to her and to make of life a poetic ecstasy of love. And what woman, even though born under a less fiery sky, does not seek the sublime creation of her virginal imagination when with timid step she enters the harsh spheres of life? What woman has not envisioned in her solitary ecstasy a protector who will sustain her in weakness, defend her innocence, and receive the cult of her adoration? . . . This being has no name, hardly a definable form, but is present in all that nature shows as great and beautiful. When a young woman regards a man, she seeks in him the traits of the angel of her dreams. . . . Oh, how difficult it is to find him! And woe to her who is seduced by a deceptive likeness! Nothing must be as painful as to see such sweet delusion shattered, and unfortunately it is destroyed all too soon. The illusions of an ardent heart are like the flowers of summer: their perfume is headier but their existence more fleeting.

Carlota loved Enrique, or perhaps we should say that she loved in Enrique the ideal object of her imagination as she wandered through the woods or by the banks of the Tínima, enraptured by the scents, the brilliant light, the gentle breezes—all those splendid gifts, so close to the ideal, which youthful nature, bursting with life, bestows under that tropical sky. Enrique was handsome and pleasant, and Carlota delved into her soul to adorn him with the most brilliant hues of her imagination. What more did she need?

When George Otway was apprised of his son's successful suit, he boldly asked for Carlota's hand, but his vanity and that of Enrique suffered the humiliation of a refusal. The family de B—— was among the most distinguished in the country and, as they still remembered the peddler he had been, did not receive the wealthy merchant's offer without indignation. Furthermore, although the elder Otway might have declared himself a true apostolic Roman Catholic from the time of his establishment in Puerto Príncipe and had educated his son in the rites of this same church, the abandonment of his former religion had not saved him from being called a heretic, which was how the old women of the country usually designated him. Even if the entire de B——— family did not hold the same views on this point, there was no lack of persons who opposed the marriage of Carlota to Enrique, motivated less by disdain of the peddler than by fear of the heretic.

Señorita de B———'s hand was, therefore, denied the young Englishman, and she was strictly ordered not to think any further about her suitor. How easy it is to give such orders! It seems that experience still has not proven their uselessness. Carlota loved all the more from the time she was forbidden to love, and even though there was certainly no great drive in her character, much less a cool perseverance, the agitation of an obstructed love and the dismay of a young girl who for the first time finds her desires thwarted were more than sufficient to produce an effect which ran contrary to expectations. All the de B——— family's efforts to separate her from Enrique failed, as her unfortunate suitor became all the more interesting to her. After repeated and painful scenes in which she showed a steadfastness that amazed her relatives, love and sadness caused her to succumb to a dangerous illness—the factor that determined her victory. A doting father cannot bear for long the sufferings of such a lovely creature, and he gave in, to the dismay of all of his relations.

Don Carlos was one of those peaceful and indolent men who do not know how to do evil, nor to go to great lengths to do good. When he opposed the union of Carlota and Enrique, he had followed the advice of his family, for he himself was fairly indifferent to the problems of lineage and, accustomed as he was to the pleasures of abundance without knowing their price, lacked ambition for either power or wealth. He had never aimed for a husband of high social position or immense fortune for his daughter: for him it was enough to want someone who would make her happy. Yet he did not take much trouble to study Enrique in order to know if the latter were capable of achieving this.

Inactive by temperament, docile by character and the habit of inertia, Don Carlos opposed his daughter's love only to appease his siblings. Subsequently he gave in to her less because he was convinced that this marriage would give her happiness than because he lacked the strength to maintain the stance which he had taken. Carlota, on the other hand, knew how to take advantage of his weakness to further her own cause, and before the family had time to influence Don Carlos's opinion again, the marriage had been agreed to by both fathers and the wedding set for the first of September of that year, as that was the date of the girl's eighteenth birthday.

This agreement was decided upon at the end of February, and from then until the beginning of June—which is when our story begins—the two lovers had all the time to see and speak to each other that was permissible.

But fortune, mocking the calculations of the covetous Englishman, had in this short time upset all of his hopes and schemes. The family of Señor de B——, deeply offended by the latter's decision and not bothering to hide the disdain with which they viewed Carlota's future husband, had publicly broken off all friendly relations with Don Carlos, and his brother Agustín drew up a will in favor of the children of another brother in order to take away from Carlota all hope of her inheritance. Another, even more devastating blow followed this one and made George despair. Contrary to all probability and expectations, the lawsuit in question was ultimately decided against Don Carlos. Justly or unjustly, the will that had designated his wife as the heiress was annulled and the unfortunate gentleman had to hand over to the new owner the large landholdings which for the past six years he had viewed as his own. Many persons judged the verdict to be biased and unjust and urged the injured party to appeal to the supreme court of the nation, but Don Carlos's character was unsuited to this. Accepting his fate, Don Carlos appeared almost indifferent to a misfortune which deprived him of a considerable part of his property. It would seem that such stoicism, such noble detachment from wealth, ought to have earned him general praise, but this was not the case. His indifference was judged to be more the result of egotism than of selflessness.

"He is still sufficiently wealthy," they said in the town, "to be able to enjoy all imaginable comforts while he is alive, and doesn't care about a loss that only will harm his children."

Nevertheless, those who judged Don Carlos in this fashion were deceived. Certainly the indolence of his character and the dejection which any unexpected blow produced in him influenced in no small measure the apparent stoicism with which he immediately bowed to misfortune without making an energetic attempt to counter it. Yet he loved his children and had loved his wife with all the ardor and tenderness of a sensitive yet apathetic soul. He would have given his life for each one of those loved ones, but even for the benefit of these very persons, he would not have been able to impose on himself the discipline of an active and purposeful life: his temperament, his character, and his ingrained habits opposed it. Resignedly and philosophically he surrendered a fortune on which he had counted to assure a brilliant future for his children, yet he was by no means untouched by this disappointment. He complained to no one, perhaps because of apathy, perhaps because of a kind of pride that was nonetheless compatible with the most perfect goodness, but the blow grievously wounded his paternal heart. At this point he rejoiced inwardly at having Carlota's fortune assured and no longer saw in Enrique the son of the peddler but the sole heir to one of the country's most prosperous firms.

It was quite the opposite with George. Carlota, deprived of her uncle's bequest and of the maternal inheritance which the suit had effected, Carlota, with five siblings who would share with her the diminished property they might inherit from their father (who was still young and promised to live a long life), was no longer the woman George wanted for his son. The avaricious Englishman would have perished of rage and pain if the misfortunes which struck the house of de B—— had occurred after Enrique's marriage, but fortunately for him it had not yet taken place, and George was determined that it never would. Too base to feel any embarrassment at his conduct, with neither reticence nor courtesy, he might abruptly have broken off the engagement he already disdained, had his son, by means of gentleness and patience, not convinced him to adopt a course of action that was more reasonable and less ill bred.

What happened in Enrique's soul when he saw his brilliant hopes of wealth suddenly destroyed was a secret to all, for although the young man was as covetous as his father, he was at least much more able to dissemble. His conduct did not alter in the slightest, nor could one detect even a hint of coolness in his courtship. People who had been of the opinion that only gain had led him to ask for Carlota's hand subsequently thought that some more noble and generous sentiment had made him decide not to give her up. Carlota was perhaps the only person who neither appreciated nor noticed the apparent selflessness of her suitor. Not suspecting that any other motive than love might prompt him to ask for her hand, she scarcely thought about the unfavorable turn which her fortune had taken, nor was she surprised that it did not affect Enrique's conduct. Alas! Only cold and frightful experience teaches noble and generous souls the merits of the virtues which they possess. . . . Happy is the one who dies without having come to know this!

Chapter Four

There is no evil for love which is returned,
There is no good which is not evil for one who is absent.
—Lista

The afternoon after Enrique had arrived at Bellavista, Carlota and her suitor were seated tenderly on the trunk of a palm tree, at the end of a long drive of orange and tamarind trees, engaged in a conversation which appeared very lively.

"I repeat," said the young man, "that pressing matters of business require me to leave you so soon, much to my sorrow."

"So you only wanted to stay at Bellavista for twenty-four hours?" answered the maiden with a certain air of impatience. "I had hoped that your visits would be longer; I would not have consented to come here otherwise. But you can't leave today, you just can't. Four days more, two at the very least."

"You know that I left you eight days ago to go to the port of Guanaja because a ship which was consigned to my firm had just docked. The cargo has to be transported to Puerto Príncipe, and it is indispensable that I be there. At his age and with his ailments, my father is no longer able to attend to all these affairs with the necessary dispatch. But listen, Carlota, I promise to come back within two weeks."

"Two weeks!" exclaimed Carlota with childish fretfulness. "Oh, no, Papá has planned an outing to Cubitas, with the dual purpose of visiting the *estancias*[1] he has there and for Teresa and me to visit the famous caves[2] which you haven't seen either. This trip is in eight days, and you must come along to accompany us."

Enrique was about to answer when they saw the mulatto (whom we introduced to the reader in the first chapter) coming toward them.

"It's time for tea," said Carlota, "and doubtless Papá sent Sab to tell us."

"Do you know that I find this slave pleasing?" replied Enrique, happily taking advantage of the situation to change the subject. "He has nothing of the degradation and the coarseness which is the norm in people of his sort; quite the contrary, he has a very fine air and manners, and I would venture so far as to call them aristocratic."

"Sab has never mixed with the other slaves," answered Carlota, "for he has been raised with me like a brother, has an immense love of reading, and his natural talent is astonishing."

"All of that is of no benefit to him," replied the Englishman. "For what use is talent and education to a man destined to be a slave?"

"Sab will not be one much longer, Enrique. I think my father is only waiting until he turns twenty-one in order to free him."[3]

"According to a certain account he gave me of his birth," added the young man, smiling, "I suspect that this boy, with good reason, flatters himself by presuming that he is of the same blood as his masters."

"I think so, too, because my father has always treated him with special consideration and has let on to the family that he has compelling reasons to believe him the son of his late brother Don Luis. But hush! Here he comes."

The mulatto bowed deeply before his young mistress and informed her that she was expected for tea.

"Besides," he added, "the sky is getting very dark and a storm seems to be threatening."

Carlota raised her eyes and, seeing the truth of this observation, ordered the slave to leave, telling him that they would return to the house presently. While Sab disappeared down the tree-lined drive, she turned to her suitor and gazed at him with a pleading look.

"Well, then," she said to him, "are you going to accompany us to Cubitas?"

"I shall return in fifteen days; aren't fifteen the same as eight?"

"The same!" she echoed, a noticeable expression of surprise appearing in her lovely eyes. "Why, no! Aren't there seven days' difference? Seven days, Enrique! I have just been seven without seeing you during this first separation, and they have seemed an eternity to me! Haven't you felt how awful it is to see the sun rise one day and another and another without it being able to dispel the darkness of the heart, without bringing us a ray of hope . . . because we know that while it shines we will not glimpse the beloved countenance? And then, when night comes, when nature sleeps amidst the shadows and the breezes, haven't you felt your heart fill with a sweet tenderness, as indefinable as the scent of the flowers? Haven't you felt the need to hear a beloved voice in the silence of the night? Haven't you been overwhelmed by absence, by that constant unease, that immense emptiness, that agony of a pain that manifests itself in a thousand different guises but is always piercing, inexhaustible, unbearable?"

A tear dimmed the eyes of the impassioned *criolla,* and rising from the trunk on which she had been seated, she walked in among some orange trees which formed a small wood on the right, as though she felt the need to control that excessive sensitivity that made her suffer so deeply. Enrique followed her slowly, as though he feared to lose sight of her yet did not

entirely want to catch up either, while his pale brow and blue eyes registered a peculiar expression of doubt and indecision. One might say that
two opposing feelings, two hostile powers divided his heart. Suddenly he
stopped, remained motionless while looking at Carlota from afar, and a
word escaped his lips, but a word which revealed a thought carefully hidden until now. Frightened by his indiscretion, he looked around to make
sure that they were alone, and simultaneously a light tremor shook his
body. Two eyes, burning like coals of fire, had shone from among the dark
green of the leaves, glaring at him with a frightful gaze. Because it was
important to know the mysterious spy who had just witnessed his secret—
necessary as it was to punish the intruder or make him keep silent—he
darted toward this spot. But he found nothing. The spy had no doubt
slipped away among the trees, taking advantage of the first moment of
surprise and confusion which the sight of him had caused.

Enrique thereupon began to hurry and caught up to his fiancée just as
she crossed the threshold of the house where Don Carlos waited for them,
tea having been served.

Meanwhile night was coming on, not serene and lovely as the evening
before but threatening to be one of those stormy nights which in Cuba
can be very frightening.

The heat was suffocating, with no breeze to temper it; the electrically
charged atmosphere weighed on one's body like a leaden canopy; the
clouds, so low as to merge with the shadows of the woods, were dark gray
with broad bands of a fiery hue. No leaf moved, no sound broke the dreadful silence of nature. Great bands of *auras*[4] filled the air, darkening the
reddish light of the setting sun; the dogs, their bristling tails tucked low,
their mouths agape with tongues parched and burning, huddled close to
the ground, instinctively sensing the fearful outbreak which nature was
about to unleash.

These stormy portents, familiar to all Cubans, were one more reason to
beg Otway to delay his departure at least until the following day. But it
was to no avail, for he was determined to leave before the storm broke.
Two slaves received the order to bring him his horse, and Don Carlos
offered to have Sab go with him. Even beforehand it had been decided
that the mulatto was to leave for the city on the following day in order to
attend to some of his master's affairs, and having him leave a few hours
earlier would give Don Carlos's future son-in-law a companion experienced on the roads he would travel. Enrique appreciated this gesture, and
rising from the table where according to the Cuban custom of the times
tea had just been served, he approached Carlota. From a window she
stared at the sky, uneasily examining the signs of the fast-approaching
storm.

"Good-bye, Carlota," he said to her, lovingly taking one of her hands.

"Our separation will not be fifteen days, for I will return to accompany you to Cubitas."

"Yes," she answered, "I will wait for you, Enrique . . . but, dear God!" she added, trembling and turning her beautiful eyes from her beloved to the sky, "Enrique, it will be a terrible night. The storm will break at any moment. Why are you determined to go? If you yourself are not afraid, do it for me, out of pity for your Carlota . . . Enrique, don't go."

The Englishman looked at the heavens for an instant and repeated the order to bring him his horse. He was not unaware of the proximity of the storm, but it was in his commercial interest to be in Puerto Príncipe that night, and when matters of this kind were under consideration neither lightning bolts nor the pleas of his beloved could make him waver. Trained as he was in the ways of covetousness and speculation, surrounded since infancy by an atmosphere of commerce, he was punctilious and inflexible in carrying out those responsibilities which the interests of his business imposed upon him.

Lightning flashed in split-second intervals, followed by the detonation of two fearful rolls of thunder. A deathly pallor spread over Carlota's face, as she regarded her beloved with unspeakable anxiety. Don Carlos came over to them, imploring the young man ever more earnestly to delay his departure, and even Carlota's small sisters gathered around him and embraced his knees, begging him not to leave. Only one individual of those who were in the room at that time remained indifferent to the storm and to all that surrounded her. This person was Teresa who, leaning on a windowsill, appeared profoundly buried in thought.

When Enrique, eluding the pleas of the master of the house, the little girls' fussings, and the mute supplications of his beloved, approached Teresa to bid her farewell, she turned toward him with a convulsive movement, startled at the tone of her own voice.

On taking her hand, Enrique noted that it was cold and trembling and even thought he perceived a light sigh, stifled with an effort between her lips. He regarded her with some surprise, but she had resumed her earlier position; her icy countenance and fixed look, almost corpselike in its lack of expression, revealed nothing of the emotions which filled her mind and agitated her soul.

Enrique mounted his horse, only waiting for Sab to depart, but Sab had been detained by Carlota, who, filled with anxiety, begged him to look after her beloved.

"Sab," she said urgently, "if the storm is as bad as these black clouds and frightful silence portend, you, who know every inch of this country, will know where to find shelter with Enrique. Because as solitary as these lands are, there will always be a *bohío*[5] where you can seek shelter from the storm. Sab! I leave my Enrique in your hands."

A bolt of lightning brighter than the previous ones and an almost simultaneous crash of thunder tore a weak cry from the timid maiden, who, in an involuntary movement, covered her eyes with both hands. When she took them away and glanced around, she saw her little sisters close to her, huddled together and trembling with fear, while Teresa remained standing, calm and silent in the same window where she had received Enrique's farewell. Sab was no longer in the room. Carlota rose from the chair into which she had dropped almost faint with fear at the crash of thunder; she attempted to run to the patio where she had seen Enrique mount his horse a moment before and where she supposed he still was, but at that instant she heard her father's voice wishing the travelers a good journey and the rhythmic gallop of the departing horses. Then she slowly sat down and exlaimed in anguish: "Oh, God! Does one always suffer so when one loves? Do all hearts love and ache the same way mine does, or have You planted in mine a more fertile seed of love and pain? Ah, if this terrible ability to love and suffer is not universal, what a cruel gift You have given me! Because it is a misfortune, it is a grave misfortune to feel this way."

She covered her brimming eyes and moaned because she suddenly felt in the most hidden corner of her heart some terrible instinctive revelation of a truth which heretofore she had not clearly understood: that there are loftier souls on the earth who are endowed with feelings unrecognizable to more common ones, souls rich in sentiment, rich in emotions for which are reserved terrible passions, terrible virtues, immense sorrows . . . and that Enrique's soul was not one of these.

Chapter Five

The shadowy storm
stirs up an Ocean in the winds
which buries all . . .
—Heredia

—— • ——

Deepest night cast the ground into mourning. As yet not a drop of rain had fallen, nor did the slightest breath of air cool the scorched earth. A dreadful silence reigned over nature, which appeared to be watching the sky's anger with dismay while it waited for the fulfillment of its threat with sad resignation.

Nonetheless, in just such an awful night two daring men crossed those scorched savannas on horseback, without the least indication of fear. These two men (already known to the reader) were Enrique and Sab—one mounted on his fiery sorrel and the other on a pony, black as ebony and more agile than strong. On the front of his saddle the Englishman carried two pistols and a short saber with an engraved silter hilt; the mulatto had no other weapon but his machete.

Neither one spoke a word nor did they take notice of the lightning, because each one was absorbed by a thought which completely dominated any others. Doubtless Enrique Otway loved Carlota de B——; how could he not love a creature so lovely and ardent? Whatever were the particular aptitudes of the Englishman's soul, the height or depth of his feelings, and the greater or lesser degree of his sensitivity, there was no doubt that his love for Don Carlos's daughter was one of the strongest emotions he had ever experienced. But this sentiment was not the only one he felt, as it was evidently counterbalanced by another rival and at times victorious passion: greed.

As he left his beloved, he thought of the joy of possessing her, then weighed this against the satisfaction of being richer, perhaps marrying a less beautiful, less tender woman, but one whose dowry could reestablish the credit of his somewhat debilitated business and appease his father's cupidity. Agitated and indecisive in this dilemma, he remonstrated with himself for being neither sufficiently covetous to sacrifice love to self-gain nor sufficiently generous to defer his personal advantage to his love.

Doubtless other more gloomy and more terrible thoughts preoccupied the soul of the slave. But who would dare to try to discern them? In the reflected illumination of the flashes of lightning, he fixed his eyes intently on his companion as though by means of them he could search the innermost recesses of the latter's heart; and by some inconceivable miracle he seemed at last to have achieved this, for he suddenly looked away and a bitter, scornful, inexplicable smile momentarily twisted his lips.

"Scoundrel!" he murmured in an audible voice, but this exclamation was drowned out by a crack of lightning.

At last the storm broke. Suddenly, at the impetuous gust of the unleashed winds, the dust of the fields rose in suffocating spirals. The heavens opened, spewing fire through innumerable openings. Lightning described a thousand fiery angles, its bolts shattering the thickest trees, and the burning atmosphere was like a huge conflagration.

The Englishman turned to his companion with a gesture of terror. "It's impossible to go on," he told him, "absolutely impossible."

"Not far from here," the slave calmly responded, "is the farm of an acquaintance of mine."

"Let us go there at once," said Enrique, who knew he had no alternative.

But the words were hardly out of his mouth when a cloud was rent above his head and the tree under which he stood fell, seared by lightning. His horse, which bolted from under the trees shaking as they were lashed by the wind, snapped the reins by means of which his distraught rider was vainly attempting to control him. Striking his head against the branches and severely jolted by the terrified animal, Enrique lost his seat and crashed to the ground, bloodied and unconscious, in the deepest part of the forest.

A long, painful moan brought the mind of the mulatto back to the situation at hand, and dismounting, he advanced rapidly and with admirable skill in spite of the profound darkness. He found poor Otway pale, unconscious, his face bruised and bloody; Sab stood before him, motionless as stone. Nevertheless, the light which was given off at this instant by the jet pupils of his eyes was as dark and sinister as the flashes of the storm, and but for the clamor of the winds and the thunder, one could have heard the beating of his heart.

"Here he is!" he exclaimed at last with a terrible smile. "Here he is!" he repeated with a deep, muffled voice that in a fearful way was in harmony with the roars of the hurricane. "Unconscious, dying! Tomorrow they would mourn Enrique Otway, dead of a fall, victim of his own rashness. No one could ever tell if his head had been shattered by the fall or whether the hand of an enemy had finished the deed. No one would be able to discern if Heaven's decree had been abetted by a human hand. It is very dark and we are alone. He and I alone in the night and the storm! Here he is at my feet, silent and unconscious, the man I loathe. One act would reduce him to nothing, and that decision is mine . . . mine, that of the poor slave whom he does not suspect of possessing a soul superior to his own, capable of loving, capable of hating . . . a soul which might be great and virtuous and at this moment even criminal! Here is the inert body of a man who should never rise again!"

Sab gnashed his teeth and with a powerful arm he lifted up the young Englishman's slender and delicate body as though it were a weightless piece of straw.

But at that instant a sudden and inexplicable change took place in his soul, for he remained immobile and breathless, as though the power of some mysterious spell restrained him. Doubtless an invisible spirit, Enrique's guardian, had just murmured Carlota's parting words in his ear: "Sab, I leave my Enrique in your hands."

"Her Enrique!" he exclaimed with a troubled and sardonic smile. "He! This heartless man! And she would mourn his death! And he would take her love and dreams to his grave! . . . Because if he died Carlota would never know how unworthy he was of her fervent love, her feminine, virginal love . . . by dying he would live on in her memory, because Carlota's soul would give him life, the soul that this wretch will never be able to understand. But shall I permit him to live? Shall I allow him to desecrate this angel of innocence and love? Shall I tear him from Death's arms only to place him in hers?"

Otway gave out a faint moan which caused the slave to tremble. He allowed Enrique's head, which he had been supporting, to fall, drew back a few steps, and crossed his arms over his chest, shaken by a tempest more awful than that of nature. He regarded the sky which resembled a sea of fire, looked in silence at Otway, and violently shook his rain-drenched head, grating his ivory teeth against each other. Rapidly he approached the wounded man, and it was evident that his vacillations were over and that he had reached a firm decision.

The next day dawned a beautiful morning, as frequently happens in the Antilles after a tempestuous night. The atmosphere was cleansed, the sky blue and splendid, and the sun poured torrents of light over the restored landscape. Only a few shattered trees bore witness to the recent storm.

Carlota de B—— saw that longed-for day begin as she leaned against her bedroom window (the same one at which she was first presented to our readers). Her red eyes and pale cheeks bore witness to the worries and tears of the night, as she glanced toward the road to the city with an expression of melancholy and fatigue.

Suddenly an indescribable spasm appeared on her countenance, and her eyes, without changing direction, took on a more pronounced expression of anguish and suffering. Letting out a cry, she would have fallen to the floor had not Teresa caught her in her arms. But hardly had she reached the fateful window when Teresa, as though jolted by an electric shock, turned as pale and agitated as Carlota herself. Her knees buckled, and a cry just like the one that had drawn her there issued from her choking breast.

But no one came to their aid: there was general alarm in the house, and Señor de B—— was too disturbed to attend to his daughter.

The object which caused such consternation was nothing more than a horse with an English saddle and torn bridle which had just arrived, led by his instinct to the place from which he had departed the previous night. It was Enrique's horse! When Carlota regained consciousness she broke out in hopeless cries. In vain Teresa cradled her in her arms with unusual tenderness, begging her to calm herself and not to give up hope; in vain her excellent father ordered all of his slaves to go in search of Enrique. Carlota paid attention to nothing, heard nothing, saw nothing but the fateful messenger of her beloved's death. She questioned him with sharp cries and in a fit of desperation flew from the house and ran wildly toward the fields, sobbing distractedly in her grief.

"I myself will search for him! I want to find his body and breathe my last upon it."

She darted as swiftly as an arrow, and when she reached the gate found herself face to face with the mulatto. His clothing and hair were still wet from the previous night's rain, while down his forehead ran burning drops of sweat, proof of the fatigue of a rapid journey.

On catching sight of him Carlota shrieked and had to lean on the gate so as not to fall. Devoid of the strength to question him, she stared at him with unutterable anxiety, and the mulatto understood her, for he took a paper from his belt which he gave her. The hand which tendered it shook just as much as the one receiving it . . . Carlota began to devour the message with her anxious eyes, but the degree of her agitation did not let her finish. Handing it to her father, who with Teresa had just reached her, she fell to the ground in a faint.

While Don Carlos took her in his arms, showering her with kisses and tears, Teresa read the letter aloud.

Beloved Carlota,

I am leaving for the city in a carriage which my father has sent for me and at present am out of all danger. A fall from my horse has forced me to stop at the farm of one of Sab's friends, from where I am writing to you to calm you and to prevent the shock which my horse's arrival might cause, as Sab presumes will happen. I am indebted to this young man for the most unflagging care. He has walked four leagues each way in less than two hours and has just brought me the carriage in which I will travel to Puerto Príncipe very comfortably. Farewell.

Carlota, barely conscious, had the slave approach and, in a paroxysm of joy and gratitude, threw her lovely arms around his neck. "My friend! My consoling angel!" she exclaimed. "May Heaven bless you! . . . You are free now, I wish it so."

Sab bowed deeply at the maiden's feet and kissed the delicate hand which was voluntarily placed near his lips. But her hand was withdrawn in a trice and Carlota shivered, for the slave's lips had burned on her hand like coals.

"You are free," she repeated, glancing at him in surprise, as though she wished to read in his face the cause of an emotion which she could not attribute to the pleasure of the freedom long offered and many times withdrawn. But Sab had himself under control; his look was sad and calm and his appearance serious and melancholy.

In response to his master's questions, he related in few words the details of the evening, concluding with assurances to Carlota that her beloved was in no danger and that the head wound he had received was so minor it should not cause her the least anxiety. Sab wished to leave for the city immediately to take care of the orders his master had given him, but the latter, judging him to be very tired, told him to rest that day and to leave the next, with the coolness of dawn. The slave obeyed, withdrawing immediately.

The varied and intense emotions which Carlota had experienced in very short order upset her to such a degree that she was forced to retire to her room. Teresa made her lie down and sat by her bed, while Señor de B——, smoking cigars and rocking to and fro in his hammock, thought about his daughter's excessively sensitive nature; attempting to quiet the anxiety which this acute sensitivity caused his fatherly heart, he said to himself, "Soon she will be the wife of the man she loves. Enrique is good and kind and will make her happy, as happy as I made her mother, whose beauty and tenderness she has inherited."

While he was reflecting on this, his four little daughters played around him. From time to time they came over to swing the hammock, and Don Carlos kissed them, holding them in his arms.

"My darlings," he told them, "at present a stronger feeling than filial affection holds sway over your sister Carlota's heart, but you as yet know nothing sweeter than a father's caresses. When a husband comes to claim all of her tenderness and care, you will devote yours to brighten the last days of your aged father."

Carlota, resting her lovely head on Teresa's breast, spoke to her also of those whom she loved: of her excellent father, of Enrique, whom she adored even more at that instant, for who can ignore how precious the beloved becomes when we regain him after having feared him lost?

Teresa listened to her in silence. Her fears dispelled, she had recovered her icy mien, and in the caresses which she bestowed on her friend there was more of solicitude than of tenderness.

Exhausted at last by the many upheavals she had suffered since the previous day, Carlota fell asleep on Teresa's bosom about noon, when the heat was the most intense. For a long while Teresa regarded that beautiful head and superb, sweetly closed eyes, whose long lashes shadowed the purest of cheeks. Gently she placed the head of the lovely sleeper on her pillow, and a tear, long held back, sprang from her eyelids.

"How beautiful she is!" she murmured between her teeth. "Who could not love her?"

Subsequently she regarded herself in the mirror, and a bitter smile played over her lips.

Chapter Six

And tenderly regarding
the noble animal
he repeats: "While I live
you will be my faithful friend."
—Anonymous ballad

——— • ———

Having rested most of the day and all of the night, Carlota awoke at sunrise and, seeing that all still slept, got up out of bed, wishing to breathe the pure dawn air outside. Her indisposition, brought on solely by the fatigue of a sleepless night and the emotional upheavals she had undergone the day before, had disappeared completely after a long and deep sleep, and when she awoke at the sun's first light she felt happy and fortunate, saying to herself: "Enrique is alive and out of all danger; in a week I will have him beside me, loving and happy, and within a few months I will be joined to him by indissoluble bonds."

She put on a light dress and went out silently so as not to wake Teresa. Dawn was fresh and lovely, and the countryside had never seemed to her quite so picturesque and colorful.

When she emerged from the house carrying some kernels of corn in her handkerchief, she was immediately surrounded by innumerable tame birds. The Berber doves, her favorites, and the small, colorful American hens came to pick at the kernels in her skirt and landed fluttering on her shoulders.

A little farther away a peacock ruffled his neck feathers of gray and blue, proudly displaying his magnificent iridescent tail to the first rays of the sun, while the peaceful gander slowly came up to get his portion. The young girl felt very happy at this moment, like a child who encounters her toys after waking from an innocent sleep on her mother's bosom.

Fear of a great misfortune makes us less sensitive to smaller trials. Carlota, having believed her beloved lost to her forever, felt his momentary absence much less keenly. Her soul, exhausted from so many acute pangs, rested with delight on the things which surrounded her, and that incipient, pure day seemed to the maiden's eyes like the peaceful times of her earliest youth.

At the time our story takes place, no great importance was given to gardens in places like Puerto Príncipe; they were hardly known, perhaps because the entire country itself was like a vast and magnificent garden which nature had made and with which no artifice dared to compete. Nevertheless Sab, who knew how much his young mistress loved flowers, had created a small and delightful garden next to Bellavista's main house, toward which the young woman, having fed her favorite birds, now turned her steps.

This little garden adhered neither to the French nor to the English fashion: in laying it out, Sab had followed only his own fancy.

It was a small enclosure protected from the hot south wind by a triple row of tall reeds of a handsome dark green known as *pitos,* which, when gently ruffled by the breeze, produced a soft and melancholy murmur, like that of a gently purling brook. The garden was a perfect square, the other three sides of which were formed by arches of rushes covered by showy festoons of vines and garden balsam, where buzzing hummingbirds[1] as brilliant as emeralds and topazes sipped from red and gold blossoms.

In this small enclosure, Sab had assembled all of Carlota's most beloved flowers. An *astronomía*[2] displayed sumptuous clusters of deep purple blossoms. There were lilies and roses, *clavellinas*[3] and jasmine, the modest violet and the proud sunflower, enamored of the eye of heaven, the changeable pink *malva,*[4] wood sorrel with its pearly blossoms and the *pasionaria,*[5] whose magnificent calyx bears the sacred marks of the Redeemer's passion. In the center of the garden, there was a little pond in which Sab had collected some small, brightly colored fish; encircling the pond was a bench shaded by the broad green leaves of the banana trees.

Carlota ran about the garden filling her white batiste handkerchief with flowers; from time to time she interrupted this task to pursue the colored butterflies which hovered over the blossoms. When fatigued she sat down at the banks of the pond. Her beautiful eyes gradually took on a pensive expression, and she distractedly plucked apart the blossoms she had just chosen so happily, then tossed them into the pond.

Once she was roused from her daydreaming by a slight sound which to her seemed to have been made by the footsteps of someone approaching. Thinking it was Teresa, who had woken up and noticing her absence was coming to fetch her, she called to her several times. No one answered and unconsciously Carlota fell back into her reverie. Not for long, however, for the loveliest and whitest of the butterflies she had seen that morning daringly came to land on her skirt, subsequently fluttering off with provocative flight. Carlota shook her head as though to expel from it a troublesome thought and followed the butterfly with her eyes, seeing it alight on a jasmine whose whiteness it excelled. The young woman got up and darted over to it, but the swift insect evaded her skilled advance and escaped from between her lovely fingers; rapidly fluttering off and stopping at intervals, it led its pursuer on for a long time, mocking her attempts at the very moment that she thought them successful. Tiring a little, Carlota redoubled her efforts, lay in ambush for her swift opponent, kept after it tenaciously, and throwing her handkerchief over it, finally managed to catch it. With the expression of triumph her face became even more beautiful, and with childish glee she peered at the prisoner through an opening in the handkerchief; but with the same inconstancy of the young, she was suddenly no longer amused by the misfortune of her captive. Opening her handkerchief, she took delight in seeing it fly away freely, just as a moment before she had taken pleasure in capturing it.

Seeing her so young, so childlike, so lovely, unreflecting men would never guess that the heart which beat with joy at the captivity and the release of a butterfly would be capable of feelings as strong as they are deep. Ah, they do not know that for superior souls it is necessary to descend from time to time from their elevated heights, that those extraordinary spirits, left unsatisfied by the greatest that the world and life offer them, also need trivial things. If at times they become frivolous and flighty, it is because they feel the need to respect their great gifts and fear to be consumed by them.

In the same way, the current gently spreads its waters over the plants of the field and caresses the flowers which in its impetuous flood it is capable of destroying and uprooting in an instant.

Carlota was interrupted in her innocent amusement by the bustle of the slaves going off to work. She called to them, asking their names one by one and inquiring with enchanting kindness about each one's particular situation, position, and state of being. Delighted, the blacks responded by showering her with blessings and extolling Don Carlos's goodness and Sab's devotion and benevolence. Carlota enjoyed listening to them and, with words of compassion and affection, divided among them what money she had in her pockets. The slaves went off still blessing her, and she looked after them with brimming eyes.

"Poor unfortunate souls!" she exclaimed. "They judge themselves fortunate because they are not receiving blows and abuse, and they calmly eat the bread of slavery. They judge themselves fortunate, yet their children are slaves before they leave their mother's womb, and they see them sold off like unthinking beasts . . . Their children, their flesh and blood! When I am Enrique's wife," she added after a moment of silence, "no unhappy soul around me will breathe the poisonous air of slavery. We will give all our blacks their freedom. What does it matter to be less wealthy? Will we be any less happy because of it? A hut with Enrique is enough for me, and for him there will be no greater riches than my gratitude and my love."

When she finished these words the reeds trembled as though a strong hand had shaken them, and Carlota, startled, left the garden and hurried toward the house.

She had just reached the threshold when behind her she heard a familiar voice wishing her good morning and saw that it was Sab.

"I thought you would have already left for the city," she said to him.

"It seemed to me," said the young man with some agitation, "that I should wait for Your Grace to get up to ask if you had any orders for me."

"I appreciate that, Sab, and will go right now to write to Enrique; I'll give you my letter in a moment."

Carlota went into the house where her father, her sisters, and Teresa slept soundly. As Sab saw her disappear from view, he exclaimed with a deep and melancholy voice, "Why can't your innocent and fervent dreams come true, angel of Heaven? . . . Why did He Who placed you into this world of wretchedness and evil not give this handsome foreigner the mulatto's soul?"

Deeply distressed, he bowed his head and remained lost a while in unhappy thoughts. Subsequently he went to the stable in which were housed his black pony and Enrique's handsome sorrel. Placing his hand on the pony's back, he looked at him with tender eyes.

"Loyal and peaceful animal," he said to him, "you gently carry the weight of this wretched body. Not even the tempest frightens you or induces you to shake it off against the crags. While you respect your worthless burden, this handsome animal rids himself of his, throwing and trampling the fortunate man whose life is cherished and whose death would be mourned. My poor pony! If you were as capable of understanding as you are of affection you would know how much good you could have done to hurl me against the rocks during the storm. No tears would be shed at my death . . . the poor mulatto would be no loss to anyone and you could gallop free over the land or carry a more worthy rider."

The horse lifted its head and looked at him as though wishing to understand him and thereupon licked Sab's hands; by this the animal seemed to be saying "I love you a great deal so as to please you; from no other hand but yours do I gladly accept food."

Sab received the pony's affection with obvious emotion and began to saddle him, saying in an increasingly mournful voice, "You are the only being on earth willing to caress these rough, sunburned hands; you are the only one not ashamed to love me; just as I, you were born to servitude . . . but oh! poor animal! Your fate is kinder than mine. Destiny has been less cruel to you, for it has not given you the unfortunate privilege of thought. No voice cries from within you that you deserved a more noble fate, and so you endure yours with resignation."

Carlota's sweet call brought him out of his dark musings. He took the letter the girl gave him, bade her farewell respectfully, and departed on his pony, leading Enrique's sorrel on a halter.

By this time the whole family had gotten up, and Carlota went in to breakfast. She had never been prettier or more pleasant: her happiness put everyone in good spirits, and even Teresa seemed less cold and aloof than usual. So that day passed in agreeable conversations and short walks, as did the others which marked Enrique's absence.

Carlota spent a considerable part of these imagining the anticipated pleasure of a delightful excursion with her suitor. Such is love! It longs for an unlimited future but does not scorn even the shortest moment. Carlota expected a lifetime of love, yet was enraptured by the prospect of the next few days, as though these were the only ones in which she might be able to enjoy her beloved's presence.

She anticipated the pleasure of traveling through a colorful and magnificent country with her chosen man, and it is true that there is nothing more pleasant to the heart than to be able to travel in that way. Nature becomes more beautiful in the presence of the beloved, and this person in turn is embellished by nature. There is some inexplicable, magical harmony between the cherished voice, the whispering of the trees, the current of the stream, and the murmuring of the breeze. In the excitement of the trip everything passes before our eyes like the landscapes of a panorama, but the beloved is always there, and in his glances and his smile we once again encounter the delightful feelings which created the vivid—yet fading—imaginings of the heart.

Should a man wish to experience fully these indescribable feelings, let him travel through the Cuban countryside with someone he loves. Let him cross with her over its gigantic mountains, its immense savannas, its picturesque meadows: let him climb the steep hills, covered with rich and unfading green; let him listen in the solitude of the forests to the sound of its streams and the song of its mockingbirds. Then he will feel that immense, powerful vitality that those who live under cloudy northern skies have never felt: then he will have experienced in a few hours a whole spectrum of emotions . . . but let him not try afterward to find them in the heavens or the earth of other lands. He will never encounter their equal.

Chapter Seven

What I want
are sacks and not rubbish. . . .
first the doubloons.
                    —Cañizares

—— • ——

At ten in the morning of a hot day, eight days after he had left Bellavista, Enrique Otway and his father were breakfasting amicably in a room on the first floor of a large house, located on one of the best streets of Puerto Príncipe.

The young man's face still bore some purple blotches from the bruises he had received in his fall, and on his forehead was the recent mark of a wound which had barely healed over. Nevertheless, his figure seemed most attractive and beguiling because of the ease and informality of dress occasioned by the heat. A shirt of transparent batiste scarcely concealed the whiteness of his back and left entirely bare a throat that seemed cast from a beautiful Greek mold, around which floated the golden curls of his blond hair.

Opposite this graceful figure could be seen the gross and repulsive one of the old peddler: bald head covered here and there by tufts of reddish hair now streaked with gray, highly flushed cheeks, sunken eyes, furrowed forehead, thin, clamped lips, pointed chin, and a tall, spare body enfolded in a white, starched dressing gown.

While Enrique eagerly consumed a large mug of hot chocolate, the old man stared at him out of cavernous eyes and said with a deep, harsh voice: "Even with her father's inheritance I doubt that Carlota de B—— will have more than a modest fortune: and that in run-down, worthless property. . . . Bah, these damned islanders know more about imitating wealth than acquiring or keeping it. But in any event, there is no lack of substantial fortunes in the country; no, while there are others from whom to choose, as good and richer than she, you are not going to marry Carlota de B——. Have you any doubts that any one of these island girls, even the most distinguished, would be happy to have you? Ha, I'll take care of that. Thanks to Heaven and to my discretion, our bad situation is not generally known, and in this new land the so-called nobility is not yet conversant with the ancient prejudices of the old European aristocracy. If Don Carlos de B—— had some objections, you see that later on he considered it wise to take another tack. I guarantee that you can marry whomever strikes your fancy."

The old man grimaced in an approximation of a smile and continued, rubbing his hands and opening as wide as possible the eyes that were shining with avarice.

"Oh, if the dream I had last night would only come true! I know you make fun of dreams, Enrique, but mine was remarkable, plausible, prophetic. I dreamt that I had won the big lottery! Forty thousand pesos in gold and silver! Do you know what a fortune is? Forty thousand pesos to a businessman in difficulty! . . . That's a boneless tidbit, as they say here. The post from Havana was supposed to have arrived last night, but the confounded mail seems to be intentionally slow in order to prolong the agony of this wait."

And indeed, the old man's face showed extreme anxiety.

"If your hopes are going to be dashed," said the young man, "the later the better. But in any case, even if we win a sixth, the amount would be enough to rebuild our business and I could marry Carlota."

"Marry Carlota!" exclaimed George, setting down the mug of chocolate he was about to bring to his lips and which he left untouched when he heard his son's remark. "Marry Carlota when you would have forty thousand pesos more! When you would be a match for the richest girl in the country! How can you even think about it, you fool? What spell has that woman cast over you to impair your judgment like this?"

"She is so lovely!" replied the young man, not without a trace of shyness. "She is so good, her heart is so tender, her talent so captivating!"

"Bah, bah!" interrupted George impatiently, "and what does a husband do with all of that? I've told you a hundred times, he becomes associated with a firm: for investment, for profit. The beauty and the talent that a man of our class looks for in a woman to marry is wealth and thrift. What a pretty acquisition you would have had with your fastidious beauty, penniless yet accustomed to the luxury of affluence. Marriage, Enrique, is—"

The old man was about to continue to expand on his commercial theories about matrimony when he was interrupted by the loud rap of the door knocker, and the familiar voice of one of his slaves shouted twice:

"The mail . . . the letters which came by mail are here."

George Otway got up with such force that he spilled chocolate all over the table and crashed his chair to the floor; he ran to open the door and with a trembling hand snatched the letters which the bowing servant proffered. He opened three in succession and threw them down angrily, saying between clenched teeth: "Nothing but business!"

Finally he tore open an envelope and found what it was he was looking for: the newspaper from Havana which contained the account of the winning numbers. But his excessive agitation prevented him from reading those lines which would fulfill or destroy his hopes, and he handed the paper to his son.

"Take it," he said. "You read it. I have three tickets: numbers 1750, 3908, and 8004. Read it quickly; I want to know the grand prize, the forty thousand pesos, hurry up."

"The grand prize was won in Puerto Príncipe," exclaimed the young man with joy.

"In Puerto Príncipe! Come on . . . the number, Enrique, the number!" and the old man scarcely breathed.

But the door, which he had left open, allowed the figure of a mulatto to enter (a figure well known to our readers) and Sab, who did not realize the bad timing of his arrival, stepped forward with his hat in his hand.

"Damn you!" George Otway shouted furiously. "What the hell do you want, you mulatto scoundrel, and how dare you come in here without my permission? What is that imbecile black doing? Where is he and why has he not thrown you out with a sound thrashing?"

Sab stopped with astonishment at such an abrupt reception. He stared at the Englishman while his brow furrowed and his lips trembled convulsively, as happens when a chill precedes a fever. One might assume that he was intimidated by George's enraged aspect, were it not for the flush which instantly altered the yellowish whiteness of his eyes and the fire which shot from his jet pupils, imbuing his silence more with menace than respect.

Enrique was acutely embarrassed by the rough language his father directed toward a young man whom he regarded with affection since the night of his fall. He courteously attempted to ease the affliction he must feel at George's unpleasant welcome and informed his father that as this was his own room and he had given Sab permission to enter it at any time with no previous announcement, the slave was not guilty of the impudence of which he was accused.

But the old man did not listen to these excuses, for having snatched the desired page out of Enrique's hands, he devoured it with his eyes. Sab, apparently mollified by the young man's kindness and recovered from the initial shock which George's boorishness caused him, was just opening his mouth to state the reason for his visit when a new outburst drew the attention of both young men to him again. In rage and desperation George had impulsively torn the printed page which he was reading to shreds.

"Damnation!" he repeated twice. "8014! 8014 and I have 8004! The difference of one digit! Only one digit! Damnation!" Furiously he threw himself into a chair.

Enrique could only share in his father's disappointment, uttering the words "destiny" and "bad luck" between his teeth. Turning to Sab, he ordered the slave to follow him to an adjoining room, wishing to leave George alone to rid himself of the bad mood brought on by a dashed hope.

When he looked at the mulatto and saw an expression of vivid joy shining in his eyes, he was surprised and offended, for he naturally thought that Sab rejoiced in his father's disappointment. He consequently shot him a reproachful glance, which the mulatto did not notice, or pretended not to have seen, for without attempting to explain himself, Sab said quickly, "I came to tell Your Grace that I am leaving for Bellavista in an hour."

"In an hour! The heat is at its worst and the hour inconvenient," Enrique said, "else I should go with you, for I had promised Carlota to accompany her on the excursion to Cubitas which your master is planning."

"At a good clip," replied Sab, "we could be at the plantation in two hours and could leave for Cubitas this afternoon."

Enrique thought for a moment.

"Very well," he replied, "tell a slave to get my horse ready and wait for me in the patio. We shall go together."

Sab bowed as a sign of obedience and went out to comply with Enrique's orders, while the latter returned to his father, whom he found stretched out on a sofa with an expression of profound discouragement.

"Father," said the young man, giving his voice an affectionate tone which harmonized perfectly with his gentle countenance, "if I have your permission, I will leave immediately for Guanaja. Last night you told me that a ship which is consigned to you is due to dock in that harbor at any moment, and my presence there might be necessary. On my way I will stop in Cubitas and attempt to find out what land Don Carlos owns thereabouts, what it produces, and its value. In short, when I return I can give you an exact account of everything. In that way," he added, lowering his voice, "you could accurately assess the advantages and disadvantages to our firm which might result in the event of my union with Carlota, should it ever take place."

George kept silent as though he were pondering the answer, and thereupon turned to his son. "Very well," he told him, "go ahead and Godspeed, but don't forget that we need gold and silver more than land, be it red or black, and if Carlota de B—— does not bring you a dowry of forty or fifty thousand pesos in hard cash, your marriage with her cannot take place."

Making no reply, Enrique bade his father farewell and went out to meet Sab, who was waiting for him.

When the old man saw him leave, he sighed heavily and murmured, "The foolishness of youth! That idiot is as calm as though he had not seen forty thousand pesos slip through his fingers!"

Chapter Eight

He sang, and lovingly
his soft voice surpassed
the song of the birds
that herald the dawn.
　　　　　　—Lista

———　•　———

For a second time the two travelers crossed those regions, but instead of a stormy night they were importuned by the heat of a lovely day. To forget the hardships of travel at such an uncomfortable hour, Enrique closely questioned his companion about the actual state of Don Carlos's property, queries which Sab answered with a show of simplicity and candor. Nevertheless, at times Sab shot him such penetrating glances that the young foreigner lowered his eyes, as though fearful that the mulatto would read in them the motive behind his questions.

"My master's fortune," he told him at one point, "is quite reduced, and no doubt it is a comfort to him to marry his oldest daughter to someone rich, who does not pay undue attention to the dowry which the young lady can bring."

Sab did not look at Otway as he spoke these words and could not see the flush which crept up Enrique's cheeks on hearing them. Waiting a moment before answering, he finally said with an unsteady voice, "Carlota has a richer and more estimable worth in her charms and virtues."

Sab glanced at him attentively with a look that seemed to ask if in fact he knew how to appreciate that intangible dowry. Enrique could not bear the wordless query and turned his head away with some irritation. The mulatto murmured between his teeth: "No, you are not capable of it!"

"What did you say, Sab?" asked Enrique, who, though he had not been able to catch the words clearly, had heard the sound of his voice. "Are you by chance praying?"

"I was thinking, sir, that the place where we are right now is the same in which I found Your Grace unconscious, in the midst of the horrors of the storm. Over on the right is the hut to which I carried you on my shoulders."

"Yes, Sab, and I have no need to see these places to remember that I owe you my life. Carlota has already given you your freedom, and I will reward the service you have done me even more generously."

"I do not deserve any reward," the mulatto answered with an altered voice. "My mistress had put your safety in my hands, and it was my duty to obey her."

"It seems that you love Carlota very much," replied Enrique, stopping his horse to pick an orange from a tree which was bowed down with fruit.

The mulatto shot his eagle's glance at him, but the expression on his companion's face assured him that those words held no hidden purpose of sounding him out. He finally answered quietly while Enrique used a knife to peel the orange he had picked. "And who that knows her cannot love her? In the eyes of her humble slave, Señorita de B—— is what she should be to any honorable man: an object of worship and tenderness."

Enrique impatiently discarded the orange and continued on without looking at Sab. Perhaps the secret voice of his conscience was at that moment telling him that if he were to exchange his own heart for that of this lowly human being, he would be more deserving of Carlota's fervent love.

Upon hearing the gallop of the two horses they knew to be Enrique's and Sab's, the de B—— family ran out to welcome them, and Carlota, trembling with love and happiness, threw herself into her beloved's arms. Señor de B—— and the little girls showered him with the tenderest affection and welcomed him into the house with obvious pleasure.

Only two people remained on the patio: Teresa, upright, motionless on the threshold which the two lovers had just crossed without seeing her; and Sab, just as upright and motionless before her, standing by the black pony from which he had just dismounted. Both regarded each and both trembled, each having seen, as though in a mirror, in the glance of the other the painful feeling which at that moment possessed them. Surprised, they both exclaimed at the same time: "Sab!" "Teresa!"

They understood each other, and each one avoided the other's glance. Sab disappeared into the cane fields, running like a stag who has been mortally wounded by the hunter's steel shaft. Teresa shut herself in her room.

Meanwhile joy reigned in the household, and Carlota had never felt greater happiness than now, when she had her beloved by her side after having feared she had lost him. She looked at the scar on his forehead and shed tears of compassion. She told him of all her fears, of all her past anguish in order to revel in her present good fortune, and her tenderness was so fervent and eloquent that Enrique, captivated by her in spite of himself, felt his heart beat with an unknown feeling.

"Carlota!" he said to her once, "a love like yours is such a gift that I fear I do not deserve it. My soul is perhaps not great enough to be filled with the love which I owe you."

And he pressed the girl's hand over his heart, which beat with such pure and ardent feeling that perhaps that moment, in which he confessed himself undeserving of his good fortune, was one of the few in his life when he truly did deserve it.

In the emotions of spirited and fervent souls there is something akin to a magnetic force which moves and has sway over everything which approaches them. In this way an ordinary soul can feel itself lifted up to the level of the superior one with which it has contact, and only when it recedes, when it finds itself alone and back in its accustomed place, can it comprehend that the strange force which moved it and gave it a vitalizing strength came from without.

Señor de B—— came over to interrupt the two lovers.

"I hope," he said, sitting down beside them, "that you have not forgotten the excursion we had planned to Cubitas. When do you want to leave?"

"As soon as possible," said Otway.

"This very afternoon, then," replied Don Carlos. "I will advise Teresa and Sab to take care of everything necessary to our departure, for I see," he added, kissing his daughter on the forehead, "that my Carlota is far too busy to attend to it."

He left immediately, and the little girls, delighted at the idea of the outing, skipped after him.

"I'll be with you for two or three days in Cubitas," Enrique told his sweetheart, "then I have to go to Guanaja."

"Hardly do I have the pleasure of seeing you," she replied with her sweetest voice, "when you already announce some new absence. Nevertheless, Enrique, at this moment I am so happy that I cannot complain."

"Soon the day will come," he replied, "when we will be joined, nevermore to separate."

Yet as he said this he secretly asked himself if this day would actually ever come, and if it would be possible for him to renounce the joy of possessing Carlota. He looked at her and she had never seemed lovelier. Upset and unhappy with himself, he got up and began to pace about the room, trying to hide his confusion. Carlota, however, could not help but notice it and asked him the reason with timid glances. Oh, if she could have guessed it at that instant! . . . She would have had to die or to cease loving him.

Enrique avoided meeting the girl's eyes and leaned on a windowsill at some distance from her. Carlota was hurt by that rapid change of mood, yet her womanly pride immediately told her to feign indifference toward such strange behavior. Since her guitar stood near her, she picked it up and attempted to sing. Emotion caused her voice to waver, but in a moment she steadied it, and purely by chance, without conscious choice, she sang this song, hardly suspecting how applicable it might be to their own situation:

Nise is young and gentle,
and her tender heart
bestows undying devotion
on the handsome Damon.
Another time her tenderness
was proudly returned by the shepherd,
but alas! a new beauty
has offered him a new love.
Nise is a poor lass
and Laura a rich beauty,
and though she is not Nise's equal in love
she exceeds her in rank.
With gold Laura gratifies
her lover's ambition;
Nise gives him her heart
as a tender treasure.
The bewitched shepherd
succumbs to the power of wealth,
and Nise watches him fall
on his knees before Laura.
Seeing herself spurned
by the ungrateful shepherd,
the unhappy maiden
damns the accursed love.
She sees not that awful vengeance
takes hold of the faithless lover
and in his cup of hope
is mingled the gall of woe.
Belated repentance
now poisons his life
and though a wealthy man,
he begins to feel the tedium of life.
He lives among cares and sorrows,
rich yet without pleasure;
sleep steals from his eyes,
and his soul is deprived of peace.
His beloved Nise remembers
and emits a sigh of pain;
in a deep and angry voice
this is how she speaks to him of love:
"One day men will rue
the wrongs they do me,
and only in this way, Damon,

do they satisfy my vengeance;
for I bestow greater contentment
in a poor and humble abode
than you, fool, with untold riches,
will ever be able to know.

The young woman finished her song, but Enrique seemed to hear her still. Carlota had just responded clearly to his secret doubts, to his hidden thoughts. Had she perhaps guessed them? Could Heaven itself have spoken through the mouth of that tender beauty?

A powerful and involuntary impulse made him fall at her feet, and he was just about to speak, perhaps to vow that she would be preferred above all the treasures on earth, when Don Carlos reappeared. Sab followed him, but out of respect he stopped at the threshold of the door while the flustered Enrique arose from kneeling at his beloved's feet, already ashamed of the strange impulse of generous tenderness which had momentarily overcome him. Carlota's cheeks were also deeply flushed, but through her embarrassment could be glimpsed the secret satisfaction of her soul; although Enrique had not spoken a word when he fell at her feet, she had, with the admirable perspicacity of her sex, seen in his eyes that she had never been loved as deeply as at that moment.

Don Carlos poked a few jokes at the two lovers, but as he noticed their increasing discomfort, he hurriedly changed the subject.

"Here is Sab," he told them. "Tell him the hour of departure because he is in charge of all the arrangements for the journey and, as he knows these roads, will be our guide."

The mulatto then approached, and Don Carlos sat down between Carlota and Enrique. Turning to the latter, he continued, "I have not been to Cubitas in ten years, and even before that I used to visit the farms I own there very infrequently. They were practically abandoned, but according to what I am told ever since Sab came to Bellavista, his frequent visits to Cubitas have been very advantageous, and I think that I will find them in much better condition than when I saw them last."

Sab observed that these properties were still far from the state of improvement and utility which they might attain if they were better cared for. He then inquired after the hour of departure.

Carlota indicated five o'clock in the afternoon, an hour in which the breezes begin to refresh the air and the summer heat is less unbearable. Sab withdrew.

"He is an excellent young man," said Don Carlos, "and his zeal and devotion have been most useful to this plantation. His natural intelligence is extraordinary, and he has admirable skill in anything he wishes to do; I am very fond of him and he could have had his freedom some time ago had he so desired. But now it is imperative that he should have it, and I hasten to carry out my resolution, for my Carlota wishes it so. I have written to my lawyer in Puerto Príncipe on this subject and you, Enrique, will go and see him on your return and bring our good friend Sab his letter of freedom yourself."

Enrique nodded his head in agreement, and Carlota, kissing her father's hand, exclaimed passionately, "Yes, let him be free! He has been my childhood companion and my first friend. It was he," she added with greater tenderness, "who lavished his care on you the night of your fall, Enrique, and who like a consoling angel came to restore peace to my distressed heart."

At that moment Teresa entered the room; the meal was served immediately, and conversation centered on nothing else but their departure.

Chapter Nine

Where is the innocent and pure race
which dwelt in the Antilles? The conqueror's steel
furiously wounds it, it trembles, moans, perishes
as mist at the rising of the sun.

—Heredia

—— • ——

When one is young a journey is the source of great pleasure and happiness. Movement and variety are absolute necessities at an age in which the soul, still free from disquieting passions but sensing the unfolding of latent desires while yet lacking an object on which to focus, projects itself outward, seeking in new occupations and activities a release from the feverish vitality which excites it.

No sooner had Sab appeared with the carriages and horses which had been readied for their departure than he was surrounded by the four pretty little girls, Carlota's sisters, who joyously showered him with affection. The mulatto responded to their childish caresses with a melancholy smile.

Ten years ago, he thought, Carlota would leap up just like that to throw her arms around my neck when she saw me again after a short absence. Just like that her rosy lips would sometimes press a sisterly kiss on my forehead, and her lovely alabaster countenance would bend over my dark one, like the small white flower which curves over the dark crag of the riverbed.

Sab hugged the little girls, and a tear, coursing slowly down his cheek, fell on the angelic head of the youngest and loveliest of the four.

At that moment Carlota appeared. An English riding habit gave a regal air to her graceful figure, and a few small curls escaped from the beaver hat which covered her head, shadowing a face which glowed gently with happiness. Fire rushed to Sab's cheeks, drying the recent trace of his weeping, and he trembled as he handed Carlota the handsome white horse which had been readied for her.

The travelers gathered around the lovely *criolla,* and Sab subsequently laid out his route of travel. He announced that he was going to guide them to Cubitas not by the regular road but by a little-known path which, although somewhat longer, would provide them with more pleasant vistas.

That plan having been unanimously approved, the only thought was to depart.

There were two *volantes* (a kind of carriage which was widely used in

Cuba at that time), one of which was occupied by Señor de B—— with the two older girls, while Teresa and the two younger ones took the other. Carlota, Enrique, and Sab were on horseback. And thus the company departed, amid the happy shouts of the girls and the neighing of the horses.

Without any schooling in equitation, the women of Puerto Príncipe are generally splendid riders, but when she rode Carlota stood out among them all for the grace and nobility of her bearing. That afternoon she cantered by her suitor's side with exceptional sureness and elegance, and the incipient breeze, alternately filling and blowing the white veil which descended from her hat and fluttered about her slender figure, made her look like one of the mysterious sylphs, daughters of the air and sovereigns of the earth.

The countryside through which they traveled was beautiful. Enrique drew near the step of the carriage in which Don Carlos was riding and struck up a conversation with him about the prodigious fertility of this exceptional country and the degree of profit that could be gained from it. Sab followed Carlota closely and alternately glanced at the land and at her, as though he were comparing them; there was in fact a certain harmony between the landscape and the woman, both so young and so beautiful.

In the meantime Teresa was having some trouble controlling her two young companions. A *campanilla,*[1] a bird which flew overhead—any object at all—excited their childish desires and made them want to get out of the carriage to possess it.

Meanwhile night was falling, and its dark shadows progressively obscured the pastoral landscape which surrounded the travelers. The rich vegetation no longer showed its various tints of green, and the distant hills appeared to the eyes like great shadowy masses.

As they approached Cubitas, the countryside became more stark: soon the black earth's abundant and varied vegetation practically disappeared, and the red earth produced nothing more than scattered *yuraguanos*[2] and here and there an unpleasant *jagüey,*[3] which appeared in the night like capricious figures from a fantastic world. The sky, notwithstanding, was more beautiful in these places: it was studded with innumerable stars, and the air was filled with glowing *cocuyos,*[4] the lovely fireflies of the tropics, which seemed like a second army of wandering stars.

Suddenly Carlota reined in her horse and pointed out to the mulatto a brilliant, pale light which flickered far away on the summit of a steep hill.

"Is Cubitas over there?" she asked. "Might that light, which looks so small in the distance, be some beacon which is placed up there to help orient travelers?"

Before Sab could answer, Señor de B——, whose carriage had drawn level with Carlota's horse, burst out laughing. Enrique, however, who had never traveled this path at night, shared his sweetheart's wonder and curiosity and like her asked about the source of that peculiar light. But at that instant the light disappeared, and one could see nothing more than the great mass of the hill, which, like a giant of the air, projected its enormous shadow on the distant horizon.

"It appears," said Don Carlos laughing, "that the disappearance of the pretty light has disappointed you, but wait . . . I will call up the genie of this place, and the mysterious beacon will shine again."

Hardly had he uttered these words than the light reappeared with greater brilliance, and Enrique and the two ladies showed as great a surprise as the little girls. Señor de B——, who had witnessed this phenomenon[5] many times before, was amused at his young companions' astonishment.

"Naturalists," he told them, "would give you a less amusing explanation of the phenomenon you are witnessing than Sab can give you, for he often takes this road and has contact with all the people of Cubitas. Undoubtedly he will have heard some very curious explanation with respect to the light which has so caught your attention."

The little girls shouted with joy, elated at the prospect of hearing a wonderful story, and Enrique and Carlota brought their horses around on either side of Sab's mount so as to hear him better. The mulatto turned his head toward his master's carriage and said, "Your Grace cannot have forgotten old Martina, the mother of one of the overseers of Cubitas, who died and left her in dire poverty, as she inherited the care of his wife and three children. Four years ago through my intervention Your Grace's generous compassion came to her aid, for when I informed you of the desperate conditions in which this family found itself, you gave me a purse full of silver to help them."

"I remember old Martina," responded the gentleman. "Her late son was an excellent person, and she, if I remember correctly, is a bit mad. Doesn't she claim to be a descendant of the Indian race and puts on ridiculously majestic airs?"

"Yes, sir," Sab replied, "and she has managed to inspire a certain deference among the farmers of Cubitas, in part because they really believe her to be a descendant of that unfortunate race, now almost extinct on this island, and in part because of her immense wisdom, her knowledge of medicine from which they derive great benefit and the pleasure they feel when listening to her tell her incessant stories about vampires and ghosts—all this gives her real importance among the local people. It is this woman, this old Martina, whom I have often heard refer—in a mysterious manner and interrupting herself from time to time with exclamations of sorrow and dire prophecies of divine vengeance—to the savage and horrible death which, according to her, the Spaniards meted out to chief Camagüey, the ruler of this province and the one from whom our poor

Martina claims to descend. Camagüey, despicably treated by the invaders whom he had welcomed with generous and open hospitality, was thrown from the top of this great hill, and his shattered body lay unburied on the ground, stained red with his blood. From that day on, the earth for many leagues around turned red, and every night the soul of the unhappy chief returns to the fatal hill in the form of a light, to predict to the descendants of his savage murderers the vengeance which sooner or later Heaven will cause to fall upon them. At certain times, when Martina is possessed by this fit of vengeance, she raves in a frightening manner and dares to utter terrible prophecies."

"And what are they?" asked Don Carlos with a certain uneasy curiosity which showed that he had already suspected that about which he asked.

Sab was a little troubled, but he finally said in a low and tremulous voice, "In her moments of exaltation, sir, I have heard the old Indian woman shout: 'The earth which once was drenched in blood will be so again: the descendants of the oppressors will be themselves oppressed, and black men will be the terrible avengers of those of copper color."

"Enough, Sab, enough," interrupted Don Carlos with some annoyance, for the Cubans, always in a state of alarm after the frightful and recent example of a neighboring island,[6] could never hear without fear any words in the mouth of a man of that unfortunate color which made patent the feeling of his abused rights and the possibility of recapturing them. But Carlota, who had paid less attention to the old woman's prophecies than to the sad story of the chief's death, turned her beautiful, tear-filled eyes on Enrique.

"I have never been able," she said, "to calmly read the bloody history of the conquest of America. My God, how many horrors! It still seems incredible that men were able to reach such extremes of savagery. I am sure it must be exaggerated, for it is impossible; human nature cannot be that monstrous."

The mulatto regarded her with an indescribable expression; Enrique made fun of her tears.

"You are a child, my love," he said to her. "Are you crying now about an old woman's story, about the death of someone who perhaps never existed at all except in Martina's imagination?"

"No, Enrique," the young woman replied with sadness, "I am not weeping for Camagüey, nor do I know if he ever really existed, but I do cry when I remember an unfortunate people who once dwelt on the lands we live on now, who were the first to see the same sun that shone on our cradle, and who have disappeared from this country, of which they were the peaceful owners. Here those children of nature lived in happiness and innocence: this virgin soil did not need to be watered with the sweat of slaves to be productive; everywhere it gave shade and fruit, water and flowers, and its entrails had not been rent asunder so that its hidden treasures could be torn out by greedy hands.[7] Oh, Enrique! I lament not having been born then when you, an Indian like me, would have built me a palm hut where we would have enjoyed a life of love, innocence, and freedom."

Enrique smiled at his sweetheart's fervor and caressed her; the mulatto turned away his tear-filled eyes.

"Ah, yes!" he thought. "You would be no less lovely if your skin were black or copper. Why did Heaven not will it so, Carlota? You, who understand the life and happiness of the savages, why were you not born with me in the burning deserts of Africa or in some unknown corner of America?"

Señor de B—— pulled him out of his reverie by asking him several questions with respect to Martina.

"Is she still alive?" he queried.

"Yes, sir, she lives on in spite of having suffered painful misfortunes these last few years."

"What has happened to her, then?" the gentleman asked with interest.

"Her daughter-in-law died three years ago, and her two grandsons ten months after that. Her house burned down a year ago leaving her in even greater poverty than that from which Your Grace's kindness rescued her. Today she lives in a small hut near the caves with the only grandson who is left her, a child six years of age; the sicker he gets, the more she cherishes him, for it does not appear that he will have a long life."

"We will go and see her," said Don Carlos, "and we will have her installed on one of my farms. Poor woman, as eccentric as she is, she is very good!"

"Ah yes, very good," the mulatto exclaimed with feeling, and urging on his horse with a shout, he rode ahead to announce his master's arrival to the overseer of the farm where they planned to stay.

It was nine o'clock at night when the visitors arrived in Cubitas. Although the house which had been chosen for their domicile had a poor appearance, it was spacious inside, and the overseer and his wife attempted to provide the recent arrivals with all possible comforts. The supper which was served was scanty and frugal, but happiness and a good appetite made it seem delicious. Don Carlos had never been as jovial, nor Carlota more smiling and amiable. Even Teresa seemed less aloof than usual, and Enrique was charmed.

The time came to retire. "My dearest," said Carlota to Enrique, stopping on the threshold of the little chamber set aside for her bedroom, to which he had led her by the hand, "how easily two tender and ardent lovers can be happy! In this poor village, in this sorry house, with a hammock for a bed and a field of yuca for wealth I would be happy with you, and nothing in the rest of the universe would arouse my ambition. And you, could you possibly want more?"

As his only answer Enrique fervently kissed her lovely hand, and she crossed the threshold, smiling tenderly at him. She said good night and slowly closed the door, which she proceeded to open again, to repeat "Good night" with an ineffable look. At last the door closed completely, and Enrique, motionless and thoughtful, stayed for a moment as though he were waiting for it to be opened yet again. Then he shook his head and murmured, "It can't be helped! This woman is enough to drive me mad and to convince me that riches are not necessary in order to be happy."

"Sir, I was waiting for Your Grace to take you to your room," said a familiar voice at Enrique's shoulder. The latter turned and saw Sab.

"Which one is my room, then?" he asked, somewhat ill at ease.

"That one on the left."

Enrique went in hurriedly, and Sab followed him to the door, where he stopped and bade him good night.

An hour later everyone in the house was asleep; the only thing to be seen was a motionless form at the door of Señorita de B——'s room, but at the slightest perceptible noise in the house during the nighttime silence, that form stirred, roused, and emitted agitated, deep breaths. Then it became evident that the form was a man.

Once, near dawn, a light, measured sound was heard that seemed to be made by the cautious footsteps of someone approaching. The form quivered convulsively, and in the dark the blade of a machete glittered. The steps appeared to come closer. The form spoke in a low but terrible voice: "Scoundrel! You will not carry out your wicked desires."

A prolonged barking answered this threat. The steps which had been heard were those of one of the house dogs.

The machete stopped glittering, and the form once again became immobile in its place. The dog barked twice more, but as the animal drew closer he must have recognized the man whose voice had alarmed him, and he quieted down. Thereupon everything was plunged into profound silence.

Chapter Ten

The mixture of oddness and enthusiasm which was present in his speech
rarely failed to produce a vivid impression on those who listened to him.
His words, though often fragmented, were nevertheless too clear and
intelligible for one to suspect that he was truly mad.
—Walter Scott, *Guy Mannering*

—— • ——

The caves of Cubitas are assuredly a marvelous work of nature, which
many travelers have visited with curiosity and interest and which the local
inhabitants admire with a sort of fanaticism. There are three principal
chambers, called the Great (or the Black Cimarron) Cave,[1] María Teresa,
and Cayetano. The first is under the great hill of Toabaquei and consists
of various chambers, each one with its own name, all of which are connected by narrow, rugged passages. The most important chambers among
these are one called the Vault because of its size and the Oven, whose
entrance is a small hole near the earth's surface through which one can
enter only with great difficulty, practically having to crawl on the ground.
Nevertheless, the latter is one of the most famous chambers of that vast
subterranean realm, and the discomforts which one experiences while de-
scending into it are fortunately compensated for by the pleasure of admiring the beauties which it contains. The traveler who lifts his eyes in that
cramped and dark space will be dazzled when above his head he sees a rich
silver canopy strewn with sapphires and diamonds, which is how the singular roof covering the cave appears in the darkness. However, one is able
to enjoy this beautiful caprice of nature with impunity for only a few minutes: the lack of air quickly forces visitors to the cavern outside, lest they
be stifled by the excessive heat within the chamber. Alabaster does not
surpass in whiteness and beauty the exquisite stones with which these caverns are carpeted. Water, filtered through innumerable and imperceptible
cracks, has formed beautiful petrified figures. On one side, a long row of
columns appears to decorate the peristyle of some underground palace; on
the other, a handsome head attracts the eyes; elsewhere one sees countless
formations of indefinite shape, revealing masses of blinding whiteness and
strange, whimsical forms.

In the cave called María Teresa the locals point out bizarre paintings
inscribed on the walls with exceedingly bright, indelible colors, assuring
that they are the work of the Indians. A thousand marvelous stories lend
a kind of enchantment to those concealed subterranean places; they re-

mind one of mysterious fairies' palaces, so like are they to the fabulous descriptions of the poets.

No one has as yet dared to go beyond the eleventh chamber. It is popularly held that a river of blood demarcates the visible boundary thereof and that the rooms beyond are the enormous jaws of Hell. The villagers' vivid imagination has adopted this extravagant idea with such conviction that nothing on earth could induce them to penetrate farther than the boundaries to which visitors to the caves have thus far confined themselves, and the narrow and dangerous nature of the subterranean path as one continues deeper underground appears to justify their fears.

Don Carlos de B—— and his family, with Sab as their guide, began their visit to these caves the day after their arrival in Cubitas. Carlota was afraid on the dangerous way down, and the mulatto, more skilled and stronger than Otway, was on this occasion also happier, as he practically carried the maiden down in his arms.

Teresa needed almost no help at all: confident, nimble, and courageous, she descended with the cool serenity which characterized her. Then Sab brought down the little girls with utmost care and helped Señor de B——, while Enrique brought up the rear with more enthusiasm than skill. In spite of the aid of a thick rope and the strong hand of a black slave, one of his legs buckled halfway down the incline, and he would undoubtedly have fallen and dragged the slave with him if Sab, who was behind him bearing a great torch of a resinous wood called *cuaba*, had not dared to come to his aid in the nick of time.

"Sab," the Englishman said to him when all began to explore the underground chambers, "for a second time I owe you my life and am almost convinced that you are my guardian angel here on earth."

Sab did not answer but looked at Carlota, whose glances even more eloquently expressed how grateful she was for this new service rendered her beloved.

Sab appreciated this gratitude but nevertheless could not endure it; he turned his eyes away from her, sighed deeply, and went over to his master, whom he amused by recounting some popular tales about the places which they were exploring.

The walls of the caverns were covered with the names of visitors, and the group could not suppress its great astonishment at finding Carlota's name among them, as she had until then never been to the caves. At the end of the afternoon, having spent a considerable part of the day exploring different chambers, the ladies showed signs of fatigue, and upon their urging they all left the caves.

Sab had previously arranged for them to eat with Martina (of whom our readers had already heard in the preceding chapter), and the entire group looked forward with pleasure to visiting the old Indian woman.

Her house was not far from the caves, and after a six-minute walk the travelers found themselves on the threshold of her modest dwelling.

As Sab had prepared the old woman for their visit, she came out to greet her guests with a kind of ludicrously majestic air, almost a parody of hospitality. Martina was nearly sixty years old, which showed in the many wrinkles lining her lean face and long, sinewy neck but which had not affected her hair; although it covered only the back of her skull, leaving bare a forehead and receding hairline, it was nevertheless perfectly black. This swatch of hair fell down Martina's thin back, and the bald part of her head, by virtue of its shine and pallor, contrasted singularly with the almost yellowish hue of her face. This skin color, moreover, was all that supported her pretensions of being Indian, for none of her facial features appeared to match her alleged origin.

Her eyes were extremely large and somewhat protruding, of a glassy white against which her small, jet pupils stood out. Her long, thin nose appeared to have been pinched, and her mouth was so small and sunken as to be almost invisible, buried between the protuberant nose and chin, which jutted out so far as to be almost on the same plane.

For her gender the woman's height was colossal, and in spite of her age and emaciation, she stood as erect and upright as a palm tree, proudly exhibiting the superlatively ugly face we have just described.

When she met Don Carlos she bowed her head slightly and said soberly, "Welcome, three times welcome, Señor de B——, to this your house."

"Good Martina," replied the gentleman, entering a small, square room without further greeting and sitting down in a chair (if the clumsily worked piece of wood could be called such), "it gives me the greatest pleasure to see such an old acquaintance as yourself again, but I am sorry to see you in such extreme poverty. But the years haven't touched you, for you are the same as when I saw you ten years ago. You can't say the same of me: I see in your eyes that you find I have aged a great deal."

"It is true, sir," she replied, "that you are very different than when I saw you last. That is natural," she added with a certain melancholy air, "for you have not yet reached my stage, and the years still find something they can take from you. The ancient tree on the mountain, when it is dry and without sap feeds only *curujeyes*[2] and year after year passes without affecting it. It resists hurricanes and rains, the rigors of sun and the dryness of drought while the tree that is still green suffers the ravages of time and little by little loses its flowers, its leaves, and its branches. But I have here," she added, throwing a glance at Enrique and the two young women, and subsequently at the four little girls who surrounded her, "I have here three handsome trees in the prime of their youth, with all the freshness of spring, and four little saplings who are growing exuberantly. Are they all your children? I didn't think you had so many."

Don Carlos took Enrique by the hand.

"This young man is not my son," he said to her, "but he will be shortly. Let me present to you, my dear Martina, my Carlota's betrothed."

"Your Carlota's betrothed!" repeated the old woman with a tone of surprise and disquiet; she shot a careful glance around her which appeared to rest on the mulatto, standing respectfully behind her master. Then she turned to the two young women and studied them both.

"One of these is my daughter and the other my ward," said Don Carlos, noticing the scrutiny. "Let's see if you can guess which one is Carlota. I have not forgotten, Martina, that you pride yourself on being a physiognomist."

The old woman looked intently at Teresa, whose eyes were casually studying the cramped quarters of the small room in which she found herself. Slowly deflecting her glance, Martina caused it to rest on Carlota, who smiled and flushed deeply. The eyes of the Indian woman (because we have no intention of disputing this name with her) met those of the beautiful *criolla*.

"This is she," Martina exclaimed instantly, "this is Carlota de B—— I have recognized this look . . . only these eyes could—" She broke off as though confused, then added quickly, "Only she can be so beautiful."

Carlota was embarrassed by a compliment she found tactless in the presence of her friend, but Teresa was paying no attention to the conversation. At that moment her eyes were fixed on a strange and piteous object, which no one had seen save her.

In a dark corner of the room, on a kind of platform made of cedar and covered by a palm mat, there lay huddled a child, who at first could hardly be recognized as human. On closer scrutiny one could observe that he was a young boy, but the dreadful sickness which consumed him had almost totally deformed his body. His huge head, covered by scanty, coarse hair, was held erect by a neck so thin that it seemed about to snap under the weight, and his small, sunken eyes appeared rimmed by a scarlet aureole extending all the way down to his pale cheeks. The unfortunate being smiled and played with a little dog who lay between his two thin legs, his head resting on the child's distended stomach.

Teresa's glances had directed the gaze of all the others toward the corner, and Martina, noticing this, exclaimed sadly, "That is my grandson! My only grandson! I have no one else left in the world . . . my son, my daughter-in-law, my two grandsons, so handsome and robust—all have died! This poor sickly creature is the only one remaining . . . the last withered leaf that will fall from this old trunk."

Moved, Don Carlos and his children drew near the sick little child, but the latter let out a penetrating shout of joy when he spied Sab, and the dog jumped up, yelping as well. The child dragged himself off the platform in order to reach the mulatto, a gleam of joy in his dulled eyes. The dog leaped about wagging his tail, yelping and looking alternately at the child and Sab, as though calling the mulatto over to his master. Sab did so and instantly the poor child clung to his neck. The animal, redoubling its cries as if in approval of such tenderness, scampered around the two and raised itself on its hind feet, putting its paws now on the thighs of the mulatto, now on the child's back.

Martina looked at this scene with visible emotion: the ridiculous gravity with which she had welcomed her guests had disappeared, and she turned her black eyes, in which quivered a tear, on Don Carlos. "You see," she said to him, "his body is almost dead, but there is still life in his heart. Poor unfortunate child! He still lives in order to love: he loves Sab, his dog, and me, the only beings who understand and return his love. Poor unfortunate child!" And with her apron she wiped away the tear, which had run down her cheek.

"Martina," said Don Carlos to her, "you have suffered much affliction, I know."

"It could even have been worse," she replied. "One after the other of my children and grandchildren died in my arms until now there is only one left . . . This one! A fire burned down my house, and my poor only grandson would have perished in the flames without the courage, the compassion—"

Martina stopped suddenly. The mulatto, who had just disengaged himself from the child and the dog, stepped in front of her, and an imperious look stifled the words her lips were about to utter. Don Carlos and his children begged her in vain to continue the story she had begun; Martina changed the subject, asking Don Carlos if he wanted her to serve the meal. As soon as Sab had left to see to it, the old woman turned to her guests and with a low, cautious voice and a profoundly moved tone continued, "Yes, it was he who saved my poor Luis, but one cannot speak of it in his presence: he is offended by my expression of gratitude. But, why do I have to repress it? Why? It feels so sweet to me to repeat: 'I owe him the life of my last grandson!'"

Upon hearing these words Carlota brought her chair closer to Martina's, listening to her with the keenest interest. Enrique himself was all ears; only Teresa remained somewhat aloof. Martina continued:

"A happy chance brought Sab to this village a few days before the dreadful fire that reduced me to poverty. He used to visit us often, and I loved him because he helped during my son's final moments, because he was our comfort when I still had others who shared my sorrow. When I lost them he stayed with me and we mourned together. He accompanied my two little grandsons to their final resting place, and the day on which we buried the last of them he came back to the house with his eyes full of tears and embraced me, moaning. 'Sab,' I said to him in my sorrow, pointing to my poor Luis, 'I only have him left in this world . . . I have no other son.' 'You still have one more, Mother,' he exclaimed, mingling his tears with mine and with a tone I can still hear today. 'I, too, am a poor orphan: I never gave any man the sweet and holy name of father, and my unfortunate mother died in my arms; I, too, am an orphan like Luis; be my mother, take me for your son.' 'Yes, I will take you,' I said, raising my trembling hands heavenward. He knelt at my feet, and in the sight of Heaven I then adopted him as my son."

Martina stopped for a moment to dry the tears which trickled from her eyes; Carlota wept as well, Don Carlos coughed to hide his emotion, and even Enrique showed signs of having been affected. As usual Teresa paid no attention to what was being said, seemingly absorbed in cleaning a very beautiful stone with her handkerchief, a piece she had picked up in the caves.

"Sab was in Cubitas when my house burned down," Martina continued, "the house which I owed to your generosity, Señor Don Carlos, and to the efforts of my adoptive son. The flames devoured my abode, and I, only half-conscious in the arms of some neighbors who had come out of pity or of curiosity, saw the rapid progress of the fire. Vainly I screamed with all my strength, 'My grandson! My Luis!' because the child, whom I had abandoned in the first moment of fear and surprise, was going to be consumed by the flames I observed steadily approaching the place where the unhappy child lay. 'Let me go,' I cried, 'let me save him or die with him.' But they held on to me, hindering my desperate attempts, and although all felt immense compassion, no one dared to risk his life in order to save that of a poor sick child."

"And Sab saved him!" exclaimed Señorita de B—— with ardor and emotion. "Didn't you say so, good Martina? Sab saved him!"

"Yes," replied the old woman, forgetting her caution and raising her voice in the rush of her enthusiastic gratitude. "Sab saved him! Through the flames, his feet burned, his hands bloodied, choking from the smoke and the heat, he fell unconscious at my feet after placing Luis and Leal[3] in my arms . . . this dog which then was very young and slept in my grandson's bed. Sab saved them both; yes, his compassion extended even to the poor little animal."

And Martina with trembling hand stroked the little dog, who, upon hearing his name, had run over to lie at her feet.

Carlota still wept and Don Carlos still coughed, but Enrique's attention wandered from the old woman's story to the stone which Teresa was polishing, the extraordinary shine of which both were admiring.

"It's beautiful," said Enrique.

"Oh, yes, it's beautiful!" echoed Martina, who had not noticed the distraction of two of her listeners. "Sab's soul is beautiful, very beautiful! When I was left without a house, with no other possessions than my sick grandson and his dog, I had no shelter than these caves, sometimes a refuge for runaway black slaves and perennial home to bats and kestrels. There I would have ended my sad days in misery without my life's guardian angel. Sab, Sab himself built this hut for his adoptive mother, in which I have the honor of receiving you; with his own hands he built the rustic furniture I needed; he gave me all his many years' savings in order to ease my poverty. He, with his affection, his goodness, has brought about the rebirth of delightful feelings of pleasure and gratitude in this lacerated old heart. Yes, this heart beats higher when it sees him cross the threshold of my humble dwelling; these eyes still shed tears of tenderness and of joy when I hear him call me his mother, his dear mother. Oh, my God, my God!" she added, raising her thin hands heavenward, "Why does he have to be so unfortunate when he is so good?"

At this moment Sab appeared carrying a small cedar table which was to hold the meal, and his presence increased the effect that Martina's story had produced. Don Carlos, forgetting that the story of Sab's good deeds had been entrusted to him behind the mulatto's back, stretched out his hand and bid him approach his chair. "Sab, . . . Sab," he repeated with increasingly acute feeling, "you are a remarkable young man!"

The mulatto appeared to guess what had transpired and shot Martina a reproachful glance.

"Yes, my son," exclaimed the old woman, "you can scold me for not keeping the promise which you demanded of me: but why, dear Sab, why do you wish to deprive your old mother of the pleasure of blessing you and of saying to all good and generous hearts, 'What do you think of my son?' Sab, my friend, forgive me, but I cannot humor you."

Carlota increased her weeping and covered her lovely face with her hands, as though to hide the excess of her emotion, but Sab had already seen her tears and fell to his knees.

"Mother," he burst out with shaking and softened voice, "yes, I forgive you and I thank you; I owe you Carlota's tears," he added, but these last words were uttered so softly that no one except Martina could catch them.

"Sab," said Señor de B——, raising him up and embracing him with extraordinary kindness, "I am proud of your beautiful heart: you know that you are free and henceforth I offer to provide you with the means to follow the generous impulses of your charitable heart. Sab, you will continue to be the overseer of Bellavista, and I will assign you wages commensurate to your work, by means of which you can begin to create an independent life. As far as Martina is concerned, I will be responsible for her, her grandson, and his faithful Leal. When I leave Cubitas I want her installed on the best of my farms, and I will assign her a lifetime pension, which she will receive annually from you."

Once again Sab threw himself on his knees before his former master, showering his hands with kisses and tears. Carlota clung to her father's neck, kissing his hair and his forehead as well, and her dress, which at that instant brushed the mulatto's face, was caught at shyly and also received a kiss and a tear. And who could refrain from weeping at such a tender scene? Teresa, only Teresa. That peculiar creature had drawn back coldly from the pathetic spectacle which met her eyes and appeared to be closely examining the deformed body of the poor child. Enrique, less cold than she, was moved and looked now at Don Carlos, now at his sweetheart. Then, giving the still-kneeling Sab's shoulder a tap, he said, "Get up, good fellow, get up for you have done well and I also wish to reward you."

Saying this, he put a gold coin in his hand, but the hand remained open and the coin clattered to the floor.

"Sab," said Carlota tenderly, "Enrique undoubtedly wants you to give this coin in his name to little Luis."

The mulatto thereupon picked up the coin and brought it to the child who took it with pleasure. Teresa was seated on the same platform as Luis, and Sab thought when he looked at her that her eyes were wet—but no doubt it was an illusion, as Teresa's face revealed no emotion whatever.

Martina wanted to thank Señor de B—— for his charitable promise, but the latter, wishing to cut off a conversation which had already aroused too many feelings in him, asked that dinner be served, begging Martina not to worry about anything now except to do the honors of the house in a dignified fashion. Once dinner was served, Señor de B—— absolutely insisted that not only Martina but also Sab sit down at the table with them. Once the enthusiasm of the first moment of her gratitude had passed, the old Indian woman once again adopted her ridiculously majestic air, which she believed suitable to the descendant of a chief. Without being asked she took a seat at one end of the table, and Sab was ordered by his master to sit at the other end, between the oldest of his little girls and Teresa. Martina took advantage of an opening which a number of questions from Carlota gave her in order to repeat the marvelous tales of the death of Camagüey and the appearances of his spirit in the vicinity, tales which she had already told a thousand times. The little girls listened to her, their eyes wide with interest, forgetting totally about eating. Enrique did not seem to have much appetite either, and one could see some dissatisfaction in his bearing, perhaps because of a childish sense of vanity that made him disapprove of Don Carlos's excessive generosity, seating a mulatto at his table who two weeks earlier had still been his slave. There is no vanity as ridiculously sensitive as that of those men who, because of a stroke of luck, have risen from nothing to good fortune. Carlota, on the other hand, was radiant with joy and was grateful to her father for the swift reward which he had bestowed on Luis's savior and Martina's benefactor. She was always the first to offer the mulatto something from this or that dish; she was the one who spoke to him with the sweetest and most affectionate tone, and the one who, with exquisite tact, made sure that in the general conversation not one word was uttered which might hurt the sensitivity or modesty of that excellent young man whose heart deserved so much consideration. She herself fixed the plate that was to go to Luis and did not forget Leal either. While continuing to tell her everlasting tales, Martina looked at her from time to time and then would glance at Sab as well. On one occasion, she sighed deeply and her eyes filled with tears, but since she was telling the sad story of chief Camagüey, no one remarked at her emotion.

As it was getting late it was necessary to return to Don Carlos's farm. When he said good-bye to Martina, he left her his full purse, and the old woman showered him with blessings. Enrique bade her fond farewell, and Carlota hugged both her and little Luis with tears in her eyes. Then she patted Leal, telling him to take good care of the boy, and went outside to join the group that was waiting for her in order to depart.

Sab's farewell was longer: three times Martina embraced him and repeated this gesture with even greater affection several times more. Luis, clinging to his neck, appeared imbued with new life because of the affection that he felt for his adoptive brother. Sab was about to tear himself from his arms, giving him a last kiss with fatherly affection, when the boy clung to him with extraordinary tenacity.

"Listen," said Luis, "I have something to ask you for, something very pretty that they gave me for you, but which you, who are so kind, will be sure to let me have."

The mulatto heard his master's voice calling him so that the group could leave, and began to let go of Luis.

"Yes," Sab answered him, not paying attention to the object which aroused the child's desire and which the latter clutched in his tightly closed right hand, "all right, I'll give it to you."

"I knew it," said the sick boy with childish pleasure. "Ah! How good you are: I knew it from the time that lady gave me this gift—she was crying when she gave it to me for you—but you won't cry because you are giving it to your brother: you are nicer than she is."

"What! A lady gave you this gift for me?" exclaimed the mulatto, kneeling down near Luis's platform once again.

"Yes, one of those who was at our house today, and she said you would love it dearly: I believe it! It's so pretty! But you love your brother more, and that's why you have given it to him." The child caressed Sab's head, but the latter paid no more attention to his caresses.

"One of the ladies gave it to you—for me! Oh, give it to me, give it to me!" And he tore the object, which the child defended with all his strength, from the boy's hand, an object which aroused his most ardent desire.

"Don't take it away from me, you gave it to me. It's mine, it's mine," shouted Luis, crying, and Sab, who ran up to the table where a candle was burning, devoured the mysterious gift with his eyes. It was a bracelet made of chestnut hair of exceptional beauty, with the clasp formed by a small portrait in miniature.

"It's mine! Give it to me!" repeated the child, lifting his thin arms and transparent hands.

"It is she!" exclaimed the mulatto without hearing him. "It is her portrait! Her hair! My God, it is she!"

Once again he fell to his knees by the sick boy's bed, and transported, convulsed, beside himself he folded the bracelet and the child in his breast, crying constantly, "It is she! It is she!"

The child, almost suffocated in his embrace, tried to pull away while still repeating: "It's mine! It's mine!"

"In the name of Heaven," Sab told him, "in the name of Heaven, repeat to me what you said. Luis, tell me again, tell me that it was she who gave you this for me."

"Yes, but you have given it to me," said the poor creature.

"Oh! I'll give you my life, my soul, anything you wish, Luis, only tell me: was it she?" and he crushed the child's delicate hands between his own.

"You're hurting me!" he cried, frightened by the ecstasy of his adoptive brother. "Sab, let me go! I'll not ask you for this pretty thing any more. Let me go—you're breaking my hands!" the child cried, yet Sab was indifferent to his weeping.

"It was she! It was she!" he repeated, each time more enraptured.

"Yes, she," responded Luis stammering, "the lady, the smaller of the two grown-up ones, the one with the green eyes and—"

"Teresa! Teresa!" Sab interrupted him sadly, letting the child's two hands go. "It was Teresa."

"See, she gave it to me wrapped in this paper, and I took it out to look at it. Take the paper and give me that, give it to me, dear Sab, you promised."

Sab took the paper on which he read these words, written in pencil: "Luis, to him who has twice saved Enrique Otway's life give this token in return for the kindness which she owes him."

"Teresa! Teresa!" exclaimed Sab. "You have looked into this heart and know its secrets. You know how much I despise the life I have twice saved and understand the full price of my generosity. Oh, Teresa! This present of yours is the most precious thing you could give me, and perhaps I can pay you back very soon. Yes, I will do it, I will do it, and I will bless you as long as my heart beats, from which this inestimable treasure, which you deemed me worthy of possessing, will never be parted."

Señor de B——'s voice, by this time impatient with the mulatto's delay, could now be heard calling him to depart. Sab hid the precious bracelet in his breast and, tearing himself from the arms of the child who still repeated "Give it to me!" hurried out of the room. He ran into Martina who was coming to fetch him; the travelers were already in the saddle and were waiting only for him.

Sab, still unsettled, murmured some trivial excuse. Mounting his pony, he rode ahead at a quick pace, resuming his role as guide to the travelers.

Chapter Eleven

What is your intention?
What means this mysterious speech?
—Shakespeare, *Macbeth*

——— • ———

The handsome bracelet, which was woven from the hair of Don Carlos's beautiful daughter and whose clasp was her portrait, had been given to Teresa by her friend a few years ago, and from that time on she had almost never taken it off. Even though her arid and unsociable disposition made her show but little affection for Carlota, her noble and grateful heart knew well how to appreciate the precious gift of friendship which her charming companion offered her.

Sab, possessor of such a priceless jewel, pressed it to his breast a thousand times, blessed Teresa, and tried to meet her eyes, wishing her to read in his own the immense gratitude of his heart. But his efforts were in vain. During the journey Teresa, buried in the rear of the carriage, never raised her eyes from a book she was apparently reading, and they reached the farm at nightfall without Sab having been able to convey by either a word or a glance his gratitude to her.

Afterward he looked in vain for an opportunity to speak with her for a moment; Teresa avoided him so carefully that it was impossible for him to do so.

Our travelers spent two further days in Cubitas, which were used by Don Carlos to acquaint his future son-in-law with all of the property he owned and to show the ladies other natural curiosities of the area. Among them were the Máximo River, also referred to as that of the "*canjilón*,"[1] whose limpid waters flowed gently between two symmetrical walls of beautiful stone and on whose picturesque banks grew pinks and an infinite variety of rare and lovely plants. Sab had them look at the mighty rock formations, high stony hills between which ran a path of some twelve to fourteen meters in width. The traveler who journeyed by this path could not lift his eyes on high without feeling vertigo and a certain fear at the imposing spectacle of those great parallel and admirably symmetrical masses, which no mortal hand has erected.

Carlota would have liked to have stayed in Cubitas to await the return of her suitor, who had had to go to Guanaja for a few days, but Señor de

B—— had already arranged their return to Bellavista the same day that Otway left for Guanaja. The good gentleman was anxious to send Sab to Puerto Príncipe and to go there himself in order to receive some news he wished to know as soon as possible. In the last mail from Havana, he had failed to receive a letter from his son or from his tutors. As the reader knows, Sab had gone to that city on various errands, one of which was to pick up the mail from the post office. Upon returning the same day they left for Cubitas, he had reported that there was no letter at all for Señor de B——. This silence from his son was odd, as the latter never failed to write him every time the mail came, and it was also strange that contrary to custom his business correspondent had not sent the Havana newspapers, all the more so as they were to contain the results of the drawing of the big lottery; Don Carlos already knew through Enrique that the first prize had been awarded in Puerto Príncipe. With all of the impatience of which his character was capable, he desired to have news of the son whose silence made him uneasy—and to know which was the winning number. As we have said before, although Don Carlos was neither avaricious nor overly attentive to wealth, he could not fail to be painfully aware of just how much his own fortune had decreased and what a beautiful stroke of good fortune it would be for him to win forty thousand pesos in the lottery. On finding out that the grand prize had been won in Puerto Príncipe, his heart beat hopefully, recalling that he had two tickets and Teresa and Carlota one each; who knew, he said, if one of these four might not be the winning number? Oh, if it could be Carlota's! What happiness! But no, added the generous gentleman quickly, I would rather it be Teresa's: she needs it more. Poor orphan, who has received only a very meager inheritance! Even without the lottery Carlota would be quite rich, especially when she married Enrique Otway.

Having spent three days in Cubitas, Enrique left for Guanaja and the de B—— family for Bellavista, leaving Martina installed in her new home, showering her with gifts, and receiving her blessings in return.

How things lose their beauty when viewed with the eyes of sadness! On her return to Bellavista, Carlota looked indifferently at those same fertile and lovely fields that had produced such an agreeable impression on her when she admired them with Enrique. She was going to be separated from the object of her total affection for eight days, and her sadness was the greater as for the first time a vague unease, an indefinable apprehension tormented her imagination.

During the three days spent in Cubitas, her sweetheart had often seemed sad and troubled, and his good-byes had been cool. When Carlota spoke to him of their impending marriage, Enrique was silent or answered with a degree of confusion; when Carlota reproached his aloofness, En-

rique excused himself with childish pretexts. For the first time an indefinable but cruel distrust lay heavily upon her open and trusting heart. He
does not love me as much as I love him, Carlota dared to confess to herself:
something is bothering him that he does not dare to entrust to me.

"Enrique has secrets from me, from me who have given him my entire
soul, from me who will soon be his wife!"

In vain she tried to find out the secret cause of Enrique's mistrust and
questioned her own heart. Ah! How could that noble and selfless heart
reply? Carlota heard her father say that Otway had been surprised to find
out the low value and few products of his holdings in Cubitas, but could
she even remotely suspect that that discovery could produce her beloved's
melancholy and coldness? If some base instinct could have revealed this to
her, Carlota might not have been able to go on loving, or perhaps living,
either.

Depressed and worried, she arrived at nightfall at the plantation from
which she had departed three days earlier with such a smiling disposition.
Knowing that Sab was to leave the next day for the city, she shut herself
in her room—on the pretext of having to write several letters to some of
her acquaintances—in order to surrender completely to her sadness and
unease; Don Carlos followed her example by retiring to his study, with
the real objective of writing a number of letters which Sab was to take to
the post office, and the tired little girls did not take long to fall asleep.
Thus, a quarter of an hour after arriving at the plantation, Teresa was the
only one left in the living room. She thereupon got up out of the chair in
which she had been sitting, and cautiously approaching the door of the
room which was their bedroom and into which Carlota had shut herself,
she put her ear to the keyhole and listened attentively for the space of a
few minutes. Slowly she returned to her chair.

"There is no doubt," she said in a low voice: "I have heard her sobs.
Carlota, what can be troubling you? You are so fortunate! Everyone loves
you! Everyone wants your love! Leave your tears for the poor orphan
without riches, without beauty, whose love no one seeks, to whom no one
offers happiness."

Languidly she lowered her head and was lost in such long and profound
meditation that for two hours she hardly moved, her breathing hardly
detectable. Without her being aware of it, the tallow candle which burned
on a table at her side had almost gone out. At last, gradually emerging
from a kind of lethargy, she gave a deep sigh, slowly raised her head, and
glanced at the table clock next to her.

"Ten o'clock!" she exclaimed, "Ten! I have been alone here for two
hours."

She glanced at the door of the room where Carlota was, which still remained shut, and at last fixed her eyes on the guttering candle which now barely illuminated anything, though at times it still gave off bright flashes of light.

"Like a heart consumed by cares," she remarked sadly, "every now and then it still emits spirited flashes before going out forever: just like my poor heart, worn out by bitterness, rent by sorrows, which still lights the final days of my youth with the sinister brightness of a delinquent and terrible flame."

At that moment the light sent out a flash even brighter than the previous ones, but it was the last: Teresa was left in profound darkness, and her voice was heard to say in an even sadder tone, "This is how you will be extinguished, unhappy fire of my heart; this is how you will go out, too, for lack of sustenance and of hope."

"No, Teresa, there is still hope for your love, you can still be happy," responded another, no less melancholy voice, which Teresa heard practically at her ear. She let out a small cry, one almost stifled by a hand placed opportunely over her mouth.

"Quiet! Quiet!" the same voice repeated. "Keep quiet if you don't want to ruin us both. Teresa, I owe you a great deal and perhaps I can repay you: you have guessed my secret and I, in turn, possess yours. We must explain things to each other: you must hear me. Do you understand, Teresa? Tonight, when the clock you looked at a moment ago strikes twelve, I will wait for you by the riverbank, in back of the southern cane fields. Tomorrow I have to leave, and you must hear me before that, because I swear to you that this talk will decide my destiny and yours; perhaps also that of others. Do you swear in the name of all that you love most to meet me?"

"Sab," replied Teresa with a trembling and frightened voice, "what do you mean? I am a wretched being whom you should pity."

"And for whom I care and can make happy," replied her companion fervently, "I beg you in the name of your mother, Teresa, promise to grant me what I ask of you. My life, and perhaps yours, depend on this favor."

"At twelve, alone, so far away!" the young woman observed in a low voice.

"What? Are you afraid of the poor mulatto whom you thought worthy of receiving Carlota's portrait? Are you afraid of me, Teresa?"

"No," she replied in a firmer voice. "Sab, I promise I will meet you."

"God bless you, woman! Fine then, at twelve, by the riverbank behind the southern cane fields."

"I'll be there."

"Teresa, do you swear it?"

"I swear it!"

A profound silence followed this dialogue, uttered in complete darkness, and when Don Carlos emerged from his study three minutes later to call Sab and hand him the letters he was to take to the city, he found Teresa in the same chair in which he had seen her when he left the living room, apparently sound asleep. At the sound of Señor de B——'s voice and that of the door of Carlota's room which opened at almost the same instant, she woke up, and stretching, she heard the gentle voice of her friend, who said while she embraced her, "Dear Teresa, forgive me for having left you alone such a long time. I had so much to write!" And instantly, as though regretting her lack of truthfulness with her friend, she added in a lower voice, "I needed so much to be alone!"

Ignoring this excuse, Teresa looked about her, as though after such a long sleep she hardly recalled where she was.

"What time is it?" she asked immediately.

"Look at the clock," responded Carlota. "It's past ten, and I think it would be good if we went to bed, all the more so since it seems to me that you are just about to fall asleep again. But here is Sab, ready to receive orders and letters; tomorrow at daybreak he leaves for the city. I am going to give him two letters I have written to our girlfriends. Do you want anything from Puerto Príncipe?"

"Nothing," answered Teresa, getting up and moving toward the bedroom. Carlota followed her, once she had put her two letters in the mulatto's hands and received a kiss and a blessing from her father.

"You must have been very annoyed, my dear Teresa," her companion said to her affectionately, after closing the door and while undressing to go to bed, "all alone like that. What did you do?"

"Slept, just as you saw," answered Teresa, who was already in bed and seemingly about to fall asleep.

"I was very sorry to leave you alone," replied Carlota, "but you see, I had such a need of solitude and silence! I was so sad! So upset!"

"You were sad—what was the matter, then?" said Teresa, sitting up a little on her pillow.

"I had—how can I put it?—a heavy heart . . . I needed to cry. I cried a great deal and I already feel better."

"You cried?" repeated Teresa, stretching out a hand to her, with more gentleness in her voice and her look than Carlota was accustomed to seeing in her. Moved by the sight of this unexpected compassion, the poor girl thereupon threw herself into her friend's arms and began to weep again. Teresa did not have to insist greatly to elicit a confession of the reasons for her sadness. Unaccustomed to pain but endowed with a soul great enough to bear it in all its intensity, Carlota had suffered so much that night with her apprehensions and misgivings that she felt an enormous need to ask for consolation and compassion. Given her habitual coolness, Teresa generally received these confidences with few demonstrations of interest, but Carlota had acquired the habit of telling her anyway, and on this occasion Teresa's heart rebuked her for the reserve she had shown her friend. Thus, with her arms about her cousin's neck and her eyes full of tears, Carlota told Teresa candidly and precisely all of the things for which she reproached Enrique. Teresa listened to her attentively.

"Poor Carlota!" she said to her after she had finished. "How you cause yourself so much worry!"

"What do you mean?" she exclaimed with an anxiety born of fear and hope. "Do you think I am being unfair?"

"You undoubtedly are," replied Teresa.

"Do you think he loves me as much as before?"

"And why should he not love you more each day, dear Carlota? You are so good, so beautiful!"

"Are you flattering me, Teresa?" asked Carlota, who at her friend's first words had raised her lovely head, drying her tears and stifling her sobs in order to hear her better.

"Certainly not; you are loved and deserve to be so. Why do you worry about mere possibilities just to hurt yourself, when undoubtedly these worries are caused by the same love which you doubt? Do you think it strange that Enrique is sad and ill humored when he has been accustomed to seeing you every day for three months and hopes soon to see you all the time yet is at present obliged by tedious business affairs to leave you frequently and to spend entire weeks away from you? This coldness of which you complain is a misgiving of yours, and besides, can you expect a man deeply involved in business matters to be as devoted to love as you are? Do you want him to do nothing but sigh with love at your feet? Oh, you are unjust, no question about it, Carlota! Enrique does not deserve the misgivings of your suspicious love."

Carlota listened to these words with inexplicable joy. It is so easy to persuade ourselves of that which we desire, and this persuasion was so sweet that the ardent girl needed no more than Teresa's few words to dispel all of her anxieties; if she did not appear to be convinced, it was for the pleasure of having Teresa repeat that she was unjust and that Enrique loved her. How much good those words did her heart! How she congratulated herself for having confided her worries to Teresa, reproaching herself for not having done it before! That night Teresa seemed to her adorable, eloquent, sublime. Carlota convinced herself with pleasure that Teresa was a thousand times more just, more sensible than she herself and subsequently wept at having offended her beloved with unfounded mistrust.

"I have certainly been very unfair," she said between smiles and tears, "but I deserve forgiveness. I love him so! For my heart one word, one look from Enrique is life or death, happiness or despair. You don't understand that, Teresa, for you have never loved."

Teresa smiled sadly to herself.

"You are so unaccustomed to suffering," she told Carlota, "that the slightest mishap, finding your heart unprotected, can enter and trouble it. Oh, Carlota! Even supposing that the tragedy which you have unreasonably feared were to happen, should you surrender to pain in this cowardly fashion? If Enrique turned out to be fickle, treacherous, would you not have enough pride and strength to despise him, judging the loss of an inconstant heart unworthy of your tears?"

Carlota took her arms from around Teresa's neck with a convulsive movement, and a sudden, sorrowful fear appeared in her eyes.

"What? Are you by any chance trying to warn me? Did you deceive me when you assured me that he loved me? Have you, too, noticed his inconstancy? Do you know it? Tell me, oh, in Heaven's name tell me, you cruel woman!"

"No, poor girl," exclaimed Teresa. "No! I have not found out anything but that you are going to be unhappy, in spite of your beauty and your charms, in spite of your husband's love and that of everyone who knows you. You will be unhappy if you don't moderate your overly sensitive nature, always on the point of becoming alarmed."

"Yes," replied Carlota, with a deep sigh, as she sadly, pensively sat down on her bed. "Yes, I will be unhappy; I know not what secret voice unceasingly tells me this, but at least I will no longer lament the misfortune against which you want to prepare me. If Enrique were treacherous, ungrateful, then all would be over; I would no longer be unhappy. The fears that one knows one cannot survive are not the most frightening."

When she had finished speaking, she let herself fall dejectedly onto the pillow. Teresa gazed at her with profound emotion; with a certain astonishment and the most tender compassion, she beheld that exceedingly young and pure brow on which neither time nor passions had as yet etched their painful marks and reproached herself for having disturbed that delightful serenity even for a moment. Misfortune should be the lot of those who spill the first drop of gall on a happy soul, she said inwardly. Of those whose faces are furrowed by years or cares, what kind of people are the ones who dare approach confident and happy youth to snatch from them their bright and innocent dreams? Cold, hard beings, souls without compassion who pretend to be doing good while awaiting the fatal moment of disillusionment when they offer sad reality to those they have despoiled of their sweet chimeras. Cruel men who freeze the smile on innocent lips when they rend the brilliant veil covering inexperienced eyes and who, when they say "this is the truth," destroy in one instant the happiness of an entire lifetime.

Oh, those of you who have already seen everything, who understand and judge it all, who already know life and are hastening to its final limit, guided by discretion and accompanied by distrust, respect those pure brows on which disillusion has not yet set its mark, respect those souls filled with trust and faith, souls rich in hope and strong because of their youth. Leave them their errors; they will do them less harm than the fatal prophecy you wish to give them.

Reflecting on these things, Teresa had bent over her cousin and held her in her arms with unusual tenderness. Carlota was so upset that she received her caresses without returning them until Teresa, resuming her conversation, attempted to quiet her by repeating with conviction in her voice that Enrique loved her, that he would love her always, and that she did him wrong in doubting his sincerity and constancy even for one moment.

Seeing her finally less upset, Teresa begged her to try to sleep, and she herself pretended she needed rest. However, it was impossible for Carlota to fall asleep for some time; although her fears had been allayed, she felt exceedingly upset, and Teresa seemed to have already been asleep for more than half an hour while she was still tossed in her bed unable to calm herself. After this turmoil ended, longed-for sleep at last closed her eyes, and Carlota fell asleep just as a distant clock chimed twelve.

Chapter One

Listen to me for I will not be long; the story
of a passionate heart is always very simple.
—Alfred de Vigny, *Cinq-Mars: A Conspiracy*

—— • ——

It was a beautiful night in the tropics: the firmament shone, picked out with stars, the breeze whispered in the immense cane fields, and an infinite number of *cocuyos* stood out against the dark green of the trees; they flew over the ground, their brilliant breasts like beacons of light. The solemn quiet of midnight was broken only by the melancholy rippling of the waters of the Tínima, which glided along among blue and white boulders at the edge of the cane fields and watered the wildflowers which adorned its solitary banks.

At that hour a woman, dressed in white and all alone, crossed the great cane fields of Bellavista with quick, careful steps and, guided by the sound of the waters, proceeded to the banks of the river. At the light sound of her footsteps, which could be clearly heard in the nighttime silence, the figure of an exceptionally tall man suddenly rose from among the boulders of the river, and one could distinctly hear these exclamations, uttered by the two individuals as they simultaneously recognized each other: "Teresa!" "Sab!"

The mulatto took her by the hand and, making her sit down on the rocks from which he had just risen, fell on his knees before her. "God bless you, Teresa! You have come like an angel of salvation to give life to a poor wretch who implored you; but in exchange I, too, can give you hope and consolation: our destinies touch and our fate will be the same."

"I don't understand you, Sab," answered Teresa. "I have come to this place because you told me that your happiness and perhaps that of others depended on it. As far as my own is concerned, I no longer desire nor hope for it while on earth."

"Nevertheless, in creating my happiness you will also be creating your own," the mulatto interrupted her. "An extraordinary coincidence has joined our destinies. Teresa, you love Enrique and I worship Carlota: you can be that man's wife, and I will be content so long as he does not marry Carlota. Do you understand me now?"

"Sab," the young woman replied with a sad smile, "you must be mad. Did you say I could be Enrique's wife?"

"Yes, you can, and I am the one who can give you the means to do it."

Teresa looked at him with fear and pity; undoubtedly she thought he was unbalanced.

"Poor Sab," she said, involuntarily drawing away, "calm yourself, in Heaven's name; you are not in your right mind when you think . . ."

"Listen to me!" Sab interrupted quickly, without giving her time to finish the sentence she had begun. "Listen to me! Here, in the presence of Heaven and this magnificent nature I am going to open my entire heart to you. There is only one thing I ask of you: promise me that not one word you will hear tonight will pass your lips."

"I promise you."

"Teresa!" he continued, sitting down at her feet. "You know that this unfortunate soul dares to love her whose footprint he is not worthy of kissing, but what you cannot know is how great, how pure this foolish passion is. God himself would not scorn such worship! I have rocked Carlota's cradle, while sitting on my knees she learned to say 'I love you,' and it was to me that her angelic lips said these words. You know this, Teresa; I spent the days of my childhood and the first of my youth at her side. Happy at seeing her, hearing her, adoring her, I forgot about my enslavement and my shame and considered myself more fortunate than a king when she would say to me: 'I love you.'"

The mulatto, whose voice was muffled by emotion, was silent for a minute, and Teresa said to him, "I know, Sab. I know you grew up with Carlota. I know that your heart has not voluntarily given itself up to a foolish passion and that the fault lies with those who exposed you to the perils of that kind of intimacy."

"The perils!" the mulatto echoed sadly. "They did not foresee them because they never suspected that the poor slave had a man's heart. They did not believe that Carlota was anything more in my eyes than an object of veneration and worship. In fact, when I looked at that child, so pure, so lovely, who was always at my side and would look at me with an ineffable glance, then it seemed to me that she was the guardian angel whom Heaven had sent me, and her mission on earth was to guide and save my soul. The first sounds of that silvery, pure voice, those sounds which seemed an echo from the eternal melody of Heaven, were not unknown to me: I fancied having heard them somewhere else, in a previous world, and that by means of the same sounds the soul which breathed them had communicated with mine before either one descended to earth. That is how I loved her, adored her from the first moment I saw her newly born, rocked on her mother's knees. I watched the child grow and the bewitching little creature turned into the most beautiful of virgins. I no longer dared to catch a look from her eyes nor a smile from her lips: tremulous before her, a cold sweat covered my brow while through my veins coursed a burning lava which consumed me. Even in my sleep I saw her, girl and angel resting at my side or slowly ascending to the heavens from whence she had come, encouraging me to follow her with that divine smile and ineffable look which she had cast on me so often. But when I awoke it was the woman and not the angel whom my eyes saw and my heart loved. The most beautiful, most adorable woman who had ever caused the heart of a man to beat: it was Carlota with her lily skin, the great eyes which had robbed Cuba of the sun's fire, her palmlike bearing, her neck, slender as a swan's, her youthful brow . . . and when I saw her so beautiful, I thought that it was impossible to see her and not love her, that among the many who would offer her their hearts, she would find one which would make her own tremble, and that for him alone would be the heartbeats of that lovely breast, the glances of those heavenly eyes, and the smiles from her honeyed lips.

"Teresa!" he added, lowering the voice which up to then had been full, sonorous, and clear and which now took on a sadder and darker timbre. "Teresa! Then I remembered that I was the offspring of a defiled race, then I remembered too that I was a mulatto and a slave . . . then my heart, seared by love and jealousy, first began to throb with indignation, and I cursed nature which condemned me to worthlessness and shame. But I was unjust, Teresa, for nature has not been any less our mother than yours. Does the sun hide its light from the regions where the wild black makes his home? Do the streams dry up in order not to quench his thirst? Do not the birds sing for him and the flowers emit their perfume? But human society has not imitated the equality of our common mother who has told them in vain: 'You are brothers.' Idiotic society, which has reduced us to the necessity of hating it and of founding our happiness on its total destruction!"

He was silent for a moment, and Teresa saw his eyes glitter with a sinister fire.

"Sab," she said with quivering voice, "have you perhaps summoned me to this place to reveal some plan of a conspiracy among the blacks? What danger threatens us? Are you one of the—"

"No," he interrupted her with a bitter smile, "calm yourself, Teresa, you are not threatened by any danger. The slaves patiently drag their chains: in order to break them they might only need to hear one voice which cries out to them 'You are men!,' but I assure you that voice will not be mine."

Teresa stretched out her hand to Sab with great feeling; he fixed his eyes on her and proceeded with a calmer kind of sadness. "My love was as pure as the first ray of sunlight on a spring day, pure as the object which inspired it, but it was already an unbearable torment for me. When I went with Carlota on a walk or to church, I noticed that all eyes were on her and anxiously followed the direction of her own. If for one moment they rested on some gallant white gentleman, I, anxious and tormented, wanted to penetrate her heart, uncover within a secret of love, and die. If I saw her at home and she let the book she was reading or the handkerchief she was embroidering fall in a thoughtful and melancholy way, if the uneven movement of her breast revealed a secret emotion, a thousand pains clawed at mine, and I said to myself furiously, 'She feels the need to love: she will love, and it will not be I.' I could not long endure that state of suffering: I felt the need to flee from Carlota and hide my love, my jealousy, and my desperation in solitude. You know this, Teresa: I asked to come to this plantation and for two years have buried myself here, returning only very seldom to see the house where I spent such happy and yet such bitter days and that adorable being who has been my only love on earth; but what you cannot know, nor can I tell you, is how much I have suffered in these two years of voluntary absence. Ask these mountains, this river, these crags. On them have I shed the tears which the river has borne along in its waters. Oh, Teresa! Ask Heaven as well, which raises its eternal canopy above us: it knows how often I begged it to take away the burden of an existence I had not asked for and for which I could not be grateful; a brazen wall always came between it and me, and the echo of the mountains returned my sorrowful laments, which Heaven did not deign to accept."

A large, burning tear dropped from Sab's eyes and fell on Teresa's hand, which he still retained between his own. Simultaneously another tear fell and ran down the mulatto's face: this was Teresa's tear, who, leaning toward him, fixed on him a look of affection and pity.

"Poor woman!" he said, "I know that you, too, have suffered! When men saw your cold exterior and your perennially serene countenance, they may have thought that you hid an unfeeling heart and perhaps have said, 'How happy she is!' But I, Teresa, I have known better because I know that in order to stifle tears and hide under a tranquil countenance the pain that is tearing at your heart, it is necessary to have suffered a great deal."

A new interval of silence followed these words, and then he continued, "Under a torrid sky, endowed with a passionate heart and doomed never to be loved, I have seen many days of my barren and unhappy childhood go by. In vain I attempted to banish Carlota from my imagination and extinguish the mad flame that consumed me: everywhere I encountered the same image, the same thoughts led me back to the same place. If at daybreak in springtime I wished to breathe the pure air of the country and awaken with nature to the initial light of a new day, it was Carlota I saw in the dawn and the land: the breeze was her breath, the light her glance, the sky her smile. The birds which sang in the forest and the brook which

murmured at my feet spoke to me of love, as did the great animate principle which gives life to the universe. If fatigued from work I came at
sunset to rest my limbs on the banks of this river; here, too, the same
dreams awaited me: because that time of afternoon, when the mocking-
bird sings while circling his nest, when in stages darkness steals away light
and color from the fields, that time, Teresa, is the hour of nostalgia and of
memory. All things inspire one with an indefinable tenderness, and involuntarily the heart's sigh mingles with the breeze. Then I would see an
ethereal and pure Carlota wandering among the clouds, which the sun
gilded with its last rays, and I imagined that in the scents of the night I
was drinking in the perfume of her mouth. Oh, how many times in my
blind delirium have I stretched out my arms to that enchanting spirit and
have begged it for one word of love, even though at the sound of that
word the heavens would have descended on my head or the earth collapsed
under my feet!

"Searing winds of the South: when you answered my desperate pleas by
bringing the tempests of heaven on your wings, you, too, have seen me
run out to welcome you and mingle my cries with the roars of the hurricane and my tears with the waters of the storm. I have prayed to the lightning bolt and have begged it in vain to strike me; the proud palm, the
queen of this land, has crashed down beside me, rent by the lightning, yet
the son of misfortune has remained standing! And nature's storm has
passed by, but never the one in his heart!"

"Oh, Sab, poor Sab, how much you have suffered!" exclaimed Teresa,
profoundly affected. "How worthy of a better fate is a heart that has
known how to love as yours has!"

"It is true that I am most unhappy," he replied in a dark voice, "but you
do not know everything: you don't know that there have been moments
when desperation has almost made me a criminal. Yes, you have no idea
what guilty desires I have thought of, what dreams of cruel happiness have
sprung from my feverish head . . . to snatch Carlota from her father's arms,
to tear her away from this society which comes between the two of us, to
flee into the wild bearing in my arms that angel of innocence and love . . .
Oh, and that is not all! I have also thought of arming the chained hands
of their victims against our oppressors, to fling the terrifying cry of freedom and vengeance into their midst, to bathe in the blood of the whites,
to trample their bodies and their laws under my feet and perish among the
ruins so long as I could take Carlota to my grave, because life or death,
Heaven or Hell . . . if she were with me it would be all the same to me."

Another interval of silence followed these words. Sab appeared to have
slipped into a profound state of distraction, and Teresa, her eyes fixed on
him, felt new and extraordinary stirrings in her heart. Teresa, who had
never heard the declaration of an ardent passion from a man's mouth,

found herself as though intrigued by the power of that immense, incomparable love, whose passionate description she had just heard. There was something contagious in the terrible emotions of the man with whom she found herself: perhaps the air he breathed, emitting in flames from his breast, spread out and seared all it touched. Teresa trembled and a strange sensation took possession of her heart. She forgot Sab's color and class, she saw his eyes filled with the fire which consumed him; she heard the voice which came from that throbbing, impassioned, penetrating heart, and perhaps she no longer envied Carlota so much for her beauty and the joy of becoming Enrique's wife as for the glory of having inspired a passion such as this. It also seemed to her that she was capable of loving in the same way and that a heart such as Sab's was the one that her own heart needed.

The mulatto, so absorbed in his own thoughts that he barely noticed her, finally raised his head and continued speaking with greater calm.

"The few times I went to Puerto Príncipe I hardly saw Carlota, but I questioned all of her maids with ill-concealed anxiety, wishing to know the state of her heart and always trembling at finding out; but my fears remained groundless. Belén, who as you know is her favorite slave, told me that although Carlota was the recipient of a thousand attentions and aspirations, she gave no man the slightest encouragement. She used to say that her young mistress was averse to marriage and would not listen without weeping when her father made even the slightest mention of this subject to her. These sweet words were repeated to me so many times that little by little my anxieties dispelled and . . . do I dare confess it, Teresa? To you, only to you can I make the painful confession of my foolish pride. I dared to formulate absurd expectations! I dared to think that that woman, whose soul was so pure, so passionate, would never find in any man the soul that was worthy of her own: I convinced myself that a secret instinct, which had revealed to her that in all the universe there was only one soul able to love and understand her, would also have told her that this soul was imprisoned in the body of a debased being, outlawed by society, reviled by men . . . and Carlota, doomed not to love on earth, would keep her virgin soul for Heaven, for that other life where love is eternal and happiness is boundless, where there is equality and justice, and where souls which men have separated on earth will be united in the heart of God for all eternity! Oh, you ravings of a burning heart, I owe you the only moments of happiness I have felt since I was four years old!

"One of the times I was in the city I could not see Carlota, though I stayed for three days with this intention. Belén told me that her mistress hardly left her room, that she was slightly indisposed and very despondent and avoided receiving even your visits, Teresa, or those of her relatives. As Belén confessed to me later, no one in the house ignored the reason for

Carlota's sadness: her hand had not been offered to Enrique Otway, but back then no one told me these things. As impenetrable as I thought my secret was, Belén had guessed it and, according to what she told me later, begged the other slaves not to speak of her mistress's affairs of the heart in my presence. Uneasy with what I was told of her ill health but unable to see her, I spent the nights glued to that window of her room which opens onto the patio, and there dawn would find me, happy if in the silence of the night I had been able to hear a sigh, a movement of Carlota's.

"The last night I spent in the city I was more attentive than ever to the slightest sound which might be heard in that beloved room. When the night was already far spent, I thought I heard Carlota walking about and a little later come over to the window against which I leaned; I thereupon redoubled my attention and distinctly heard her sweet voice. I was surprised by this because I knew that she slept alone; concentrating my entire soul into my hearing, I shortly realized that she was reading aloud. It was undoubtedly the Gospel which she was pondering, for after reading for some minutes in a low voice which did not permit me to catch her words distinctly, she finally said more audibly: 'Come unto me ye who travail and are heavy-laden, and I will give you rest.'[1] After repeating these tender and comforting words, I could no longer hear her silvery voice and only perceived several sighs. Trembling, moved to the very depths of my soul, I repeated to myself the words of consolation I had heard and, foolish as I was, thought that they had been directed at me! Suddenly I heard the lock on the window being unfastened and barely had time to hide behind the rosebush which shades it when Carlota appeared. Although it was one of the coolest nights of the month of November, her head was uncovered, and her lovely tresses floated in a mass of curls over her breast and shoulders. She was wearing a dress of purest white; the paleness of her face and the shine of her moist eyes gave her figure an ethereal and supernatural quality. The full moon was suspended like a circular lamp from the somber blue of the firmament, and its rays glimmered on the virginal brow of that melancholy beauty.

"I dragged myself along the ground until I was once again next to the window and, lying flat on the earth, fixed my eyes and my heart on Carlota. She, too, seemed agitated, and a minute later I watched her fall to her knees by the grille. At that point we were so close that I could kiss the border of the sash which tied her dress at the waist; this ribbon hung outside the grille on which she rested her two lovely arms and her angelic head. She remained in this position for a moment, during which time I felt my heart about to burst and opened my dry lips eagerly to drink in the air which she breathed. Then she slowly raised her head and lifted her tear-filled eyes heavenward. I can still see her! Releasing the grille, she lifted up her hands as well, and the moonlight which bathed her brow appeared to form a divine halo. Never have the eyes of man been offered such divine beauty! There was nothing earthly or mortal in that figure: it was an angel about to fly to Heaven, its portals already wide to receive her, and I was on the point of crying out to her: 'Wait! Wait for me! I will leave this despised body on earth and my soul will follow you!'

"Carlota's voice, which sounded sweeter and more celestial than the voice of the cherubim, stifled this indiscreet exclamation on my lips. 'Oh You,' she said, 'You who have said come to me all ye who travail and I will refresh you, receive my soul which seeks You so that You can take away the pain which afflicts it!' I added my supplications to hers, Teresa, and in the most secret recesses of my heart I repeated with her: 'Receive my soul which seeks You.' I believed absolutely that at that very moment both of us were going to die and appear together before the God of love and mercy. A confused feeling of vague, indefinite, celestial happiness filled my soul, lifting it to a sublime ecstasy of divine and human love, to an indescribable ecstasy in which God and Carlota fused in my soul. The loud click of a lock shattered this vision—I searched for Carlota but did not see her. The window had shut, and Heaven and the angel had disappeared. There was only the wretched slave, pressing to the earth a heart seared by love, jealousy, and desperation!"

Chapter Two

What shall I do? What way shall I find
where there is no way to be found?
But if the solution is to die
I shall find the solution in death.

—Lope de Vega

—— • ——

"Poor Sab!" exclaimed Teresa, "How you must have suffered when you found out that this angel of your dreams wanted to give herself to a mortal!"

"Unworthy of her!" the mulatto added sadly. "Yes, Teresa, a hundred times less worthy than I, in spite of his snow-white skin and golden hair. If he were not unworthy, if this man deserved Carlota's love, believe me, the heart which is here in my breast would be generous enough not to despise him. 'Make her happy!' I would say, and even as I died of jealousy I would bless him. But no, he is not worthy of her: she cannot be happy with Enrique Otway . . . this is the cause of my desperation! Carlota in a man's arms is anguish, terrible anguish! But I would have found within me the strength to bear it. But to have Carlota handed over to a scoundrel . . . Oh, God! appalling God! This is too much! I had accepted my cup with resignation, and You wished to poison the gall.

"I did not return to the city until the month before last. Carlota's marriage had been settled for almost two months, yet I had been told nothing; since I was in the city for only three days and was always occupied on my master's business, I never saw Otway and returned to Bellavista without suspecting that Señorita de B—— was entering into an indissoluble union. Neither my master nor Belén nor you, Señora . . . no one told me that Carlota would soon be the wife of a foreigner. Destiny wanted me to receive the blow from the despised hand itself!"

Sab was referring here to his first meeting with Enrique, and as though the memory of that fateful afternoon were a greater burden than all of his other sorrows, he plunged into deep despair after the abovementioned account.

"Sab," Teresa said to him with a troubled voice, "I pity you, you know that. But what can I do for you?"

"A great deal," he answered, lifting up his face, which suddenly came alive with a forceful expression, "a great deal, Teresa: you can prevent

Carlota from falling into the Englishman's arms and, inasmuch as you love him, become his wife."

"I? What are you saying, you poor young man? I, the wife of Carlota's suitor?"

"Your suitor!" he repeated with a sardonic smile. "You deceive yourself, Señora: Enrique Otway does not love Carlota."

"Does not love her? Then why has he asked for her hand?"

"Because at that time Señorita de B—— was rich," replied the mulatto with a tone of inner conviction, "because her father had not yet lost the suit which deprived her of a large part of her fortune, because she had not been disinherited by her uncle. Now do you understand me, Teresa?"

"No, I don't understand," she said, "and I think you unjust."

"No," replied Sab. "When I judge this foreigner it is not because my jealousy or my aversion are influencing me. For many days I have been the shadow that has constantly dogged his steps. I am the one who at all hours has studied his conduct, his glances, his thoughts, the one who has caught words which escaped him when he believed himself alone and even those he uttered in his dreams while he slept, the one who has won the confidence of his slaves to find out from them the conversations held between father and son, conversations which rarely escape the notice of the house slave who wishes to hear them. But all this was not even necessary! From the first time that I looked at that stranger I realized that the soul which dwelt in his handsome body was a shabby guest in such a magnificent abode."

"Sab," said Teresa, "you astonish me; so you think—" The mulatto did not let her finish.

"I think," he replied, "that Enrique regrets the betrothal which links him to a woman who is no longer anything more than an undistinguished match; I think his father will not happily give his approval to this union, above all if a more advantageous marriage for his son comes along, and I believe, Teresa, that you are the match that both the young and the old man will accept without hesitation."

Teresa thought she was dreaming.

"I?" she repeated three times.

"You," responded the mulatto. "George Otway would prefer a dowry in cold cash (I have myself heard him say as much) to all the property that Señorita de B—— could bring to his son, and along with your hand you can offer Enrique a dowry of forty thousand pesos in gold."

"Sab!" the young woman exclaimed bitterly, "it is certainly not right for you to mock an unfortunate soul who has pitied you and wept over your misfortunes, not even her own."

"I do not mock you, Señora," he replied solemnly. "Tell me, don't you have a lottery ticket? I know you have one. I have seen that you are keeping two in your desk: one has your name on it and the other Carlota's, both written by your hand. She, too embroiled in her love, hardly even remembers these tickets, but you have carefully kept them because without a doubt you thought, 'If I were rich, I would be beautiful, I would be happy, for no woman fails to be loved if she is rich.'"

"All right!" exclaimed Teresa anxiously, "it's true. I have a lottery ticket."

"I have another."

"Well, then!"

"Destiny can give forty thousand pesos to one of the two of us."

"And you expect—"

"That they will be the dowry you bring Enrique. Look, here is my ticket," he said, taking a paper from his belt, "which bears the number 8014, and 8014 has won forty thousand pesos. Take this ticket and tear yours up. When I return from Puerto Príncipe in a few hours, Señor de B—— will receive the list of winning numbers, and Enrique will know that now you are richer than Carlota. Now you see that I was not deceiving you when I told you that there was hope for your love; now you see that you can still be happy. Will you agree to it, Teresa?"

Teresa did not reply: not a single word escaped from her lips, but words were not necessary. Her eyes had suddenly taken on that forceful expression which so rarely enlivened them. Sab looked at her and demanded no other answer: he lowered his head with embarrassment, and a long silence prevailed between them. Sab finally broke it with a troubled voice.

"Forgive me, Teresa," he said to her, "I already know . . . you will never buy a debased heart with gold nor would you bequeath the possession of your own to an ignoble man. Enrique is as unworthy of you as of her; I acknowledge that. But, Teresa, you could pretend for several days that you would be willing to give him your dowry and your hand; and when he is vanquished by the lure of the gold, which is his god, and the scoundrel falls at your feet, when Carlotta realizes the baseness of the man to whom she has given her soul, then let your disdain and hers crush him, then send this man who is not worthy of looking at you away from both of you. Are you willing, Teresa? I ask this of you on my knees, in the name of your friend, the daughter of your benefactors, of this infatuated Carlota who deserves your compassion! Don't allow this angel of innocence and goodness to fall into the arms of a scoundrel . . . do not allow it, Teresa."

"In this heart which has fed for so many years on bitterness," she replied, "the sacred feeling of gratitude has nevertheless not been extinguished. No, Sab, I have not forgotten the angelic woman who protected this helpless orphan, nor am I ungrateful for the kindnesses of my worthy benefactor, Carlota's father. Carlota, whom I have envied in the bitterness of my heart, but whose happiness—although it makes me suffer—it would be my obligation to secure at the cost of my life's blood! But oh! Is it really happiness you wish to give her? Sad happiness which is founded on the ruin of all her dreams! You are deceiving yourself, poor young man, or I know Carlota's soul better than you do. That tender and passionate soul has given herself wholly: her love is her existence, and to take away the one is to take away the other. It is true that a base and covetous Enrique would no longer be the idol of such a pure and generous heart, but how will you tear out the unworthy idol without destroying her noble heart?"

Sab fell at her feet as though struck by lightning.

"My God!" he cried with a choking voice. "Does Carlota love that man that much?"

"So much," responded Teresa, "that perhaps she would not survive the loss of her love. Sab!" she continued with a strong, firm voice, "if it is true that you love Carlota with that sacred, boundless love you have described to me, if your heart is really capable of feeling this, cast away forever a thought based solely on jealousy and egotism. Barbarian! Who gives you the right to snatch her dreams from her, to deprive her of the moments of happiness that these can give her? What will you have attained when you awaken her out of this dream of love that is her sole existence? What are you going to give her in exchange for the hopes of which you rob her? Oh, how despicable is the man who hastens the terrible day of disillusionment for someone else!"

She paused for a moment, then seeing that Sab stood motionless listening to her, continued more gently, "Your heart is noble and generous; if for a moment passions led it astray, it should return even greater and more just. At present you are free and rich: this time luck has been just and has given you the means whereby you can raise your destiny to the height of your soul. Martina's benefactor has gold to distribute among the poor, and the joy of virtue awaits him as well at the end of the road which Providence has opened."

Sab looked at Teresa with wild eyes, as though awakening from an anguished sleep.

"Where am I?" he exclaimed. "What are you doing here? What have you come for?"

"To console you," the young woman responded compassionately. "Sab! Dear Sab—come to."

"Dear?" he repeated with a tormented smile, "dear . . . no, I have never been nor ever shall be. Do you see this face, Señora? What does it tell you? Don't you see this sinister, opaque color? It is the mark of my accursed race. It is the seal of shame and misfortune. But nevertheless," he added, pressing Teresa's hands convulsively against his breast, "nevertheless, the fertile seed of noble sentiments lives in this heart. If my destiny had not stifled them, if a man's physical degradation had not been in constant opposition to his moral development, perhaps I could have been noble and virtuous. Enslaved, I have had to think like a slave, because a man deprived of rights and dignity cannot keep hold of noble feelings. Teresa! you should despise me. Why are you still here? Flee, lady, and—"

"No," she exclaimed, bending her head over the mulatto's, "I will not leave you unless you swear to respect your own life."

A cold sweat ran over Sab's forehead, and the burden his heart bore choked his voice; nevertheless, at Teresa's gentle tone he raised his eyes, which were brimming with gratitude.

"How good you are," he told her. "But who am I that you should concern yourself with my life? . . . My life! Do you know what my life is? Who has need of it? I have neither father nor mother . . . I am alone in the world; no one will weep at my death. I have no homeland to defend, because slaves have no country. I have no obligations to perform, because the obligations of a slave are those of a beast of burden who walks while he is able and collapses when he can go no farther. If only the whites, who expel from their social order the man born with skin of a different hue, would leave him alone in the wilderness; then he would have both a homeland and love . . . because he would love a woman of his own color, as untamed as he himself, who, just like him, would never have seen other climes nor other peoples, nor known ambition, nor admired the talents of others. But, ah! the black is denied that which is granted the wild beasts to which he is compared, for they are permitted to live in the place where they were born, whereas the black is torn from it.

"A vile slave, he passes on to his children an inheritance of slavery and degradation, and these unfortunate children will plead in vain for the sylvan life of their fathers. To torment them even more, they will be condemned to see fortune and ambition facilitate a thousand ways to glory and power for men no better than themselves, while they may harbor neither ambition nor hope for the future. In vain will they feel in their minds the capacity for thought, in vain in their breasts a heart that beats. Power and will! In vain an instinct, a conviction which cries out to them 'Rise up and walk!' because for them all roads are barred, all hopes dashed. Teresa! This is my lot. Above my station because of my nature, below all men because of my fate, I am alone in the world."

"Leave this place, leave it!" exclaimed Teresa forcefully. "Poor young man! Search out other heavens, other climes, another life; look also for another love, a wife worthy of your heart."

"Love? Wife?" echoed Sab sadly. "No, Señora, there is no love or wife for me either. Haven't I told you as much already? A terrible curse weighs on my life and has marked my brow. No woman can love me, none will want to join her fate to that of the poor mulatto, to follow his footsteps and console his sorrows."

Teresa stood up. In the quivering starlight Sab could see the gleam of her proud, pale forehead. A passionate fire sparkled in her eyes, and her whole figure had an inspired air about it. At that moment she was beautiful: beautiful, with a beauty which comes from the soul, and which the soul knows better than the eyes. Sab looked at her with surprise. She stretched out her two hands to him and raised her eyes heavenward:

"I!" she exclaimed, "I am that woman which entrusts herself to you: we are both orphans and unfortunate souls . . . we two are alone on earth, and each of us needs compassion, love, and happiness. Allow me, then, to follow you to remote climes, to the heart of the wilderness. I will be your friend, your companion, your sister!"

She stopped speaking, yet the mulatto seemed still to be hearing her. Surprised and motionless, he looked at her as though to ask if she were not deceiving him and really meant that which she had offered. But ought he to doubt it? Teresa's look and the hand which pressed his own were enough to convince him. Sab kissed her feet and in the rush of emotion could only exclaim, "You are an angel, Teresa!"

A flood of tears burst from his eyes; sitting at Teresa's side and pressing her hands against his chest he felt rid of the enormous burden which weighed on him. His eyes lifted to Heaven to give thanks for the moment of calm and consolation which had been conceded him. Then he kissed Teresa's hands effusively.

"Sublime and incomparable woman!" he said to her, "God will know how to reward you for what you have done for me. Your compassion gives me a moment of sweetness that is almost like happiness. I bless you, Teresa!"

And kissing her hands anew, he added, "The world has not understood you, but I who know you should worship and bless you. You would follow me! You would offer me consolation when she is sighing with pleasure in a lover's arms! Oh, you are a sublime woman, Teresa! No, I will not link my own shattered heart to one such as yours. . . . My entire soul would not suffice to repay one sigh of compassion which yours would extend to me. I am unworthy of you. My passion, this irrational love which consumes me, began my life and will end with it: the sufferings which it causes me are my existence. I have nothing apart from it: I would be nothing if I ceased to love. And you, generous woman, you do not know the nature of your commitment; you fail to foresee the torments you create for yourself. Fervor can prompt and bring about great sacrifices, but later on these weigh heavily on the afflicted soul. I absolve you of keeping your generous and rash promise. God, God alone is worthy of your great soul! As for me, I have already loved, I have already lived. . . . How many die without being able to say as much! How many souls depart this world without having found someone on whom to bestow their capacity to love! Heaven put Carlota on this earth so that I could experience to the fullest the supreme happiness of loving fervently. It does not matter that I alone have loved: my flame has been pure, immense, inextinguishable! It does not matter that I have suffered because I have loved Carlota—Carlota who is an angel! Carlota, a worthy recipient of my total adoration! She has been less fortunate than I: my love enhances my heart, and she . . . ah, she has profaned her own! But you are right, Teresa, it would be an act of cruelty to tell her 'The idol of your love is a scoundrel incapable of understanding and loving you.' No, never! Let her have her illusions, which I will respect with religious fervor. . . . Let her marry Enrique and may she be happy!"

For a moment he was silent, then convulsively grasped Teresa's hands again. Tremulous and profoundly moved, she remained at his side, and he exclaimed with new and more pained agitation, "But will she be happy? Can she be when after a few days of misconceptions and rapture she will see the veil of her illusions rent and find herself joined to a man that she must come to despise? Can you understand just how hideous this union of Carlota and Enrique's souls is? It would be like joining the eagle to the serpent, or a living being to a corpse. And she must vow love and obedience to that man! She will surrender her heart, her future, her entire destiny! She will make it her duty to respect him! And he, he will take her to wife like a piece of merchandise, calculatingly, for profit, transforming into shameful speculation the most holy bond, the most solemn pledge! She, who will give him her soul! And he will be her husband, the one who possesses Carlota, the father of their children! Oh no, no, Teresa! This thought is hell . . . you see, I cannot bear it . . . it's impossible!"

And so it was, for an icy sweat ran over his forehead, and his distorted eyes showed that his reason wandered. Teresa spoke to him tenderly, but in vain, as he was seized by a kind of fit.

It seemed to him that the earth trembled under his feet and that the river, the trees, and the rocks spun chaotically round him. The very air stifled him, and he felt a violent physical pain as though his heart were being torn apart by two iron claws while an enormous leaden weight descended on his head.

Carlota Enrique's wife! Showering him with her caresses! She, besmirching her pure heart, her unblemished charms with the uncouth love of a scoundrel! This was his only thought, and it weighed on his soul and on his limbs. He had no idea where he was, nor heard Teresa, nor remembered anything save this one idea, fixed in his mind and his heart. Terrified himself by what was happening to him, he for a moment doubted that any human being could resist all this. A confused and strange thought passed through his mind: he imagined that he had died and that his soul was suffering those inconceivable torments that the wrath of God has in store for unrepentant sinners. There are pains whose agonizing intensity man's perceptions cannot measure: the body is destroyed at their onslaught, and only the soul, because it is infinite, can bear and understand them.

At this juncture the unfortunate Sab attempted to rise, perhaps to flee from the horrible thought that was driving him mad, but his attempts were in vain. His body was leaden, and as though in a nightmare, his efforts so exhausted him that he was unable to move from that hellish crag to which he appeared to be chained. He uttered inarticulate cries which bore no resemblance to human speech, and Teresa saw him cast deranged glances about him and finally look at her with terrifying intensity. Teresa's heart broke with sorrow at the sight of that unhappy being, and she wept over his tormented head, murmuring words of consolation. At last Sab appeared to listen to her, because with a shaking hand he groped for that of the young woman; grasping it, he pressed it to his breast and looked at her with burning eyes. Making a last convulsive effort to stand up, he collapsed at Teresa's feet as though his muscles had totally given way.

Bent over him and cradling his head on her knees, the poor woman looked at him and felt her heart tremble. "Poor, wretched young man!" she thought. "Who will remember your skin color when they see how greatly you love and suffer?" A thought passed swiftly through her mind, and she asked herself what this man, endowed with such searing and deep feelings, might have been had barbarous prejudices not closed all means of noble ambition to him. But his powerful soul, obliged to squander all its immense treasures, had surrendered to the only passion it had experienced thus far, and that sole passion had vanquished it. "No," Teresa thought, "you should not have been born a slave . . . a heart which knows how to love in this way is not a common heart."

When the mulatto came to, he looked at her and knew who she was.

"Señora," he told her with a faint voice, "are you still here? Did you not abandon me because of my cowardly soul, one which has been crushed by the misfortune for which it ought to be well prepared?"

"No," she replied feelingly, "I am here to pity and console you. Sab! You have suffered greatly tonight."

"Tonight? Ah, no . . . it hasn't only been tonight! What I have undergone before your eyes this one night I have suffered another thousand, without one word of consolation to fall like a drop of dew upon my burning heart. And now you weep, Teresa, may God bless you! No, this has not been my worst night. Teresa, come closer so that once again I can feel your tears fall on my brow. Had it not been for you, I would have passed through life as through a wilderness, alone with my love and my misfortune, without ever encountering a kind glance or a word of compassion."

Both remained silent for a moment, while Teresa wept and Sab, seated at her feet, appeared sunk in profound dejection. At last Teresa dried her tears and, gathering her strength, pointed out to the mulatto the edge of the horizon on which light-tinged clouds were becoming visible.

"We must part," she told him. "Sab, take your ticket, it will make you rich . . . some day may you be able to find peace and happiness!"

"When I bought this ticket," he replied, "and wanted to try my luck, Martina, the poor old woman who calls me her son, was in a state of poverty; at present she is comfortably off, and gold is useless to me."

"But why? Aren't there other unfortunate beings?"

"No one on earth is more unfortunate than I, Teresa, and I can pity only myself. Yes, I pity myself because I know that in my heart there is only one desire, only one hope: death!"

"Sab, don't give in to your distress; perhaps Heaven will see fit to spare you the torment of seeing Carlota as Enrique's wife. If old Otway is as greedy as you think and if his son loves Carlota only a little, they are both aware of the fact that she is not as rich as they thought, and this marriage will not happen."

"But you told me," exclaimed Sab sadly, "that she will not survive her love . . . you said it, you know it . . . but what you don't know is that I, who offered you the gold to buy this man's hand, would never forgive you had you accepted it, nor would I ever forgive either him or myself. You don't know that blood extracted drop by drop from his veins and my own blood as well would not be sufficient revenge for me, nor would a thousand lives taken by my hand compensate for even one of Carlota's tears. Carlota scorned! Scorned by these vile merchants! Carlota, who would be a king's pride! No, Teresa, don't say it to me again . . . you cannot understand the contradictions of such a tormented heart."

Teresa stood up and listened for a moment.

"Good-bye, Sab," she said. "It appears that the slaves are already up and on their way to the cane fields: good-bye, never doubt that in Teresa you have a friend and a sister."

She waited in vain for a few minutes for the mulatto to answer. Resting his forehead on a rock, motionless and silent, he appeared sunk in deep and somber thought. Then his eyes gleamed with an expression that revealed a sudden and definite decision, and he arose: great, resigned, heroic.

The blacks approached. Sab only had time to murmur a few words to Teresa, words which appeared to startle her for she quickly exclaimed:

"It's possible! . . . But what about you?"

"I will die!" he answered, indicating with his hand that she should leave. Teresa hid in the cane as the slaves arrived for work. Only one, lazier than the others or perhaps thirsty, left his hoe and went down to the river. A violent stumble nearly caused him to fall.

"That's God's punishment, José," his companions shouted, "for being as lazy as you are."

José did not answer bur remained rooted in the place from which he had just gotten up, staring at the ground with astonishment.

"What happened, José?" one of the blacks shouted. "Did you hurt yourself when you fell?"

José called to them, not with his voice but with those expressive facial gestures often seen in the countenances of blacks. The most curious ones ran to his side, and those left behind heard many voices repeat in unison: "The *mayoral!*"

Sab lay unconscious by the river; the slaves picked him up and carried him on their shoulders to the plantation.

When Don Carlos de B—— arose two hours later, he heard the gallop of a departing horse.

"Who's going somewhere now?" he asked one of the slaves.

"It's the *mayoral,* Master, going to the city."

"What? This late? It's seven o'clock and I told him to leave at dawn."

"That's so, Master," replied the slave, "but the *mayoral* was very sick—"

"He was sick? What was wrong with him?"

"The *mayoral,* Master? I don't know, but his face was as hot as a firebrand, and later he spit blood, a lot of blood."

"Spitting blood! What? Spitting blood and he left in that condition?" exclaimed Don Carlos.

José, who walked by carrying a cane sickle, stopped when he heard him and shot the other black a reproachful glance. José was the slave most devoted to Sab, and Sab cherished him because, like his own mother, he was Congolese.

"Your Grace shouldn't pay any attention to this fool. Except for having had a nosebleed, the *mayoral* is all right and told me that by three o'clock this afternoon Your Grace would have his letters from the post office."

"Well, that's better," said Señor de B——. "This lout had me worried."

The black withdrew mumbling: "Lout? I'm a lout because I tell the truth?"

Chapter Three

*It was evident from his appearance that he had run hard,
and his message had to be of immense import.*
—Larra, *The Page of Don Enrique the Sorrowful*

—— • ——

The ship consigned to George Otway had anchored in the port of Guanaja
the day before Enrique's arrival, and after a few hours the latter could have
returned to Puerto Príncipe with the cargo, but he did not do so. The
cargo was sent on to his father with a trusted man, and although nothing
held him in Guanaja, Enrique stayed there, without being able to explain
to himself the reason for this delay. Weak natures tend to hold back when
they are obliged to take a decisive action, in a sense postponing it; one
day, one hour seems an eternity to them, during which they hope for some
major event to make up their minds for them. Enrique already envisioned
his hopes utterly destroyed: he knew without a shadow of a doubt the
exact state of Don Carlos's fortune and understood his father only too well
to hope that he would agree to his union with Carlota. Upon returning to
the city he would have to confess to his father the facts that he had learned
about the reduced value of the farms which Don Carlos de B—— owned
in Cubitas and the declaration Don Carlos himself had made regarding the
considerable arrears of his fortune. His marriage had been arranged to
take place within a month, and the young man saw that the moment had
come to make a decision and to proceed accordingly. What would this
decision be? There were moments when the idea of giving up Carlota
seemed so cruel that had he not had an avaricious father and were free to
choose, perhaps he would have given her his hand in preference to the
richest heiress in the islands, but even in these moments of transports of
love, Enrique never even remotely considered going against his father's
strong will, nor even persuading him to change his mind. In accordance
with the ideas by which he had been raised, nothing was more reasonable
than his father's opposition to a marriage which was no longer profitable
to him, and Enrique reproached himself for the censurable weakness of a
love which bid him go against the paternal will.

"It is a fact," he said to himself, "that this woman has affected my judgment. It's a good thing my father is inflexible, because were I free to follow

my own ideas, I would very likely commit the folly of marrying the daughter of a penniless *criollo*."

But in spite of reasoning in this fashion, he found himself confused and almost ashamed when he thought that Don Carlos would after all know him to be a grasping man, would perhaps abhor or despise him. How could he extract himself from an engagement that was both public and formal—without revealing the reason for his change of heart? And in the eyes of his beloved—his beloved, who was so generous and so unmaterialistic—how could he conceal the odious condition induced by his covetousness?

On the second day after his arrival in Guanaja he was walking by the seashore, agitated by these thoughts, and searched for a way to make up his mind about returning to Puerto Príncipe on the following day.

"I will go," he said. "I'll go without seeing Carlota, without stopping at Bellavista. I will tell my father the truth about everything and will beg him to conduct himself with prudence and discretion so that when he breaks my engagement he will not hurt either Carlota's pride or her sensitivity too severely. I will ask him to search for, to think up a plausible pretext which disguises the real reason for this break as much as possible, and subsequently I will ask his permission to go to Havana, to Philadelphia, to Jamaica . . . anywhere. I will travel for four to six months to get over this infatuation which has made me as helpless as a child."

But hardly had he made this decision than it seemed that some evil spirit put Carlota before his eyes—more beautiful, more tender than ever—and he envisioned her grief-stricken, reproaching him his abandonment, tossing his avarice in his face, and perhaps despising him in her heart. Subsequently (and this last image affected him the most), subsequently he imagined her being consoled from his own treachery by the fervent and selfless love of some passionate *criollo,* and he felt that the latter would be fortunate, and so would she. Then blood rushed to his head and his heart, and he felt close to suffocating. For jealousy is at times more powerful than love itself, and the man least capable of feeling noble passion in all its grandeur is still susceptible to feeling the terrible violence of jealousy. An egotist by nature, a man resents seeing another enjoy the happiness which he himself has spurned, and often, although he has stopped loving, he still believes himself entitled to be loved. Great souls as well as weak ones, higher and lower natures are susceptible to jealousy—but how differently this same sentiment manifests itself! How passions conform to the heart they rule! Sab, succumbing to the jealousy stifled for so long in the secret recesses of his heart, Sab, feeling his heart break at the dreadful prospect of an unworthy yet happy rival, only grieved because his sufferings could not obtain Carlota's happiness. Enrique was unable to bear the happiness of the woman he was abandoning, and the thought that a more worthy suitor might enjoy the good he rejected shook him out of his habitual serenity and forced him to drink the cup of bitterness and rage.

The afternoon was warm and peaceful. It was the middle of June, and the air was beginning to take on that menacing look which characterizes the Antillean summer. After the great storm went by a few days earlier, the weather had been cool and beautiful; but since his arrival in Guanaja, Enrique had noticed signs predicting the storms which in those parts occur almost on a daily basis from June to September. On the afternoon to which we are referring, the calm was so profound that the sea appeared as smooth and burnished as a mirror, with nary a breath nor a movement. The shore was deserted: there was none of the usual bustle or activity which seems essential to a seaport. In the harbor two schooners and several smaller boats lay sad and immobile at anchor, without the song or the shouts of a sailor to give life to that immense solitude. Only a few cranes appeared intermittently on the beach to feed quietly on the sea creatures, whose habitat it was.

Enrique had perched gloomily on a rock and, with his eyes fixed on the sea, let his thoughts drift. What would Carlota do now, he asked himself; would that impassioned soul have a presentiment to warn her that at that very moment her Enrique was thinking about a way to leave her, or trusting and blissful, was she enjoying making sweet plans of happiness for our upcoming union? Then he thought: look at this poor and silent port; when I am once again as rich as I was, instead of these dilapidated little craft this bay will boast elegant ships which will carry the industrial products of all of Europe to my warehouses. Yes, for if I had a middling fortune, in twenty years' time it would be multiplied a hundred times in my hands, and then I would not be an insignificant trader in a Mediterranean city. I would be a wealthy businessman in New York or Philadelphia, and my name would be known by the merchants of both hemispheres. And then, what would I care that Carlota de B—— had a husband and had forgotten me for him? She would follow her destiny as I would mine.

At that moment Enrique, like every man who feels his overriding passion gratified by hope, albeit remote and uncertain, felt strong in the face of any opposition that might present itself to foil the outcome of his desires. Love, jealousy, everything else disappeared or succumbed to a higher power, because the desire for wealth, as with all ambitions, is a strong and vigorous passion. The greedy man who thirsts after gold tramples affections and his own happiness underfoot if these obstruct the path he is following to attain it, exactly the same way that the more noble ambition, that of glory, sacrifices everything in order to pursue the deceptive illusion which conceals an ashen brow under a crown of light. Oh! both are equally vain: the man who accumulates gold in order to buy a tomb and he who sacrifices his youth to a future he never attains and dies with the hope that his name, transmitted from year to year and century to century, might last longer than he himself in the unfathomable abyss of eternal oblivion. But do not tell him who thirsts after gold that it will not bring him happiness, nor the one who is avid for glory that it will lead him to misfortune: they will rise up to say to you, "No matter, my soul has need of it."

"Carlota," said Enrique with his eyes on the ring that shone on his hand, a gift of love which his sweetheart had given him, "I cannot love another woman as much as you, and none will make me so happy as you would have, but destiny separates us. I need to be rich, and you cannot make me rich, Carlota."

Thereupon he got up, made up his mind to return to the city the following day, and cast a proud look about him, like a man who has just defeated a powerful enemy. But then he altered this look and concentrated it fixedly for a while, his head cocked like someone who is listening intently. What Enrique heard, at first indistinctly and then more clearly, was a horse racing toward him. An instinct told him that something of great interest to himself was at that instant approaching, and he took a few steps as though to anticipate it. Suddenly he stopped: he had already spied the horse and the man who rode it. The animal's speed was so headlong that the rider, in spite of visible efforts, could not control him as he wished: the horse shot by like an arrow and only gradually and apparently unwillingly came to a halt, at some distance from Enrique. The latter could, however, see that the rider sprang to the ground, and the foam-flecked horse swayed, finally collapsing at his feet. The man bent over the horse, and it seemed to Enrique that he was speaking to the poor animal which slowly raised its head, looking one last time at his master as though wanting to answer him, and then let it fall. The animal shuddered two or three times and then lay still. The man remained bent over, and Enrique, who was now approaching, could hear two deep and choking cries. He stopped, unable to avoid a kind of emotion, and as at that moment the man raised his head, he was able to recognize the mulatto.

"Sab!" he exclaimed. The mulatto instantly got to his feet and came over to him.

Enrique regarded him for a moment. Perspiration covered his head and ran down his face in thick drops: his eyes had an extraordinary brightness, and his color appeared darker than usual. In his face one could see the type of sad and strange brilliance that is often the result of a fever.

"Sab," said Enrique, "what has happened? When I left your master he didn't tell me that you were coming to Guanaja: no doubt some extraordinary and demanding reason brings you, for it appears that you have had a very rapid journey."

"There you see it, Your Grace," answered the mulatto, indicating his horse. "He is dead, ridden to death! I left Bellavista a little more than four hours ago."

"A little more than four hours," exclaimed Enrique, "you rode thirty miles in four hours and killed the pony you loved so well! No doubt the reason is very important."

"This letter will instruct Your Grace," replied Sab, handing him the paper and letting himself drop mournfully beside his horse. Enrique broke the seal with an unsteady hand, and while he read the mulatto did not let him out of his sight, smiling bitterly when he saw the evident turmoil on the Englishman's face. The letter was from Señor de B—— and ran thus:

It is two o'clock in the afternoon, Enrique, and Sab returned from the city less than an hour ago, bringing me the latest correspondence from Havana, which I did not receive at the usual time due to I know not what unhappy fate. I was expecting a letter from my son and in its stead received one from the director of his school, notifying me that the consumption which threatened my son such a long time ago that we were no longer concerned about it has suddenly flared up with great virulence. Eugenio was so ill when the mail left that the doctors gave him only a few days to live. My beloved son appeared to be resigned to death, of whose proximity he was well aware, but was tormented by the wish to see me one last time before leaving me forever. I am sure you understand, Enrique, the effect that such a wish must have on his father's heart. I am leaving for Havana tomorrow and cannot tell if I will ever return; I don't know if I can bear this blow after so many others and if I will survive my son. However it may be, when I depart I want to leave Carlota with her husband. My disdainful relatives have disowned me, and I cannot leave my daughters alone. For that reason I will not leave for Havana today, because before I go I want to see you married to Carlota. Sab is leaving immediately with all due haste to bring you this letter, and you should not delay for one minute your return to Puerto Príncipe, for which I am leaving with my family within two hours. On your arrival all will be ready so that you can be married in my home at once. Immediately thereafter I shall make my departure, leaving my family in your hands, my adored daughters who may have no other protection, no other father but you.

Come without delay, my son, to receive the sweet treasure I wish to entrust to you.

Carlos de B——

Enrique trembled, and while he read the letter an ashen paleness had taken the place of the handsome rosy hue which usually colored his cheeks.

The mulatto constantly kept his penetrating gaze fixed on him. "Well," he said, "what have you decided?"

Enrique stammered a few words, of which Sab was able to understand: "Impossible! I can't leave Guanaja without my father's permission." Sab kept silent, but his gaze, unwaveringly fastened on the Englishman, seemed to devour him. Filled with confusion and uncertainty, Enrique was almost incapable of reading the postscript which followed the last lines of Don Carlos's letter, and which the mulatto pointed out to him with an expressive gesture. The postscript said:

> Luck, by some cruel mockery, has seen fit to compensate for the fatal blow inflicted on my heart by the loss of my son by bestowing a fortune on my oldest daughter. Carlota has won the grand prize of forty thousand pesos in the most recent lottery. Enrique, you who are not losing a son, can thank Heaven for this favor.

When Enrique had finished reading these words, Sab asked him again, "Well, sir, what has Your Grace decided?"

"To leave for Puerto Príncipe immediately," answered the young man with determination.

"I had guessed as much," the mulatto said with a sardonic smile, turning his glance, which at that instant registered his profound scorn, away from Enrique.

"Come, let us leave this very moment."

"Your Grace will have to go alone," responded Sab, once more sitting down beside his horse. "I am completely exhausted."

"You are right, poor Sab; I cannot lose a minute, but you stay on until tomorrow."

"Yes," said Sab, "hurry, Your Grace. I need to rest a moment."

Enrique left; Sab followed him with his eyes until he lost sight of him and then allowed himself to fall on the body of the poor animal stretched out at his side.

"You no longer live," he said with a sad voice, "you no longer live, my poor friend: you have died carrying out your duty, as I will die carrying out mine. But this duty is terrible! Terrible! My heart is bursting as yours did, my poor friend, but you no longer suffer while I still do. This is finished!" he added immediately, raising his head and throwing a glance around him. "This is finished; there is no other way any longer . . . There is no hope! A few hours more and she will be his! His forever! Forever! In this life Heaven is for him and Hell for me: because Hell is here, in my heart and in my mind."

He rose and regarded the stretch of sea before him. Then he shuddered and violently stretched out his hands before him, simultaneously averting his eyes as though he wished to thrust an unwanted object away from him. Death! It was a terrible temptation for the unfortunate man, and the sea unfolded before him as though to offer him a grave in its profoundest depths. It must have cost him terribly to resist that awful invitation! He raised his eyes heavenward and appeared to offer God that last sacrifice, seemed to say to Him: "I accepted the cup which You ordered me to drain, and I will not cast it away before You ask me to. But now that it is empty, shatter it, God of justice."

Doubtless Heaven heard his entreaties and God sent him a merciful glance, for at that instant the unhappy man felt his entire body falter, and the coldness of death froze his heart. An inner voice seemed to call to him: "You have only a few hours of suffering left, and your mission on earth is now over."

Sab accepted that prophecy, looked gratefully at Heaven, and let his head drop on his horse's body, spattering it with a rush of blood that burst from his mouth.

A fisherman who came by shortly afterward in order to spread his nets on the seashore saw the strange sight of a man and a horse lying in a pool of blood. He thought he had just discovered a murder, and his first instinct was to flee. But a groan which he heard coming from the one he took to be a corpse made him come closer. Examining his entire body in a fruitless search for the wound from which the blood might come, with no little amazement he found the man to be uninjured. Thereupon he lifted him in his arms to take him to his nearby home. When he carefully attempted to raise him, the dying man made a convulsive effort to free himself from his arms, and with indescribable emotion the fisherman watched him get to his feet, like a pale and bloody ghost.

"A horse! Give me a horse in the name of Heaven! My good man," cried Sab, "I am not so ill that I cannot ride seven leagues in the cool of the night: get me a horse."

"If you asked me for a boat I could oblige you," replied the fisherman, still astonished, "but as to a horse, I have none. But my good friend Uncle Juan lives close by, and he can lend you his."

"Good, take me to this man."

The fisherman gave Sab his arm, to support him because he was still unsteady. Turning one last, slow gaze on the body of his horse, he allowed the fisherman to take him to Uncle Juan.

Chapter Four

Over all his limbs
which life abandons, a cold sweat
runs, and a sad trembling.
—Quintana

—— • ——

It was one o'clock in the morning, and in the village of Cubitas all lay in silence and repose; the tillers of the red earth rested from the day's labors, and a few dogs, the only ones afoot in the deserted streets, occasionally interrupted the silence of that tranquil hour with their barking. Nevertheless, a traveler passing through the village at that time would have noticed that in the general darkness and quiet one individual, at least, was not enjoying the sweetness of slumber. The main window of one of the better huts was open, and the glow which shone from it indicated that the room within was lit. From time to time this light appeared to move from one place to another, and the observer would easily have guessed that a wakeful person in that room was moving about. Yet the silence in the illuminated house was as deep as that outside, without even the slightest sound of footsteps.

We will allow ourselves to enter and find out the identity of the people who alone were awake in that hour of general tranquillity.

On a small canvas cot, between coarse but very clean sheets, appeared the emaciated and cadaverous head of a child, seemingly young in years because the shape of his body on the cot could scarcely be made out. The body was so completely still that one would have thought him dead, had it not been for the labored breath which could be heard passing between his white, parted lips. Beside the bed, seated on a wooden chair, was a very old, copper-colored woman, her eyes fixed on the ashen face of the sick child, her arms crossed over her breast in a gesture of sad resignation. A dog lay at her feet.

From time to time the woman arose and with light steps approached a small cedar table placed under the window, undoubtedly open to cool the room which, because of its smallness, was very hot; she took from it a glass and a small candlestick in which burned a tallow candle, then immediately returned to the sick child's bed. Putting the candle on the chair on which she had been sitting, she examined his face attentively and damp-

ened his lips with the liquid in the glass. The dog followed her each time
she got up to do this, and when she would put the little candlestick and
the glass back onto the table and return to her seat next to the bed, the
animal would stretch out quietly at her feet, without disturbing the silence. It must have been about two o'clock in the morning when the door
which connected this room with the main one in the house was carefully
opened. An older man entered on tiptoe until he stood by the old woman,
to whose ears he bent his lips and whispered, "How is the patient,
Martina?"

"As you see," the latter replied, pointing to the sharp features of the
child with her thin hand, "though it is already two o'clock, he will not see
the light of day."

"What? Do you think that soon . . ."

"Yes," said Martina, shaking her head sadly, "yes, *mayoral,* very soon."

"Well, then," responded the recent arrival, "go and rest a while, Martina, and I will stay and watch over him. You have not closed your eyes in
four days: go and rest and I will take your place."

"No thank you, *mayoral;* you can't afford wakeful nights because you
have enough work during the day, and Don Carlos de B—— has you here
to attend to his affairs and not to take care of my patients. Go back to
your bed and let me be. What is one more sleepless night to me? Tomorrow," she added with a sad smile, "tomorrow poor Luis will no longer
need me, and I will be able to rest."

"I will do as you wish, Martina," responded the overseer, shrugging his
shoulders, "but you know that I am in the adjoining room in the event
that I can help you."

"I thank you, *mayoral.*"

The old man tiptoed out, but as he reached the door he paused and
listened to the gallop of a horse, which could be heard distinctly in the
silence of the night. The dog became attentive as well, pricking up his ears
and listening intently.

"Do you hear, Martina?" said the overseer in a low voice.

"Well, then! What startles you? It's someone passing by on a horse,"
replied the old woman.

"But he's not passing by; either I am very much mistaken or the horse
has stopped outside our door."

Hardly had he finished these words when two successive knocks
sounded on the front door of the room adjoining Martina's. The dog began to bark and the overseer exclaimed, "It's here, it's here—didn't I say
so? But who would come to disturb us at this hour? It might be some
messenger from the master, but for him to arrive at this time something
very unusual must have happened."

"Go and open the door," Martina interrupted him, "I have recognized Sab by the two knocks . . . listen, listen! He is repeating them again; it is Sab, *mayoral,* run and open the door for him. Leal, quiet, it's Sab."

The overseer obeyed, and perhaps because of the noise of the bolts as they were being slid open to allow free entry and the dog's barks which frightened him, or perhaps because at that moment his pangs were more intense, the patient shuddered all over and stretched out his emaciated arms. Sab entered the room and came to a halt before the dying child's bed.

"My son," Martina said to him, "as you see . . . Come closer, Heaven has no doubt brought you to remind me that I still have one son. Only you will remain in this world to console this poor woman's last days."

Sab knelt down by the bed and kissed Martina's hand, while the dog jumped about him in greeting, and Luis made painful attempts to lift his head.

"Look at him, my son," said Martina, "your presence has put new life into him; speak to him, for no doubt he can still hear you."

Sab bent toward the dying child and called him by his name: Luis opened his eyes slightly, although without focusing on Sab, and stretched out his transparent little hands as though to grasp something. Sab took them between his own and, bending his face over that of the child, let a large, burning tear fall on it.

"Do you know me?" he said. "It is I, your brother."

Luis directed his glassy look toward the place from which the voice came and pressed Sab's hands slightly; immediately afterward he turned his face back to the opposite side and returned to his previous immobility, only his breathing became more labored, creating the dry, guttural sound which is the death rattle.

"You must rest, Mother," said Sab to Martina. "Your face tells me that you have not slept for many nights."

"Four!" exclaimed the overseer. "She has not closed her eyes for four nights, and not for lack of my telling her—"

The mulatto interrupted the old man and took Martina's hand:

"Tonight you will rest," he said to her, "because I am here and I will watch over my brother."

"Yes, and you will hear his last breath," the Indian woman replied with bitter resignation, "for Luis will not live two hours. Very well, very well!" she added, rising and bending over the child's bed. "I will leave him because now—now I am no longer of any use to the unfortunate creature."

"You are mistaken, Mother," Sab told her while with the aid of the overseer he made up a bed for Martina. "Luis is not as ill as you think, for he still recognizes me."

"Sab, my son, I will leave you at his side and will go away quietly, but don't try to deceive me: I know full well that he is dying. But for that very reason I can leave him. I have seen my son, my daughter-in-law, and two of my grandsons in the same state, and I have listened to their last breaths, yet in spite of all that, I feel weak by the side of this poor creature. He is the last, Sab, he is my last relative, the last link that binds me to life, and at this moment I feel weak."

Sab took the old woman's hand and pressed it between his own. Martina let her head fall to his shoulder and added in a softer voice, "I am unjust, I know! I still have a son: you! You are still with me."

"Here! This is not the time to cry and make all of us weep," said the overseer, putting the finishing touches on Martina's bed. "Come and lie down and stop thinking these thoughts: tomorrow you can speak to Sab at length and can tell him everything; what is important right now is that you sleep a bit."

Martina bent over and placed a kiss on the already icy brow of her grandson, subsequently permitting Sab to lead her to the bed which had been prepared for her. The young man laid her down carefully and covered her with a blanket. Then he turned to the overseer and told him in a voice which betrayed his emotion, "Early tomorrow I will need a trustworthy man to take a letter to my master's house in Puerto Príncipe, and I charge you to find me one."

"If you will permit me, I will go myself," the old man replied. "But tell me, Sab, has anything happened in the city? Your arrival at this hour and the letter—"

Sab did not let him finish.

"Nothing has happened, *mayoral*, which is of any import to you. Tomorrow at six you will leave to take a letter to Señorita Teresa, my master's cousin, and put yourself at his disposal; you will also explain to him the reason for my delay in Cubitas. He is about to begin a journey and may need a trustworthy man to go with him. I should be this man, but you will go in my stead."

"Oh, I assure you, Sab, that although I am old I am as capable as you—"

"I believe it," interrupted the mulatto with some impatience. "Now, *mayoral*, go to sleep: good night. Only give me a piece of paper and an inkwell. Until tomorrow."

The old man obeyed: in the voice of that mulatto there was an indefinable quality of authority and greatness that had always subjugated him.

When Sab was alone he knelt by the side of Martina's bed, who, sitting up against her pillow and fixing him with a penetrating and deeply troubled look, said to him:

"With me, Sab, you need hold nothing back. I demand that you tell me the reason for your coming and for this trip that you tell me Don Carlos has to take."

The young man embraced Martina's knees, bending his head over them in silence.

"Sab!" exclaimed the old woman, inclining her own over that beloved head and pressing it between her hands, "your head is burning . . . your brow is covered in perspiration . . . you have a fever, my son."

"Calm yourself," he told her, attempting to smile, "it's the strain of the journey: I am quite well, try to rest. Tomorrow you will know everything, Mother."

"No, no," cried Martina anxiously, "let me get the light and shine it on your face. My God! How you have changed! Your eyes are sunken and shine with a feverish light. My son! My son! What is the matter with you?"

And she knelt down before him.

"For pity's sake!" exclaimed the mulatto, raising her up almost angrily. "Be quiet, be quiet, Martina, calm yourself if you don't wish to see me die of sorrow at your feet."

Martina allowed herself to be led to her bed once more, and the poor woman made an effort to appear calm.

"Sit here at my head, my son, I will not bother you any more. I will be as silent as the grave. But come, my son, let me hear your voice, let me see your face, let me feel your heart beat next to mine. Oh, Sab! To think that I have nothing left in the world save you, that you are my only son, the only bastion of this long and shattered life."

Sab embraced her tightly, and two heavy, burning tears fell on her brow.

"Yes, Mother," he told her, "rest on my breast: my voice will lull you to sleep. I will speak to you of God, and of the angels among whom our dear Luis will dwell. I will speak to you of the eternal rest of the unfortunate and of the consoling promises of the Gospel. Rest in my arms: are you comfortable like this?"

Martina, exhausted by fatigue and sorrow, let Sab lay her down and appeared to slip into that kind of lethargy which follows great upheavals.

"Speak," she repeated, "speak, my son, and I will listen to you."

Sab murmured a few disconnected words; at that moment the poor child, too, suffered dreadfully. But Martina, resting on Sab's breast, felt calmer and finally slept, just as he was beginning to tell her of the resurrection of the righteous. Sensing her asleep, he gently laid her head on the pillow. He placed a long, silent kiss on her forehaed and fell to his knees before the table, on which the overseer had left him paper and inkwell.

Subsequently that humble room became a dramatic scene. It was a terrible sight to see, on the one hand, the sleep of old age and the tranquil death of innocence and, on the other, Sab's young life destroyed by sorrows. Compared to Luis, the fragile child who was surrendering without resistance, a delicate reed that bent without a sound, it was another matter to observe the ebbing strength of the vigorous man who succumbed like the oak before the tempests of heaven.

It seemed that while his soul was leaving his body, it was completely reflected in his countenance. Oh, what terrible agony that had no other witnesses than sleep and death! No one bore witness to the passionate soul that was revealed in its finest hour.

But Sab wrote, and the letter was his legacy.

The sublime martyr of love died unrecognized, but the letter survived and won for him the only prize that he wished for without hope of attaining it: one of Carlota's tears!

Sab wrote with a quivering hand that became progressively more unsteady. Once he put the quill aside and took an object from his breast which he contemplated for a while with melancholy interest. It was Carlota's bracelet, which Teresa had given him by way of Luis in that same room five days before.

"Here she is!" he murmured gazing intently at the portrait. "So lovely! So pure! For him! All for him!"

His convulsed fingers let the bracelet drop, and a moment later he began to write again. But it was clear that his strength was ebbing rapidly. Nevertheless, for more than an hour he wrote without respite, pausing on several occasions only to approach Luis's bed and dampen his lips as Martina had done. The latter remained in a kind of stupor, every now and again tossing about and stretching out her arms, saying, "Sab! I have no son but you."

The mulatto heard her, and his hand shook even more in those instants, but he continued writing. The light of dawn was already coming in the window when he sealed his letter.

He enclosed the bracelet within and attempted to write the address; but his hand no longer obeyed him, and at that moment he was seized by violent convulsions.

There was an instant in which overwhelming pain gave him some fleeting strength, and with a long and tormented effort he attempted to stand, but then collapsed as though paralyzed, his clenched teeth grinding convulsively.

Still he managed to drag himself laboriously toward Luis's bed, where his wild, burning glance met the dying child's glassy and motionless stare. Sab wished to bid him a last good-bye but stopped himself, aghast at the sound of his own voice which seemed to him an echo from the grave.

A multitude of ideas and sorrows flashed through his mind. He realized that he was going to die too and that at the same instant that he was suffering an agonizing end, Enrique and Carlota would exchange their vows of love. Then he no longer thought anything: his ideas became confused, his imagination clouded, his memory bewildered. His body collapsed and he fell across Luis's bed, inundating it with thick bubbles of blood which spurted from his mouth.

The *mayoral* of the farm looked up at the sun, his infallible clock, and saw that it was already five. He left his saddled horse at the door of the house and, stealthily approaching Martina's room so as not to disturb the old woman if by some chance she were asleep, repeatedly called Sab. But Sab did not answer. In vain he progressively raised his voice, and knocking at the door with greater force, he pressed his ear to the door with silent attention. Deep stillness permeated the room, and, frightened, the *mayoral* struck two monumental blows upon the door. Then the dog barked and Martina awoke, casting a terrified glance about her. She could not see Sab! With a cry she ran toward her grandson's bed. There were the two of them—Luis dead, Sab dying.

Martina fainted at the foot of the bed, and the *mayoral,* breaking down the door, entered just in time to hear the mulatto's dying breath.

Sab died at six in the morning, at the same hour that Enrique and Carlota were receiving the nuptial blessing.

Chapter Five

This is life, Garcés;
One dies, another marries,
Some cry, others laugh . . .
Sad human condition!
　　　　　　—Garcia Gutiérrez, *The Page*

—— • ——

There was great turmoil in Señor de B——'s house when, after witnessing the marriage of his daughter, he had left for the port of Nuevitas, from which he was to embark for Havana.

George, who had been present for the celebration of the marriage and Don Carlos's departure, returned to his home, leaving Enrique already installed in his wife's. The anxiety which Carlota felt because of her brother's condition, the painful sentiments produced by the first separation from a tenderly loved father, and her precipitous marriage, which had taken place under such inauspicious conditions, at first caused her to be somewhat distracted and insensitive to the assiduous endearments which her husband lavished upon her.

Her weeping little sisters surrounded her, but she was unable to give them even one word of consolation. Only Teresa kept her presence of mind, and while she was giving directions to the slaves and restoring to the house the order which had momentarily been interrupted, she also took care of the little girls and of Carlota herself. Lovingly she urged her to lie down for a few hours, fearing that so many upheavals and a sleepless night would affect her delicate health; giving in to her pleas at last, Carlota was about to obey when the *mayoral* from the Cubitas property arrived with the news of Sab's death. This tragedy, he said, was no doubt the result of a catastrophic fall, for according to Martina, who was an oracle for the good farmer, all of the chambers of Sab's heart had burst.

This news, which a few days before would have been extremely painful for Carlota, hardly seemed to affect her at a moment when she had been through so much. She had just been separated from her father, her brother was most likely dying at that very moment, and in comparison with these calamities the loss of the mulatto was very minor.

Enrique showed his surprise and sorrow much more keenly.

"The poor fellow!" he said. "These sudden deaths terrify me."

And then, as though he had had an illuminating thought, he added, "Martina is right: a fall from his horse was undoubtedly the cause of his death. Poor Sab! Now I recall how pale, how changed he was yesterday when he reached Guanaja. I attributed it to the fatigue of such a hasty journey: he rode his black pony to death."

"I have here an unaddressed letter," said the overseer, "but I think it is for the Señora."

"For Carlota! And from whom is this letter, my good fellow?"

"From the poor dead man, sir," replied the overseer, proffering it. "I think he wrote it while he was dying, as he asked me for paper and an inkwell at three in the morning, and at six the unfortunate man gave up his soul to his Maker. But it seems that it was a matter of importance, and so, as I had to come to accompany the master to Havana . . . but I already see I have come too late, and my arrival will have only served to bring this letter."

In the short time taken up by the overseer's speech, to which no one was listening, a very lively scene took place in that room. Enrique, who had appropriated the letter which was said to be for his wife, hurriedly tore open the envelope, and upon being opened out fell the bracelet, which he picked up with surprise.

"A bracelet! Carlota, . . . this bracelet—"

"Is mine," said Teresa, calmly approaching. "It is a gift from Carlota which I hold in such regard that I could only give it to the one person in the world I believed worthy of my affection and esteem. Now that it has come back to my hands, I want to keep it until I die. Give it to me, then, Enrique, and the letter as well, which is also for me."

Enrique was thunderstruck and looked at Teresa and then at Carlota, as though he wished to read in their faces the explanation for that enigma. But Teresa's countenance was pale and serene, and in Carlota's lovely features one could see at that moment only a candid expression of surprise.

"Have the goodness to give me that letter and that bracelet, Enrique," repeated Teresa firmly, "and take Carlota to her room: she needs to rest."

Enrique cast a glance at the letter, whose first line he had read, and immediately handed it and the bracelet over to Teresa, saying to her with a malicious smile, "Indeed it is for you, Teresa, but I had no idea that you corresponded with the mulatto and that he would return a gift to you that, according to what you say, you would only give to the man you loved and esteemed most."

"Well, if you didn't know it, Enrique," she replied with dignity, "now you do."

Then she embraced Carlota, pleading with her anew to go and rest with her little sisters for a few hours, as their childish faces were ashen from the strenuous night.

Carlota lifted one after the other of the four little girls in her arms.

"Yes," she said, "come and rest, poor little things, who have stayed up and wept with me the entire night. And you, Teresa," she said, fixing her friend with a look of indulgence and compassion, "you rest too, my dear, because you are affected as well."

Carlota got up, supported by Enrique and surrounded by her sisters as though by a choir of angels, and retired to her room, after having placed a kiss on the pale and resigned brow of her friend.

In order to get her sisters to rest, who did not want to leave her for even a moment, she lay down fully dressed on her bed, and the four little girls settled themselves around her, falling asleep almost immediately.

Enrique closed the curtain, advising his young wife to try to sleep as well while he busied himself with trying to straighten out some papers which Señor de B—— had left in his charge.

"Yes," said Carlota, "I will keep silent so as not to wake these poor children, but don't leave the room, Enrique, because I confess to you that I am afraid. This so sudden death of Sab's has made a deep impression on me. Oh, my love! What sad omens for our union! Deaths, farewells! Don't leave me alone, Enrique; it seems to me that I see death rising up and threatening all my loved ones and that if I fail to see you for a moment I shall never see you again."

"Calm yourself, my darling," answered her husband. "I will be here to watch over your sleep. But don't be afraid of my death, because one does not die if one is as happy as I am. Sleep peacefully, Carlota, so that the roses will return to your cheeks: don't you know that I want to see you beautiful on our wedding day?"

"Our wedding day!" she murmured. "How sad this day has been!"

But Enrique had already sat down at Don Carlos's desk, where he busied himself reading and arranging papers, and Carlota, with no hope of rest but not wishing to interrupt that of her sisters, closed her eyes and pretended to sleep. She was able to remain in this position for almost an hour; but then it was impossible to stay there any longer, and carefully freeing one of her arms on which rested the head of the youngest of the sisters, she gradually slid off the bed.

"Are you awake already?" said Enrique, coming over to give her a hand. "Don't you want to rest another hour, my sweet?"

"I can't," she answered, "because I have been thinking, Enrique, that in the confusion of the first moment of surprise and sorrow I failed to remember to look after the needs of the good man who brought us the news of our poor Sab's death, and I certainly should have ordered that he be offered refreshment, for the good old fellow, with the best intentions in the world, hurried to bring us the unpleasant news. He should also return to Cubitas immediately and take some money to Martina for the unfortunate man's burial. And Teresa, Enrique, poor Teresa! I left her at a moment . . . I must speak with her, find out what mystery is contained in that letter and that bracelet which she has received."

"It's easy to guess," said Enrique, smiling. "Teresa loved the mulatto."

"Love him! Love him!" repeated Carlota with doubt in her voice. "This thought had occurred to me, but . . . to love him! . . . Oh, it's not possible!"

"You women, my love, have such inconceivable whims and such extraordinary tastes!"

"Love him!" repeated Carlota, "Him, a slave! And also, Teresa is so cold . . . so little susceptible to love!"

"Perhaps we have been mistaken, judging her heart by her appearance, my love."

"No, Enrique, I have not judged her heart by her appearance: I know that her heart is noble, good, capable of the greatest sentiments; but love, Enrique, love is for the tender, the passionate hearts . . . like yours, like mine."

"It is for all hearts, my dear, and Teresa has a heart."

"Come then, we'll go and see her, Enrique, and if it is true that she loved this unhappy man, she deserves compassion and not censure. He was a mulatto, it is true, and was born a slave, but he, too, had a beautiful heart, Enrique, and his soul was as noble, as elevated as yours, as all noble and elevated souls."

When he heard these words Enrique's gaze, which had been fixed lovingly on his wife's beautiful eyes, wavered a little, and as though his conscience made painful for him a comparison which he well knew was not deserved, he hurriedly answered:

"Come then, Carlota, let us go and see your cousin. I don't think, after what she said when she asked me for the bracelet, that she would want to deny her love for Sab."

"I won't attempt to wrest her secret from her either, but if she cries, I will cry with her," said Carlota leaning on her husband's arm, and talking together in this fashion, they left their room and reached the door of Teresa's, which was open. Enrique stopped at the entrance, and Carlota went in, calling her friend. But she was not in the room. Carlota had Belén come and asked about Teresa.

"What?" the slave responded, surprised. "Didn't Your Grace realize she was about to go out? She left more than half an hour ago."

"Where? With whom?"

"She didn't say where, but I assume to church, because she put on her black dress and covered her head with her mantilla. The overseer who came from Cubitas went with her."

"Do you hear, Enrique?" said Carlota, sitting down sadly on a chair which stood before Teresa's table.

"Well? Why are you concerned, Carlota?"

"Why? Because Teresa does not usually go out at this hour with a man she barely knows and on foot, without telling me . . . This is very strange!"

At that moment Carlota noticed a paper with writing on it on the table upon which she leaned and, as she knew Teresa's handwriting, read it hurriedly. Bursting into tears she immediately handed it to her husband, and Enrique read it aloud. It said:

Poor, orphaned, unattractive, and nameless,[1] I have, for a number of years, regarded the convent as the only destiny to which I might aspire in this world, and today an irresistible impulse of the heart impels me toward this holy sanctuary.

I would not leave you on this day of affliction if I felt I were needed or even useful, but you now have a husband, Carlota, whom you love and who has today sworn before God and men to love you, protect you, and make you happy. I leave you with him, wishing you a future filled with love and happiness. Your destiny has been decided, and I wish to decide mine.

To spare myself the reasons which you would muster to have me change my mind about a decision I have irrevocably taken, I am leaving your house without bidding you farewell except by these lines and am going to the Ursuline convent, which I shall never leave. My inheritance, although small, covers the dowry which I need to be admitted, and within a year I hope I will be permitted to take my vows.

Good-bye, Carlota and Enrique, love each other and be happy.

Teresa

"Oh, Enrique," exclaimed Carlota, "there you are, everything conspires to trouble me, to make this day of our union sad and dismal: this day, which should be such a happy one!"

"You should no longer have any doubts," said Enrique, "of your cousin's love for Sab. It is his death which has brought on this sudden decision to become a nun. In truth, your friend has noble inclinations."

"Don't blame her, Enrique, have forebearance with the weaknesses of the heart. Poor Teresa, how unfortunate she is! But couldn't she have waited and postponed carrying out her decision to another day? Why was she so cruel as to add one more vexation to all the ones I've been through today? The ungrateful creature leaves me on the very day my father has gone: alone . . . abandoned."

"Alone! Abandoned, Carlota!" repeated Enrique, putting his arms about her. "When you are with your husband who adores you, when I am here at your side, pressing you to my heart? My darling! The loss of a brother is painful, though he is a brother you have not seen in three years, and whose weak and sickly constitution has long been preparing you for this blow; the separation from a father is painful, though it will be a very short one; painful also the death of a mulatto who was a faithful slave to your family; and painful too that a mad friend who was enamored of him would want to become a nun, even though that is certainly the best thing she could do. But is all of this sufficient motive to be grieving to such a degree, and to spoil the happiest day of my life for me? Is this not an injustice, Carlota, an act of ingratitude toward your Enrique? Instead of happiness will you give me pain, tears instead of caresses? Ah! Four days ago you loved me . . . today . . . today you don't love me."

"Not love you!" she exclaimed with a rush of emotion caused by worry and tenderness. "You say I don't love you! Ah, I don't love you, I worship you! You are my consolation, my hope, my bastion, because now you are my husband, Enrique, and today will be a day of happiness in spite of all the obstacles Destiny may cause to happen. Perhaps I needed this balance so that my mind might not succumb to too much happiness. Because I love you, Enrique!"

"Well then prove it to me, my love, and don't cry any more; prove it to me with a smile, with a look of joy. Make me happy with your happiness, Carlota—"

"Yes, yes, I am happy," she interrupted him with a kind of delirium. "My father, my brother, Teresa, Sab . . . What are all of them compared to your love? I no longer have anyone but you . . . but you are everything to your Carlota's heart. Look, don't mind that I cry: they are tears of joy, sweet tears that I shed on your breast. Because I am yours! Because I love you! Because I am happy!"

"Carlota, my dearest, say it to me again: what does anything else matter when we love each other like this?" exclaimed Enrique rapturously.

"You are right," she added. "When we love each other like this, Heaven itself cannot make us unhappy."

"Carlota, now you are mine!"

"Yours forever!"

"How happy I am!"

"And I, Enrique, and I!"

And they truly were. That was the first day of their union; and the first day of a pure and holy union, the day on which the deepest and most ardent feelings are transformed into the gravest of responsibilities, is undoubtedly a supreme day. On this day there should be an overflowing of happiness that is not of this earth, nor of this life, and which Heaven grants us for one day in order to make us understand therewith the happiness which it is saving for chosen souls in the eternity of its glory. Because heavenly bliss is nothing else but eternal love.

A terrible storm roared across the earth. It was three in the afternoon, and the sky, covered by an opaque curtain, predicted a dreadful afternoon.

At that hour Don Carlos, defying the tempest, raced for the dock at Nuevitas, thinking that one moment of delay might keep him from finding his son alive. At that hour Teresa, kneeling before a crucifix in a narrow cell, implored God's mercy for those who had died. At that hour in Cubitas two bodies were being interred, that of a man and that of a boy; an old woman wept over a bloodstained bed, and a dog howled at her feet. And at that hour Carlota and Enrique were happy, because they loved each other, because they had married that day and endlessly repeated with voice and glances: "Now I am yours!" "Now you are mine!"

Such are the contrasts we see every day in the world. Joy and Sorrow! But Joy is an exile from Heaven who does not remain in any one place. Sorrow is a son of Hell who does not release his prey until he has torn it to pieces.

Conclusion

If on man's brow could be read
The inner sorrow with which he struggles,
How many there are who arouse our envy
Who instead should move us to pity.
　　　　　　　　—Metastasio

It was the afternoon of the sixteenth of June, 18——, five years to the day after the events with which the previous chapter ended, and some movement could be detected inside the Ursuline convent of Puerto Príncipe. Undoubtedly some extraordinary event was the cause of this turmoil, which was unwonted in the grave and monotonous life of the nuns. But what new or strange thing could occur within the walls of a convent? Death! This was the important event which marked time for the solitary members of a convent: the death of one of their own, death which came to open the iron gates of that vast sepulcher for the unhappy nun, only to thrust her into another and more restricted grave.

On the day in question it was indeed death which caused the stir in the convent. Sister Teresa lay in the final hours of her life, the victim of a consumption which had afflicted her for three years; still, all the nuns felt consternation at the proximity of a death which they already knew was coming.

Sister Teresa was universally loved. Although cold and austere, her severe virtue, her elevated character, the sublime resignation with which she had accepted her long illness, and the thousand little attentions she had lavished on her companions with the unfailing though indifferent goodness which characterized her had earned her everyone's affection; they were genuinely sorry to lose her, although some of them might feel a kind of satisfaction that an event, whatever its nature, had brought some variety and change into their melancholy congregation.

It was six o'clock in the evening, and the nuns were beginning to be impatient that Señora de Otway had not yet arrived. A message, informing her of the seriousness of her cousin's illness and of the desire the latter had manifested to see her before dying, had been sent to her at the Bellavista plantation where she was staying. The delay annoyed the good nuns, because, as they said, it was ungrateful of Señora de Otway to be so slow in coming to the side of the dying woman who loved her so well and with whom she had always had such a tender relationship.

Indeed there were many times, especially in the last two years, that the nuns had secretly criticized Carlota's long visits with her cousin, perhaps because they felt annoyed at being unable to satisfy their curiosity and hear what the two friends discussed during their talks, which frequently took place in Sister Teresa's cell. It was scandalous, they said, those conversations alone which ran counter to the rules of the institution and which the abbess only permitted because Señora de Otway was a relative of hers and perchance all the more because of the Señora's frequent bequests to the convent.

Had the poor nuns been able to satisfy their curiosity by listening to those conversations, they might have gone away from that cell more content with their own lot and less envious of Carlota's, because they would have heard that the beautiful, rich, and admired woman, who had a husband and many comforts, came seeking consolation from the poor nun who had renounced the world. They would have seen that the woman they thought fortunate wept and that the nun was happy.

Teresa had indeed reached that calm and grave happiness which virtue bestows. Her proud, strong spirit had mastered her destiny, and her feelings and elevated, firm, and decided character had allowed her to reach that noble resignation which is as difficult for passionate souls as it is for those of weak character. Her passion for Enrique, that introspective and deep passion, the only one that in all her life had ever possessed that proud heart, had been extinguished under her hair shirt, in the shadow of the convent's cold walls; her ambition, which had virtue as its sole end, had been for her a useful and holy stimulus, and in spite of physical ailments and interior struggles, her noble aspiration had been crowned with success.

Carlota, on the other hand, was unhappy, and the more others believed her to be happy, the more wretched she became. Young, rich, beautiful, wife of the man of her choice who loved her, highly thought of by all— how could she have convinced anyone that she envied the lot of a poor nun? Obliged to be silent before men, she could only weep freely within the walls of the Ursuline convent, on the breast of a nun who had attained happiness of soul by learning to deal with misfortune.

But why did Carlota weep? What was her sorrow? Not all men would understand it, because very few would be able to commiserate. Carlota was a poor poetic soul thrown in among a thousand materialistic lives. Gifted with a fertile and active imagination, ignorant of life, at an age when life is no more than feelings, she found herself obliged to live calculatingly, by reflection and by measuring advantage. That mercantile and profit-oriented atmosphere, those unceasing preoccupations with interests of a material nature withered the lovely illusions of her youthful heart. Poor, delicate flower! Beautiful, useless, you were born to perfume gardens, gently caressed by Heaven's breezes!

Before she was married Carlota had enjoyed the advantages of wealth without knowing their price: she had no idea of the effort involved in obtaining it. Once married, at the cost of a thousand small and prosaic humiliations, she daily learned how one reaches a state of wealth. Nevertheless, Carlota lacked for nothing: comforts, pleasures, and even luxury—she had it all. The two Englishmen ran their home on a brilliant scale. But beautiful appearances and even real advantages of life were all founded upon and sustained by ceaseless activity, perennial scheming, and an exhausting watchfulness. Carlota could not by rights disapprove of her husband's conduct nor complain of her lot, but to her sorrow she felt oppressed by all the harshness and materialism of business life. While her father was alive—a man as sweet and indolent as she, and with whom she could with impunity be childish, imaginative, and impassioned—she could also be less in contact with her new life, and only had occasion to weep when she saw her husband more occupied with his fortune than with his love and when business interests forced him to take frequent trips, now to Havana, now to the United States of America. Yet at those times she remained with the father who adored her and whose weakened health required a thousand attentions which filled her life.

But Don Carlos survived his son by only two years, and his death, which deprived Carlota of an indulgent friend and gentle consoler, was accompanied by circumstances which once and for all rent the veil of her illusions and embittered her life forever.

During the final weeks of the poor gentleman's life, George never left his bedside, keeping vigil beside him during the nighttimes when Carlota rested. She appreciated this help with all the warmth of the noble and sensitive heart which was unable to see through his evil motives, but when she discovered them her indignation was all the more vehement for having trusted him.

As Don Carlos had a weak character, weaker still after two years of an illness which had undermined both his body and his spirit, he was malleable wax in the iron hands of the astute and covetous Englishman, who convinced him to draw up a will in which he left to Carlota the major part of his estate. Carlota knew nothing of this injustice until her father was dead and she was informed of his last will and testament, in which she saw the unequivocal proof of the avarice and vile nature of her father-in-law. She had a frank and resolute talk with Enrique, declaring her intention not to condone the injustice which had been committed and to return to the sisters who had been unjustly dispossessed those goods which avarice had wrested from weakness.

Carlota had convinced herself that her husband would think the same way she did, but Enrique found his wife's demands absurd and treated them like the illusions of a little girl who does not yet know her own mind. The will was legal, and Enrique could not understand Carlota's delicate scruples, nor why she termed it unjust and invalid.

All of Carlota's entreaties, her tears, her protests only served to alienate her father-in-law, without Enrique ever listening to her in any other way than as to a capricious child who is asking the impossible. He treated her lovingly and spoke endearing words but ended by laughing at her indignation.

Carlota fought to no avail for many months, after which she kept silent and appeared to have resigned herself to it. For her everything was over. She saw her husband as he really was: she began to understand life. Her dreams faded; her love, and with it her happiness, vanished. Then she came to know all the starkness, the pettiness of reality, understood the error of her eager ways; and her spirit, which still craved fervor and illusions, found itself alone with those two men, so earthbound and sustained by material gain. Then she became unhappy, then the long, secret talks with the Ursuline nun became more frequent. Her only comfort was to weep on her friend's bosom over her lost illusions and her restricted freedom, and when she was not with Teresa she avoided the company of her husband and her father-in-law. She frequently went to Bellavista and there spent months in absolute solitude or with only the company of her sisters, who were, however, too young to be able to console her. At Bellavista she breathed more freely: her poor heart felt the need to give of itself, and she opened it to the heavens, to the free country air, to the trees and the flowers.

Thus, on the day that this last chapter of our story begins, she was out of town, while the nuns waited for her impatiently and Teresa lay dying. The latter had already fulfilled all of her obligations as a Catholic; she seemed to listen absently as the priest who attended her spoke of wondrous things, and frequently called for Carlota.

At last she arrived. A carriage pulled up to the door of the convent, and Señora de Otway, pale and frightened, hurried to the dying woman's cell.

Teresa seemed to revive at the sight of her friend and in a weak but clear voice asked that they be left alone.

Carlota knelt down by the bed, at whose head two wax candles burned, illuminating a skull and a silver crucifix. Teresa raised herself a little on her pillows, offering her hand.

"I am dying," she said after a moment of silence, "and possess nothing, nothing that I can bequeath to the friend of my youth. But perhaps I can leave her a strange comfort, a sad but powerful weapon against the trouble that is debilitating her most beautiful years. Carlota, you are weary of life and detest the world and men . . . nevertheless, you have been a fortunate woman, Carlota; you have been loved with the kind of love that was your heart's dream and would have been the glory of my life had I been the one to inspire it. Without being aware of it, you have possessed one of those great, ardent souls born for supreme sacrifices, one of those exceptional souls that pass by like God's breath upon the earth. So, Carlota: are you wearied by a purely material existence? Do you need the poetry of suffering? Do you wish for something to worship? Untie this black ribbon from around my neck . . . on it there is a small key: unlock that small shell box with it. Good! Can you find in it a paper stained by my tears? Take that paper, Carlota, and keep it as I have kept it.

"Heaven did not give me an active imagination, nor a poetic and exalted soul; unlike you, I have not lived in the world of my dreams. To me real life always presented itself unadorned, and the sad experience of misfortune made me understand and suspect many terrible secrets of the human heart. In spite of this, Carlota, I die believing in love and in virtue, and to this paper I owe that sweet faith that has kept me from the cruelest of ills: discouragement."

Teresa's voice faltered for a moment; she asked her cousin for a glass of water and then more firmly revealed to her the mulatto's noble sacrifice.

"He gave you the gold," she told her, "which convinced Enrique to make you his wife, but don't hate your husband, Carlota: he is just like the majority of men, and there are many worse! May Heaven keep you from one day looking back with sorrow at the country in which you were born, where uprightness is still esteemed, base actions are despised, and where, in obscurity, fundamental virtues still exist. Men are evil, Carlota, but you should not hate them nor become discouraged on your road. It is useful to know what they are and not to ask more of them than they can give; it is useful to relinquish those dreams that perhaps no longer exist anymore except in the heart of a daughter of Cuba. For we have been fortunate, Carlota, to have been born on virgin soil, under a magnificent sky, not to have lived in the bosom of a feeble nature but surrounded by all of God's great works which have taught us to know and to love Him.

"Perhaps some day destiny will take you away from this land in which you had your cradle and in which I shall have my grave: perhaps, in the corrupt atmosphere of the cities of the old hemisphere, you will search in vain for a breeze to refresh your soul, a reminder of your early youth, a vestige of your dreams; perhaps you will find nothing great or beautiful to restore your weary heart. Then you will have this paper: this paper is an entire soul, a life, a death, a summary of dreams, a compendium of sorrows . . . the fragrance of a heart which died without withering. The tears this paper will elicit will not be harmful; the thoughts it will inspire in you will not be base. Whenever you read this paper you will believe, as I do, in love and virtue, and when the clamor of the living tires your soul, take refuge in the memory of the dead."

Teresa placed a kiss on her friend's forehead. Carlota took her in her arms . . . but oh, she was embracing but a corpse!

By the gloomy light of the candles which lit up the skull and the crucifix, Carlota, pale, trembling, and on her knees beside Teresa's dead body, read Sab's letter. Afterward . . . why say what she felt afterward? We who are telling the story have seen this letter: we have it firmly committed to memory. Here is what it says.

Sab's Letter to Teresa

Teresa,

My hour of rest approaches: my mission on earth is about to end. When I leave this world in which I have suffered and loved, I wish to bid farewell only to you.

I have come to die near my mother and my brother: I thought that their presence—the presence of these two people who have loved me—would ease my passing, but I was wrong. God saved His ultimate test for me here, my last torment.

The poor old woman sleeps, surrounded by death: she sleeps near two people who are dying, her two sons who are going to leave her! To you I will confess it: when a moment ago I saw her naked brow, deeply furrowed by time and sorrows, resting wearily on my breast, and when her voice—that voice which has bestowed on me the sweet name of son—said to me, "You are the only one left to me in the world," at that moment I desired life and placed my hands convulsively over my heart, to tear from it the pain which is killing me.

Ah, yes! Death was my only wish, my only hope, and when I felt its cold hand tightening around my heart, I felt uplifted by a fierce joy and raised my heart to God to say to Him: I acknowledge Your mercy.

But at the sight of this old woman, who sleeps lulled by the death rattle of a dying child, by the side of the skeletal body of her last grandson who even in her sleep reaches out her arms and tells me "You are the only one left to me in the world," then I feel a new kind of struggle, a terrible battle. I feel the desire to live and the need to die. Yes, for you, poor old woman, I would wish to live, for you have taken pity on the orphan and have told him "I will be your mother," for you, who have not been ashamed to love the servant and have told him "Lift your head, son of the slave woman, the chains which fetter your hands should not oppress your soul." For your sake I would like to live, to be able to close your eyes and bury your body and weep over your grave: the abandonment in which I leave you embitters my solemn and desired hour.

And yet, my God, I accept this new test and, with no sign of aversion, will empty the last drop of gall which You have poured into the bitter chalice of my life.

I am dying, Teresa, and I want to bid you farewell. Haven't I told you this before? I believe I have.

I want to bid you farewell and thank you for your friendship and for having shown me generosity, selflessness, and heroism. Teresa: you are a sublime woman, and I have tried to imitate you—but can the dove soar like the eagle? You rise great and strong, ennobled by sacrifices while I fall back broken. When the hurricane launches its chariot of fire across the land, the *ceiba* tree remains upright, its victorious crown illuminated by the halo which its enemy bestows on it, while the bush, which has vainly attempted to survive in the same way, is left only to attest to the force which has destroyed it. The sun comes out, and the *ceiba* greets it by saying "Here I am," while the bush exhibits only scattered leaves and broken branches.

And yet, you are a weak woman: what is this strength which sustains you and for which I vainly ask my virile heart? Is it virtue which gives it to you? I have thought a great deal about this: during my wakeful nights I have invoked that great word—Virtue! But what is virtue? Of what does it consist? I have wanted to understand it, but in vain have I asked men for the truth. I remember that when my master sent me to confess my sins at the feet of a priest, I asked God's minister what I should do in order to attain virtue. The virtue of the slave, he replied, is to obey and be silent, serve his lawful masters with humility and resignation, and never to judge them.

This explanation did not satisfy me. Well then, I thought, can virtue be relative? Is virtue not one and the same for all men? Has the supreme head of this great human family perhaps established different laws for those who are born with white skin and those with black? Don't all have the same needs, the same passions, the same flaws? Why, then, do some have the right to enslave and others the duty to obey? God, Whose supreme hand has evenly distributed His benefits among all the countries of the earth, Who makes the sun come up for all of His great family scattered all over the world, Who has written the great dogma of equality on the grave, could God sanction the iniquitous laws on which one man bases his right to buy and sell another, and can His spokesmen on earth tell a slave "Your duty is to suffer: the virtue of the slave is to forget that he is a man, to renounce the gifts God gave him, to give up the dignity with which He has endowed him, and to kiss the hand that brands him with the seal of infamy"? No, men lie: virtue does not exist among them.

Many times, Teresa, in the solitude of the fields and in the silence of night have I thought about this great word: Virtue. But for me Virtue is like Providence: an unknown need, a mysterious power which I can imagine but which I don't know. In vain have I looked for it among men. I have always observed that the strong man oppressed the weak one, that the clever cheated the ignorant, and that the rich disdained the poor. Among men I have failed to find the great harmony that God has established in nature.

I have never been able to understand these things, Teresa, as much as I have questioned the sun, the moon, and the stars, the roaring winds of the hurricane, and the gentle breezes of the night. To my sorrow the thick clouds of my ignorance obscured the flashes of my intelligence; and when I ask you now if you owe your strength to virtue, I have yet a new doubt and wonder if strength is based not on virtue but on pride. Because pride is the greatest and most beautiful thing I know, and the only source from which I have seen men's noble and brilliant actions emanate. Tell me, Teresa, the greatness and selflessness of your soul, isn't it only pride? And what if it is? Whatever the name of the feeling which calls forth noble actions, it must be respected. But what do I lack that I cannot compare myself with you? Is it a lack of pride? . . . Is it that this great feeling cannot exist in the soul of a man who has been a slave? Nonetheless, although a slave, I have loved everything beautiful and great, and I have felt my soul rise above my destiny. Oh, yes! I have possessed great and beautiful pride: the slave has let his faculty of thought range freely, and his ideas have soared higher than the clouds which bear the lightning. Then what is the difference which exists between your moral order and mine? I will tell you, I will tell you what I think. It is that within me there is an immense ability to love: you have the courage to resist, and I the energy to act; you are upheld by reason, and I am devoured by emotion. Your heart is of the purest gold, mine of fire.

I was born with a rich store of interests. When, in my early youth, Carlota would read aloud to me the ballads, novels, and histories which she liked best, I listened to her breathlessly and imagined a multitude of ideas, and a new world would evolve before my eyes. I found the destiny of those men who fought and died for their country very beautiful. Like a charger who hears the sound of the trumpet, I quivered with a savage zeal at great words like "country" and "liberty": my heart swelled, my nostrils flared, my hand groped intuitively and eagerly for a sword, and Carlota's sweet voice was barely able to wrest me from my trance. At the same time as the beloved voice, I thought I heard martial music, shouts of triumph, and songs of victory, and my spirit soared toward that magnificent destiny until a sudden and devastating reminder came to whisper in my ear: "You are a mulatto and a slave." Then a dark rage would constrict my breast, and my heart's blood coursed like poison through my swollen veins. How many times did the novels which Carlota read refer to the mad love which a vassal felt for his queen or a humble man for some illustrious and proud lady! . . . Then I listened with a violent trembling, and my eyes devoured the book; but oh! the vassal or the plebeian were free, and their faces did not bear the brand of disfavor. To them Heaven opened the gates of fortune, and courage and ambition came to love's aid. But what could the slave do, to whom destiny opened no path, to whom the world conceded no rights? His color was the mark of an eternal fate, a sentence of moral death. One day Carlota read a play in which at last I found a noble maiden who loved an African, and I felt transported with pleasure and pride when I heard that man say: *"Being an African is no blemish, and the color of my face does not paralyze my arm."* Oh sensitive and unfortunate woman! How I loved you! Oh Othello, what burning sympathy you found in my heart! But you, too, were free. You came from Libya, burning and brilliant as its sun: you never fed on the bread of servitude, nor did your proud brow ever bow before a master. Your beloved never saw the mark of irons on your triumphant hands, and when you told her of your works and deeds, no memory of humiliation ever caused your countenance to blanch. Teresa! Love soon had exclusive hold over my heart, but it did not weaken it, no. I would have won Carlota at the price of a thousand heroic deeds. If destiny had presented even one alternative to me, I would have hurled myself down its path. The tribune or the battlefield, the pen or the sword, action or thought . . . it was all the same to me: within myself I had the aptitude and the will. I only lacked the power! I was a mulatto and a slave.

Like the pariah, I have often dreamt of great, rich, crowded cities, of those immense laboratories of civilization in which the gifted man finds so many destinies! My imagination soared on fiery wings toward the world of the intellect. Take these fetters off me, I cried out in my delirium, take away this mark of infamy! I will rise above you, proud men: for my beloved I will win a name, a destiny, a throne.

I have known no other sky but that of Cuba: my eyes have never seen great cities with marble palaces, nor have I breathed the fragrance of glory: but here in my imagination, like a magnificent panorama, there took shape a world of opulence and greatness, and when I was tortured by insomnia, I envisioned crowns of laurel and mantles of purple. Sometimes I saw Carlota as a celestial vision, and I heard her call to me: rise up and walk! And I arose but fell back to the terrible echo of a sinister voice which repeated to me: You are a mulatto and a slave!

But all of these visions have slowly disappeared, and only one image has reigned in my soul. All of my fervent desires have become concentrated in one only: love! An immense love which has consumed me. Love is the purest and most beautiful of man's passions, and I have felt it in all of its omnipotence. In this supreme hour, in which as its victim I immolate myself on the altar of suffering, it seems to me that my destiny has been neither ignoble nor ordinary. A great passion fills and ennobles an existence. Love and suffering elevate the soul, and God reveals Himself to the martyrs of any pure and noble cult.

At this moment, Teresa, I see Him as great in His mercy, and I fling myself confidently on His fatherly breast. Men had disguised Him before my eyes: now I know Him, see Him, and adore Him. He accepts the lonely worship of my soul . . . He knows how much I have loved and suffered; these white stars that watch over the earth and hear the heart's cries in the silence of the night have told Him my laments and my vows. He has heard them! I die without having stained my life: I die consumed by the holy fire of love! Before His eternal throne I cannot lay claim to the virtues of patience and humility, but I do have courage, generosity, and sincerity. These qualities are good for achieving strength and freedom; in a slave they are useless to others and dangerous for him, but they have been involuntary.

Men will say that it is my own fault that I have been unhappy, because I have dreamt of things that were not within my reach, because being but a nocturnal bird, I have wished to gaze on the sun like the eagle. Judged before their tribunal such men would be right, but not before that of my own conscience. It would reply: though the nocturnal bird does not have eyes strong enough to endure the sunlight, he knows his weakness, and no inner drive but the strength of his will has thrust him into a place for which he was not destined by birth. Is it my fault that God has endowed me with a heart and a soul? That he has granted me love of beauty, desire for justice, ambition to greatness? And if it has been His will that I suffer the terrible conflict between my nature and my destiny, if He gave me the eyes and the wings of the eagle only to imprison me in the dark body of the nocturnal bird, can He hold me responsible for my sufferings?

Can He say to me: why did you not destroy the soul I gave you?
Why were you not stronger than I? Why didn't you make yourself
different and stop being the one I created?

But it is not God, Teresa, it is men who have shaped my destiny,
it is they who have clipped the wings with which God endowed my
soul, they who have constructed a wall of misconceptions and prejudices between me and the destiny which Providence had chosen
for me, it is they who have rendered God's gifts useless, they who
have said: Are you strong? Then be weak. Are you proud? Then be
humble. Do you thirst after great virtues? Well, employ your powerlessness in humiliation. Do you have an immense capacity for love?
Well, stifle it, because you should not love anything beautiful and
pure and worthy of inspiring your love. Do you feel the noble ambition of wanting to be useful to your fellow man and to employ for
the general good and for its delight the abilities which weigh heavily upon you? Well, bow down under their weight and ignore them
and resign yourself to living in a useless and despised way, like the
barren plant or the filthy animal . . . It is men who have imposed
this dreadful fate upon me, they are the ones who should fear to
appear before God: because they have a terrible explanation to give,
because they have incurred an immense responsibility.

Do they know what I might have been? Why have they, who severely punish those who take another man's life, invented this moral
death? Why do they establish hereditary greatness and prerogatives?
Do they have the power to make virtues and abilities hereditary?
Why is the man who comes out of obscurity rejected, being told
"Return to nothingness, man without heritage, waste away in your
mire, and if you have the virtues and abilities your masters lack,
stifle them because they are of no use to you"? Teresa, how many
thoughts oppress me! Death, which already chills my hands, has not
yet reached my head and my heart. My eyes, however, grow dim . . .
I think I see visions before me. Don't you see? It is she, it is Carlota,
with her wedding ring and virgin's crown . . . but a hateful, squalid
band follows her! They are Disillusionment, Tedium, Regret and behind them a monster with sepulchral voice and head of iron: the Inevitable! Oh, women! Poor, blind victims! Like slaves, they patiently
drag their chains and bow their heads under the yoke of human
laws. With no other guide than an untutored and trusting heart,
they choose a master for life. The slave can at least change masters,
can even hope to buy his freedom some day if he can save enough
money,[1] but a woman, when she lifts her careworn hands and mistreated brow to beg for release, hears the monstrous, deathly voice

which cries out to her: "In the grave." Don't you hear a voice,
Teresa? It is that of the strong who say to the weak: obedience, humility, resignation . . . that is virtue. Oh, I feel sorry for you,
Carlota, I feel sorry for you although you are happy and I lie dying,
although you fall asleep in the arms of pleasure and I in those of
death. Your destiny is a sad one, poor angel, but never turn against
God, nor confuse His holy laws with those of men. God never shuts
the doors on repentance. God does not accept impossible vows. God
is the God of the weak as well as the strong and never asks more of a
man than what He has given him.

Oh, what anguish! It is not death, it is not ordinary jealousy
which torments me, but the thought, the foreboding of Carlota's
destiny . . . to see her profaned! She, Carlota, a dawn flower who
had never yet been touched except by the breezes of Heaven! And
the solution is impossible! Impossible—what an iron word! And
these are men's laws, and Heaven is silent . . . and God allows them!
Oh, let us worship His inscrutable judgment! Who can understand
it? But no, You will not always be silent. God of all justice! *Error,
Ignorance, and absurd Prejudice: you will not always rule in the world:
your decrepitude foretells your ruin. The word of salvation will resound
over all the earth: old idols will topple from their profaned altars, and the
throne of justice will rise brilliantly over the ruins of old societies.* Yes, a
heavenly voice tells me this. In vain, it tells me, in vain will the old
elements of the moral sphere fight against the regenerative principle:
in vain will there be days of darkness and hours of discouragement
in that terrible battle . . . the day of truth will dawn clear and brilliant. God made His chosen people wait forty years for the promised
land, and those who doubted were punished by never setting foot
therein; but their children saw it. Yes, the sun of justice is not far
off. The world waits for it in order to rejuvenate in its light: men
will bear a divine mark, and the angel of poetry will shine its rays
over the new kingdom of the intellect.

Teresa! Teresa! The light which has shone in my eyes has blinded
them . . . I cannot see what I am writing anymore . . . the visions
have disappeared . . . the divine voice is silent . . . a deep darkness
surrounds me . . . a silence . . . No, it is interrupted by the death
rattle of someone who is dying and by the moans that a nightmare
wrenches from an old woman who sleeps! I want to see them for the
last time . . . but I cannot see any longer! I want to embrace
them . . . my feet are leaden! Oh, death! Death is a cold and heavy
thing like—like what? With what can death be compared?

Carlota! . . . perhaps at this very moment . . . let me die first. My

God . . . my soul wings to You . . . farewell, Teresa . . . the pen falls from my hand . . . farewell! I have loved, I have lived . . . I no longer live . . . yet I still love.

A few days after the nun's death Carlota, whose delicate health was visibly failing, indicated to her husband her wish to see if the climate of Cubitas might help her, as it was generally reputed to be very salubrious.

She indeed left the city at the beginning of the following month, accompanied only by Belén and two of her most faithful male slaves, and moved to Cubitas, where she was welcomed by the good country folk with the greatest pleasure.

Her first concern was to ask the overseer about old Martina, but to her great sorrow she had died six months earlier.

"The good old soul," added the overseer, "was barely alive after the deaths of Sab and her last grandson. Constantly ill, yellowed and thin like a corpse, she only went out in the afternoons, nearly at dark, to go on her favorite walk followed by her dog."

Carlota did not need to ask what her favorite walk was, for a farmer who was present immediately added, "What my friend says is very true: every night when I came from my farm, I saw two shapes, one large and another somewhat smaller, at either side of the wooden cross which we placed on poor Sab's grave, and where we also buried Martina's grandson. Those two shapes no longer aroused anyone's attention: we all knew that they were the old woman and her dog. From the time she died we have only seen one shape, but that one is there all the time. Day and night you can see poor Leal lying at the foot of the cross, and he only leaves his spot from time to time to come and fetch a bone or some scraps from my friend here."

"That's not exactly true," replied the overseer. "Often they're good pieces of beef that animal gets, and not bones or scraps. But who has the heart to deny a mouthful to such a faithful dog, who spends his life by the side of his master's remains, and who besides this is already old and blind?"

Señora de Otway sent the two speakers away with proof of her generosity, expressing her gratitude to the overseer for the good treatment he had accorded the poor little animal who no longer had a master.

She stayed in Cubitas more than three months, but her health continued in such poor condition and she lived in such absolute seclusion that no one saw her in the village again. In the beginning there was much talk about Señora de Otway's strange affliction which no one, not even her favorite woman slave, was able to diagnose, and there was gossip about the indifference of her husband, who left her alone in such a difficult situation. But very soon the attention of the village's few inhabitants was diverted to another matter, and people forgot to think about Carlota.

News of a miraculous event began to circulate rapidly, which reported that the old Indian woman, after having been buried for half a year, returned nightly for her habitual walk and could be seen kneeling by the wooden cross which marked Sab's grave, exactly at the same hour that she used to come while she was alive, and accompanied by the same dog. This rumor was widely believed, because in Cubitas it had always been thought that Martina was different from other human beings. The most hardened unbelievers wanted a glimpse of the alleged spirit, and there was great surprise and absolute conviction when these same people confirmed the truth of the matter; however, the only difference was the strange circumstance that when the old Indian woman returned to earth she had been transformed in a singular manner. Those who had observed her on her nocturnal visit swore that she was no longer either old, thin, or olive colored, but young, white, and beautiful—as much as could be seen of her, for she always had her face covered with a gauzy veil.

The sensation caused by this vision was the sole topic of the farmers' free evenings, and no one thought any more about Carlota until the day she was forced to return to Puerto Príncipe, her illness having taken a turn for the worse.

By a singular coincidence, Leal died that same day, and the vision was seen no more. When they went to the grave on that particular occasion, the observers of the nocturnal visitor found only the body of the faithful little animal, who by order of the overseer was buried next to his master, an honor his prodigious loyalty had rightfully earned him.

From then on it is certain that no one has come back to pray at the foot of the rustic wooden cross, the only gravestone erected to the memory of Sab. But perhaps some simple farmer who tills the red earth may recall the time when an old woman and a dog came to visit that humble grave, and the mysterious vision which subsequently was seen at that place every night for the next three months.

We would also like to give the reader news of the beautiful and afflicted Carlota, but though we have attempted to inquire into her present status, we have been unable to find this out. Logically her husband, whose wealth had increased markedly in only a few years and whose father had died, will most likely have deemed it advisable to set himself up in a more prominent shipping center than Puerto Príncipe. Perhaps Carlota, as Teresa had foreseen, is now living in populous London. But whatever may be her fate and the nation of the world in which she is residing, will the daughter of the tropics have been able to forget the slave who rests in a simple grave under that magnificent sky?

Notes

——— • ———

Introduction

1. In Spanish, "Creole" (*criollo/a*) refers to a person of Hispanic ancestry born in the Spanish colonies; it does not imply a racially mixed heritage.

2. The first woman to be admitted to the Royal Spanish Academy was the poet Carmen Conde, in 1977 (see Allison).

3. Perhaps because of personal vanity, perhaps because Avellaneda tended to attract men who were somewhat younger than herself, in her autobiographical writings she consistently shaved a few years off her real age.

4. She also omitted almost all of her 1846 historical novel, *Guatimozín, the Last Emperor of Mexico,* which dealt with the Spanish conquest of that country.

5. Schlau has an excellent discussion of Avellaneda's treatment of nature in *Sab;* in her opinion, "Despite Avellaneda's long descriptions emphasizing the magical quality of this landscape, the scientific explanations, which appear in the author's footnotes, often contradict its power" (501).

6. A possible Cuban source could be a long narrative poem, *Espejo de paciencia* (Mirror of Patience), written in 1608 by Silvestre de Balboa, a Spaniard who lived in Puerto Príncipe. In this poem, the first of known authorship to be composed in Cuba (Barreda 13–14), a courageous black African slave named Salvador saves a bishop from French pirates. Benítez Rojo underscores the importance of this text for the members of the Del Monte group. "The poem was subjected to a romantic reading by the Cuban literary critics of the 1830s, who saw in it an opportunity to legitimize their own discourse" (25). By the time the Del Monte group republished the *Espejo* (1837–1838), however, Avellaneda was already in Spain.

7. By "desert" the author actually meant "wilderness."

8. Like Avellaneda, Aphra Behn (1640?—1689) was a successful playwright, poet, and novelist, a woman who held her own in the literary world of Restoration England. Coincidentally, one of her theatrical friends was named Thomas Otway (Strange 43), the same, rather uncommon last name Avellaneda used for her English characters in *Sab.*

9. Cruz (9) and Luis (40–41) point out that the Del Monte group also read Hugo eagerly and was inspired by him; Schulman, however, feels that his influence was minimal (366 n. 20).

10. So that no one would miss the point, she herself brought the book to the royal court (Bravo-Villasante 67).

11. *Obras de doña Gertrudis Gómez de Avellaneda.* 6 vols. Havana: Imprenta de A. Miranda, 1914.

12. Two notable exceptions are Bravo-Villasante and Barreda.

13. Another novel which foregrounds the personal love story is Suárez y Romero's *Francisco,* which was written in 1835 but not published until forty years later.

14. Other Cuban abolitionist works (such as the above-mentioned *Francisco*) have similarly submissive heroes. In Schulman's opinion, this position of restraint corresponded to the fact that these writers were reformers, not revolutionaries, and also had to deal with the severe censorship on the island which would not permit a more radical stance (362).

15. Richard L. Jackson's study of the black image in Latin American literature discusses this issue at length. As Jackson noted, "when we speak of race relations in Latin America we must also speak of the mulatto, and I use this term to cover a wide range of black-white interracial mixture," as opposed to the United States, where one is classified as being either black or white and the term "mulatto" is practically never used (5–6).

16. Crossbreeding and the possibility of incest caused by a lack of knowledge of one's racial origins are frequent themes in the Cuban antislavery narrative (Netchinsky 5–6) and also surface in Faulkner, specifically in *Absalom, Absalom!*

Autobiography

1. The entire letter uses the more formal *usted* form of address, rather than the familiar and more intimate *tú*. In her love letters, both to Cepeda and to Romero Ortiz, Avellaneda would often shift between the two forms of address, depending on the state of her relationship with the man in question.

2. She was fully nine and a half years old, as she was born in March 1814 and her father died at the end of 1823. As Cepeda (1816–1906) was two years younger than Avellaneda, she was interested in making herself appear as young as possible. Note also that she never mentions the exact date of her birth.

3. Avellaneda is referring to St. Domingue (today Haiti and the Dominican Republic).

4. A walk near the Guadalquivir River, where fashionable Seville society would gather.

5. Under Spanish law a testator could leave a fifth of his estate to whomever he chose; this is the inheritance her grandfather had promised Avellaneda.

6. Curro was Cepeda's brother.

7. José María Heredia, Cuban patriot and Romantic poet, had been Avellaneda's tutor. One of his most famous poems, "To the Hurricane," is the one she cites here.

8. This paragraph is unintelligible in the original, probably because Avellaneda left out some phrases. I have attempted to give it a meaning which is consistent with the gist of her opinions about Galicia.

9. Constantina was the town in which Avellaneda's father was born.

10. She was, of course, referring to Cepeda himself.

11. Bravo was one of Cepeda's friends.

12. Avellaneda did not follow this impulse (she is already undermining it by writing the *Autobiography* itself), as her correspondence with Cepeda is voluminous and lasted from 1839 to 1854.

Sab

In order to avoid confusion between Avellaneda's original notes and my own, I have enclosed hers in quotation marks and have indicated which are mine in parentheses.—Trans.

Part One, Chapter I

1. "Only he who has been on the island of Cuba and heard these songs sung by the local folk can imagine their inimitable lilt and singular charm, by means of which they endow the most trivial ideas and commonplace language with spirit and grace."

2. As was noted previously, in Spanish the term *criollo* (Creole) denotes a person of Spanish descent born in the Americas. It does not imply mixed racial ancestry. (Tr. note)

3. "The *yarey* is an average-sized tree, of the family of the fan palm, whose large, shiny leaves are used to weave hats, baskets, etc., of quite remarkable quality."

4. In the novel the word *ingenio* is used in reference to Bellavista; according to the author's note, "'Ingenio' is the name given to the machine which crushes the cane, but it is also commonly used to designate the plantation on which these machines are found."

5. "The slaves of the island of Cuba address whites with the title of 'Su Merced' [Your Grace]."

6. "'Mayoral' is the title given to the chief administrator who directs and presides over the slaves' work. It is very rare for another slave to be assigned to this position; when it occurs it is considered the highest honor which can be given him."

7. Rendered as *vos* in the original. Avellaneda notes: "The use of *vos* was only abolished in Puerto Príncipe a very few years ago. It was used very commonly instead of 'usted,' and was even used in conversation by people who generally addressed each other as 'tú.' People of a lower class did not use it toward members of the upper class, and I only allow Sab to use it because the agitation with which he spoke at that moment would not have allowed him prior reflection."

8. This gate is called a *taranquela*, which the author defines as "thick logs, placed a certain distance apart, with crosspieces to prevent the livestock from getting out."

Part One, Chapter IV

1. "The name *estancia* is applied to small working farms, but in Cubitas the name is used particularly to designate the patches of *yuca*, a hard, white tuber from which a kind of bread called *casabe* is made. On each of these farms there are

normally cabins in which the overseer lives, and these cabins form the groups of houses of the villages of Cubitas."

2. "The caves of Cubitas are an admirable work of nature and worthy of being visited. Later on we will speak of them again more extensively."

3. Avellaneda has evidently forgotten that Sab is six years older than Carlota; if she is seventeen, this would make him twenty-three. (Tr. note)

4. "The *aura* is a bird somewhat like a crow, but larger. When a storm threatens, uncounted bands of these birds populate the air, and by their low flight the people of the country know the density of the atmosphere." The English translation of this term is "vulture" or "turkey buzzard." (Tr. note)

5. "*Bohío:* thatched hut or cabin."

Part One, Chapter VI

1. Avellaneda here uses the indigenous Carib name *colibrí* to designate a hummingbird and provides the following note: "The *colibrí* is a very small bird known only in the most torrid zones of America. Its plumage is extremely beautiful by dint of the nuance and brilliance of its colors. It sips the flowers like a bee, producing a buzzing similar to that of mosquitoes, for which reason it is known in some places as a *rezumbador* [a Cuban expression for a whirring, spinning top] and in others as the *pica flores* [flower nibbler]."

2. Avellaneda may be referring to the crepe myrtle, or *astromelia,* since her original term of *astronomía* is not a botanical term. (Tr. note)

3. "The Cuban *clavellina,* also called lily by some island people, is a plant that is not analogous to the carnation [*clavel* in Spanish]: its flower, which has a very soft scent, is white when it first blooms and later turns pink."

4. "The *malva rosa* is white in the morning and red in the afternoon."

5. "This extraordinary flower is produced by a plant similar to the wild white grape. Before it opens it is the color of a pale hyacinth and when it opens displays other, even whiter petals forming a crownlike circle. A cylindrical stem rises from the center of the flower, like a column which ends in a kind of chalice from which three nails emerge. The interior of the chalice has the shape of a hammer, and because of these markings it is called the *passion flower* or *pasionaria.*"

Part One, Chapter IX

1. "*Campanilla:* a wildflower in the shape of a bell; it is produced by a very common creeper in that area."

2. "The *yuraguano* is a tree of the family of the fan palm, whose many leaves somewhat resemble palm fronds; the ones referred to in this story, which proliferate in the environs of Cubitas, are taller than the common yuraguanos. In contrast to the palm, which grows in a straight and elegant fashion, its trunk is normally twisted and at times extends almost horizontally."

3. "At first a *jagüey* is no more than a creeper which fastens onto a tree. It grows prodigiously; its branches cover and squeeze the trunk which supports it and in the end cause it to wither. Then the creeper itself becomes a thick tree,

given a distinctive shape by the irregularities of its trunk and the great number of branches which it stretches forth capriciously, as well as the thick roots which are visible on the ground's surface."

4. "Among the fireflies the *cocuyos* are the most rare and showy, as well as the largest. They feed on sugarcane juice and for this reason abound in cane fields. They have four wings, two lights spots on the body, and two on the head."

5. "In previous times the people of Cubitas invented strange accounts relative to a light which they claimed appeared nightly in that spot and which was visible to all who traveled the road between the city of Puerto Príncipe and Cubitas. Ever since the aforementioned village has become more frequented by visitors and acquired a certain importance, this phenomenon, whose causes have never been satisfactorily explained, has not been mentioned again. One talented person recently published a newspaper article entitled 'Additional Notes on the History of Puerto Príncipe,' which addressed this topic and says that they were will-o'-the-wisps which general ignorance classified as supernatural apparitions. The same author adds that the annual brush burnings which they do in the country may have consumed the substances which caused this phenomenon.

"Without stopping to examine whether or not this conjecture is well founded, and leaving to our readers the freedom to form more exact judgments, we will for now adopt the opinion of the *cubiteros* and will explain the phenomenon in the course of this story just as it has been told and explained to us more than once."

6. The reference here is to the widespread massacre of whites after Haiti acquired political independence in 1804. (Tr. note)

7. As Mary Cruz points out in her edition of *Sab,* (Havana: Editorial Letras Cubanas, 1983, p. 243, note 15), both Indian and black labor was used in the mines to which Avellaneda refers. (Tr. note)

Part One, Chapter X

1. *Cimarrón* is a term which was used to refer to a runaway slave. Avellaneda here is talking about a cave where fugitive slaves would hide. (Trans. note)

2. "The *curujey* is a type of parasitic plant which springs from the trunks of old trees."

3. Leal, the little dog's name, means "loyal" in Spanish. (Trans. note)

Part One, Chapter XI

1. *Canjilón* is a little-known word which refers to a type of container or receptacle, generally used for storing liquids. Mary Cruz explains that the rocks in the bed of the Máximo River reportedly had shallow depressions reminiscent of these *canjilones* (p. 245, note 2). (Tr. note)

Part Two, Chapter I

1. Avellaneda erroneously attributes this quotation from Scripture to the Gospel of St. Mark, chapter 12, the passage is actually Matthew 11:28.

Part Two, Chapter V

1. This is a reference to her illegitimacy. (Tr. note)

Conclusion

1. Historian Eugene V. Genovese attests to the widespread existence in Cuba of the practice of *coartación,* or self-purchase (*The World the Slaveholders Made: Two Essays in Interpretation,* [New York: Vintage Books, 1969] 64). (Tr. note)

Works Cited

Allison, Esther M. "Carmen Conde, primera académica española." *Abside* 42 (1978): 195–199.

Ammons, Elizabeth. "Heroines in *Uncle Tom's Cabin*." In *Critical Essays on Harriet Beecher Stowe*, edited by Elizabeth Ammons, pp. 152–165. Boston: G. K. Hall Co., 1980.

Arrom, José Juan. *Esquema generacional de las letras hispanoamericanas: Ensayo de un método*. 2d ed. Bogotá: Publicaciones del Instituto Caro y Cuervo XXXIX, 1977.

Avellaneda, Gertrudis Gómez de. "Autobiografía." In *Sab*, pp. 247–290. Paris: Vertongen, 1920. (Originally published in 1841.)

———. *Cartas inéditas existentes en el Museo del Ejército*. Edited by José Priego Fernández del Campo. Madrid: Fundación Universitaria Española, 1975.

———. *Diario íntimo*. Edited by Lorenzo Cruz de Fuentes. Buenos Aires: Ediciones Universal, 1945.

———. "La mujer." In *Album cubano de lo bueno y lo bello*, pp. 34–37; 226–229; 259–261. Havana: 1860.

———. *Sab*. 1841. In *Obras de doña Gertrudis Gómez de Avellaneda*. 6 vols. Havana: Imprenta de A. Miranda, 1914. 4:400–541.

Barreda, Pedro. *The Black Protagonist in the Cuban Novel*, translated by Page Bancroft. Amherst: University of Massachusetts Press, 1979.

Benítez Rojo, Antonio. "Power/Sugar/Literature: Toward a Reinterpretation of Cubanness." Translated by Jorge Hernández Martín. *Cuban Studies* 16 (1986): 9–31.

Bravo-Villasante, Carmen. *Una vida romántica: La Avellaneda*. Madrid: Instituto de Cooperación Iberoamericana, 1986. (Originally published in 1967.)

Chesnut, Mary Boykin. *A Diary from Dixie*. Boston: Houghton Mifflin: 1949. (Originally published in 1905.)

Cotarelo y Mori, Emilio. *La Avellaneda y sus obras: Ensayo biográfico y crítico*. Madrid: Tipografía de Archivos, 1930.

Cruz, Mary. Prólogo. In *Sab*, by Gertrudis Gómez de Avellaneda, pp. 7–15. Havana: Editorial Letras Cubanas, 1983.

"Documents: The Banning of *Sab* in Cuba [Documents from the Archivo Nacional de Cuba]." *Américas* 1 (1949): 350–353.

Figarola Caneda, Domingo, and Doña Emilia Boxhorn. *Gertrudis Gómez de Avellaneda: Biografía, bibliografía e iconografía, incluyendo muchas cartas, inéditas y publicadas, escritas por la gran poetisa o dirigidas a ella, y sus memorias.* Madrid: Sociedad General Española de Librería, 1929.

Franco, Jean. *Spanish American Literature since Independence.* London: Ernest Benn, 1973.

Gold, Janet. "The Feminine Bond: Victimization and Beyond in the Novels of Gertrudis Gómez de Avellaneda." *Letras Femeninas* 15 (1989): 83–89.

Gómez de Avellaneda, Gertrudis. See Avellaneda, Gertrudis Gómez de.

Guerra, Lucía. "Estrategias femeninas en la elaboración del sujeto romántico en la obra de Gertrudis Gómez de Avellaneda." *Revista iberoamericana* 132–133 (1985): 707–722.

Harter, Hugh A. *Gertrudis Gómez de Avellaneda.* Boston: Twayne, 1981.

Jackson, Richard L. *The Black Image in Latin American Literature.* Albuquerque: University of New Mexico Press, 1976.

Kirkpatrick, Susan. *Las Románticas: Women Writers and Subjectivity in Spain, 1835–1850.* Berkeley and Los Angeles: University of California Press, 1989.

Luis, William. *Literary Bondage: Slavery in Cuban Narrative.* Austin: University of Texas Press, 1990.

Metzger, Lore. Introduction. In Mrs. Aphra Behn, *Oroonoko; or, The Royal Slave*, pp. ix–xv. New York: W. W. Norton and Co., 1973. (Originally published in 1688.)

Miller, Beth. "Gertrude the Great: Avellaneda, Nineteenth-Century Feminist." In *Women in Hispanic Literature: Icons and Fallen Idols.* Edited by Beth Miller, pp. 201–214. Berkeley and Los Angeles: University of California Press, 1983.

Morejón, Nancy. "Cuatro novelas antiesclavistas en el siglo XIX cubano." In *Fundación de la imagen*, pp. 29–45. Havana: Editorial Letras Cubanas, 1988.

Netchinsky, Jill Ann. "Engendering a Cuban Literature: Nineteenth-Century Antislavery Narrative (Manzano, Suárez y Romero, Gómez de Avellaneda, A. Zambrana)." Ph.D. diss., Yale University, 1986.

Portuondo, José Antonio. *Capítulos de la literatura cubana.* Havana: Editorial Letras Cubanas, 1981.

Rodríguez, Ileana. "Romanticismo literario y liberalismo reformista: El grupo de Domingo Delmonte." *Caribbean Studies* 20 (1980): 35–56.

Schlau, Stacey. "Stranger in a Strange Land: The Discourse of Alienation in Gómez de Avellaneda's Abolitionist Novel *Sab.*" *Hispania* 69 (1986): 495–503.

Schulman, Ivan A. "The Portrait of the Slave: Ideology and Aesthetics in the Cuban Antislavery Novel." *Annals of the New York Academy of Sciences* 292 (1977): 356–367.

Shaw, Donald C. *A Literary History of Spain: The Nineteenth Century.* London: Ernest Benn, 1972.

Sommer, Doris. "Sab C'est Moi." *Genders* 2 (1988): 111–126.

Strange, Sallie M. "Aphra Behn." In *A Dictionary of British and American Women Writers, 1660–1800.* Edited by Jane Todd, pp. 43–44. Totowa, N.J.: Rowman and Allanheld, 1985.

Tompkins, Jane P. "Sentimental Power: *Uncle Tom's Cabin* and the Politics of Literary History." In *Feminist Criticism: Essays on Women, Literature, and Theory.* Edited by Elaine Showalter, pp. 81–104. New York: Pantheon Books, 1985.
Torres-Ríoseco, Arturo. *The Epic of Latin American Literature.* Berkeley and Los Angeles: University of California Press, 1967.